Everest is Hollow

By Indigo Jones

Everest is Hollow is an adventure novel, featuring a teenage Indiana Jones-style archaeologist. His nickname is "Trouble." Together with his friends Nuru and Tattoo, Trouble climbs Mount Everest's difficult West Ridge. Fierce weather and snow leopards add to the risk of an already challenging expedition. Their risks multiply when Trouble enters a cave and realizes Everest is hollow. Inside the world's tallest mountain, he discovers an abandoned city, the key to a lost civilization built on treasures of the past. How it was done is a mystery. The only clue is a strange creature, the last of his species.

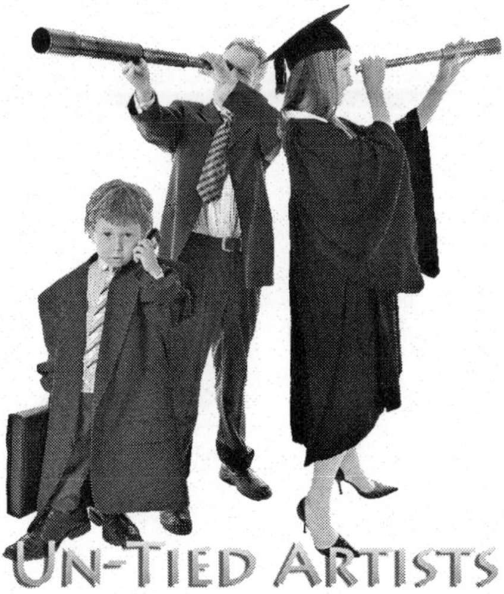

Based in Silicon Valley, these authors write comic fiction, thrillers, mysteries and adventures. Un-Tied Artists donate proceeds from sales of their books to Doctors Without Borders.

In 1999, the Nobel Peace Prize was awarded to Doctors Without Borders for their work in relieving the suffering of underprivileged countries. Why a peace prize for doctors? Because terrorists find eager recruits among the despairing millions of this world, living in unthinkable conditions.

See more about Un-Tied Artists and their books at
www.SiliconValleyNovel.com

Everest is Hollow

By Indigo Jones

This book's story and characters are fictitious. Some well known public agencies, locations and establishments are discussed. But the characters in this novel are entirely imaginary.

ISBN-13: 978-0-9817702-8-4
ISBN-10: 0-9817702-8-2

Published in the United States of America by Un-Tied Artists

The trail to Mount Everest hits an important crossroads at 11,000 feet. At this junction, the path to the world's tallest mountain weaves through a thousand-year-old trading post. Vendor stalls are simple and basic, primitive rock huts or canvas tents, perhaps just a rug spread on the ground. Visitors and locals squeeze through a tangled maze of shops, like an Arab bazaar, jammed with people and merchandise.

The market is an exotic mix of timeless ways and the latest technologies. Foil-wrapped energy bars dangle amid yak jerky and silk prayer flags, made by hand in the same way they were crafted when Manhattan was a Dutch colony. American Wave snowsuits hang next to traditional Sherpa garments, unchanged since Genghis Khan conquered Asia.

Eight hundred years after the brutal Khan and his Mongol hordes left, the trading post could still be dangerous, especially for a thirteen year old boy …

1

Inside the world's highest marketplace, Trouble darted between tables of gold bracelets and t-shirts, crouching low to hide from his pursuers. He could smell the strange men chasing after him, a weird blend of coriander, body odor and wet leather. They cursed in high-speed grunts, sounding like strangled cats. Their voices grew louder with every moment, frightening him. Trouble's pulse hammered in his ears with the fury of hummingbird wings vibrating against a microphone. Yet he continued running, pushing through the packed crowd of tourists and cattle herders, dodging racks of high-tech climbing gear and antique yak saddlebags. There wasn't a straight path anywhere and Trouble spun through a dizzying maze of furry huts and faded canvas sheltering traders. Worse, none of the ground was level, forcing him to run uphill, then down a narrow trail of steps.

His escape route came to a dead end where an old butcher, tired from a long day of work, was stacking a wall of buffalo steaks, one slab at a time. Each slab was large enough to feed a family of eight for a whole week. Trouble waited impatiently for the bulky man to step away, his thick fingers closing around the next marbled round of meat.

Trouble gestured, urging the butcher to step aside. "Please, I need to get out of here."

Suspicion pinched the man's eyes almost shut. "You buying something?"

"Um, sure." Trouble felt desperate. He tossed a wad of bills on the ground, watching the butcher stoop to pick them up, sharp knife held firm inside a bloody fist. The rotten, sickly sweet smell of blood attracted flies and a red stream clotted on the dry earth.

There was no time to lose. Trouble held his breath to shut out nauseating odors and hurdled a pile of gory flesh, jumping past the butcher.

Running again, his legs felt like heavy stones dragged from the bottom of an old well. Sprinting at 11,000 feet elevation was draining. His lungs burned from inhaling thin air stripped of oxygen. He detoured around an orange canvas tent, pausing to suck fresh air into exhausted lungs. Backpack straps cut into his shoulders, adding to Trouble's exhaustion. He needed a moment to loosen the straps and rest weary muscles.

Trouble dared a glance at his pursuers. Accustomed to the high altitude and its thin air, they were gaining speed, getting closer. Wearing dark clothes, the men blended into the twilight sky and Trouble didn't notice they were encircling him. When he tripped and fell, a painful grip squeezed his arms, jerking Trouble to his feet. Men slapped him against a stone building, knocking the air from his lungs.

They pressed him into a wall and tore off his backpack. Emptying every compartment, they ran small flashlights over the tangle of items dumped from Trouble's pack. Power bars, Kleenex packets, loose coins, a plastic Spiderman, iPod, clothing, nothing seemed to interest them. Finally, the men pinned Trouble against the wall with a choke-hold on his neck. Their breath held the rancid smells of buffalo jerky and chewing tobacco. Yellow teeth and cracked lips shouted questions in a host of foreign languages, but Trouble understood none of what they were saying.

Their leader stepped up, flaunting his cocky attitude and a sharp knife, its thick hunting blade gleaming a razor-like edge. A ski mask covered the man's face, revealing only arrogant eyes. "Where is it?" he demanded.

Trouble couldn't speak. He had no air in his lungs and the choke hold blocked any breaths. He bobbed his chin, indicating he needed to breathe and couldn't because they were holding him so tightly.

"Release him," the leader instructed his men.

No longer pinned against rough bricks, Trouble dropped on the ground, falling to his knees. He gasped for air, his throat raw, stinging with pain from their brutal treatment.

The leader grabbed Trouble by the neck of his jacket and stuck the ski mask in his face. Trouble could feel the man's breath puffing through thick, cracked lips when he spoke. "You are American. Where is your passport? We need it to contact your family. Your parents will pay money to get you back. They must send us a ransom."

"I …" Trouble stammered. He heard the heavy tromping of boots from an approaching squad of angry feet. A burst of orders were shouted.

"Soldiers," the leader hissed. He spat in contempt, releasing his grip on Trouble's parka.

Bright military flashlights darted along the wall, painting halos around Trouble. For a moment, he felt blinded by a harsh beam. When the glare disappeared, Trouble was alone. His pursuers became ghosts vanishing into the crowd, tearing off their ski masks to blend with vendors and locals.

Soldiers in green fatigues tromped past, their boots clomping on the pavement. One of them saw Trouble and pointed at him, shouting a question to his commander. Luckily, the officer ignored the comment and ordered his soldiers to follow the criminals. Trouble felt grateful the outlaws were being chased, but he knew the army patrol would soon return, frustrated and angry. They'd want to know what happened and he had no good answers to their questions.

He needed to get away, but there was nowhere to hide, no dark crevice to jam himself inside. Quickly, Trouble shoved his belongings in the backpack. He didn't have time to be careful. Clothing, food, toothpaste and soap were just tossed inside and zipped shut.

A sliver of yellow light ran over his feet. Behind him, a door slowly opened. There was a creak of ancient hinges. "In here," a boy's voice hissed. "You'll be safe inside. Hurry."

Trouble hesitated.

"Trust me," the boy urged.

But Trouble felt too uneasy to move.

"Look, you have no choice. The soldiers will return any moment. They'll also want to see your passport."

There were more orders shouted in a staccato burst of voices. A whistle blew, then tromping boots marched toward him, echoing across the rough stone and dirt alleyways. Trouble was out of time. A hand pinched his sleeve and tugged him toward the door. The tugging on his arm grew harder and he quit resisting its pull. Trouble scooped up his backpack and slid through the open door. He paused, startled by the abrupt change in his environment. With one step, he went from the ancient marketplace into a modern tavern, crowded with human bodies. Trouble's nose was assaulted by the odor of people sweating from being totally overdressed, wearing insulated jackets and pants in a heated room. Unfamiliar food scents wafted from a kitchen stove lit with propane, throwing grease, spices and hot metal smells in the already thick air.

His eyes adjusted to the dim room and Trouble discovered a place jammed with kids of all ages, most of them locals from the Himalayas. Their dark faces were painted with the eerie glow of flashing PC screens. The PCs had their sound turned up, speakers pumping out kick-boxing games and car engines revving through 3D terrain. Trouble's ears felt attacked by a hurricane of sound. The blizzard of animation and noise was disorienting. Voices argued and fingers clicked computer mice at high speed, racing to keep pace with a computer-animated rush. It took a moment to realize a hand tugged his sleeve, urging him to move into the crowd.

The hand belonged to a state-of-the-art Sherpa teenager, wearing rip-stop nylon hiking pants. In the current fashion, pockets climbed the legs from ankles to hips. His pants were topped by a fleece pullover, zipper pulled to the chin. The North Face logo decorated the turned-up collar. A New York Yankees baseball cap was fitted backwards over thick black hair, completing the teen's hip look. Trouble saw a dimpled face with curious eyes gazing at him.

He felt uneasy under the stare. "Who are you?"

"Nuru is my name." The boy smiled. "You're lucky to be alive."

"I am?" Trouble rubbed his sore neck, massaging pained muscles where they'd choked him.

"Sure. Those guys with ski masks are Maoist guerrillas. They hacked off my uncle's arms because he was a government official. That's why I helped you. I hate them for what they did to my uncle."

"Thanks. I knew they were dangerous."

"The soldiers chasing them are also a threat. And they'll be back. The soldiers will want to question you, examine your entry papers." Nuru gave him a knowing look. "From what I overheard, you don't want that, right?"

"Um …" Trouble squirmed.

"Well, there's time to discuss it after we mingle with the crowd, blend in. Here, we'll swap hats. That'll disguise you from the soldiers."

"Wait a minute. You're wearing a Yankees cap. I'm an American from New York City. Wearing a Yankees baseball hat won't disguise me."

"Sure it will. Americans buy wool hats first thing, so they look like authentic trekkers. Sherpa teens trade their wool hats for baseball caps worn by Americans. That's how I got mine. Pile your hair under my Yankees cap and the soldiers will think you're local. You've got a tan. In this light, it looks like dark skin."

They traded and Trouble snugged the baseball cap over sandy brown hair that seldom got trimmed in a barber shop. He shrugged. "It's a start, but we need to do more. The soldiers will still find me."

"We'll move into the crowd. Hurry, two guys just left. We can grab their table." Nuru slid past clumps of teens, glued to their computer screens.

Trouble followed him, ducking under souvenirs hung on ceiling beams by foreign trekkers – climbing helmets with high-intensity headlights, battered compasses, empty canteens, mesh bags with crushed aluminum cans, oxygen masks and a necklace of energy bar wrappers.

"What's all this gear doing here?" Trouble asked.

"Namche's the gateway for climbers trying their luck on Mount Everest. It's the world's highest peak, you know." Nuru gave Trouble a smug look.

"Yeah, well, everybody knows that. I meant, like why'd they hang all this stuff from the ceiling?"

Nuru shrugged. "I dunno. Guess it's to show they were here. Some guys use their knives to write a message, like how far they got up the mountain." He pointed at their table, engraved by past visitors. The carving read "E.N. made Camp 6 – blizzard, back in 2 yr."

Trouble wiped goo from his chair and sat down. "This place got a name?"

"The Khumbu Cybercafé. Twenty-four hour fax, scanner, e-mail, Internet. Surf any website. No filters. You just got to wipe your feet before you go inside." Nuru grinned. "Streets in Khumbu are too narrow for cars. I'm afraid the yak is still our truck. The Cybercafé is on the main drag, so there's a lot of yaks walking by. They leave their downloads on the street, if you know what I mean." He put a grossed-out look on his face and mimicked scraping yak dung off the bottom of his shoes. "Doesn't stop us from downloading all the MP3 we want."

Trouble laughed. "Can you download Crunk? I just got into Lil' Jon. Is there a website with *Snap Yo Fingers* and *Act a Fool*?"

"Crunk, huh?" Nuru looked a bit confused. "Don't know much about Crunk. I can ask around. Somebody will know." His eyes lit up. "We'll Google 'crunk' and find some cool downloads for you."

The owner loomed over them, a wide body topped by the bulging face of a croaking frog, his neck swollen like an inflated balloon. "You aren't gonna surf anything unless you pay last month's bill, Nuru. And you gotta order some drinks, for you and your … friend." He gave Trouble a nasty looking over, like the owner decided to hate Trouble before he ever said a word.

Nuru groaned and pulled a wad of bills from his pocket. "Here's a down payment. We'll have pearl milk tea, with extra tapioca balls." Nuru looked at Trouble. "What flavor you want?"

"You have mango?" he asked the proprietor.

"No," the owner grunted.

"How 'bout coconut?"

"Um," the proprietor growled and spun around, leaving them.

"Guess he knows what flavor you want," Trouble commented.

"Yeah, I always have the same thing," Nuru laughed.

"What's that?"

"Purple yam bubble tea."

"That's pretty exotic."

Nuru shrugged. "Not as exotic as getting to the Himalayas without a passport. How'd you do that?"

"It's a trade secret." Trouble hesitated.

"Oh, I save your life and you don't tell me how you got here. Nice thing."

"OK, um …"

"Well?" Nuru leaned over and cupped his head in his hands, prepared for a long story.

Trouble squirmed in his chair, reluctant to answer the question.

"Come on," Nuru urged. He twisted a green plastic wristband, stretching it with his fingers. Impatient, he bounced his knee against his palm like a basketball player dribbling along the court. "You can tell me. I can keep a secret."

"You can? You won't tell *anybody*?" Trouble rocked back in his chair. His eyes ran around the room, looking everywhere except at Nuru's face.

Nuru leaned over the table, pressing on Trouble with insistent body language. "Go on. Tell me. I wanna know."

"OK." Trouble exhaled a long slow breath. "It's like this …"

"Yeah?" Nuru shoveled his hands, acting like he could pry words out of Trouble's mouth.

"Well . . . um. I flew here."

"I knew that." Nuru acted disgusted. "How did you get on the plane? I mean without a passport."

"I didn't go the normal way. I wasn't exactly a passenger."

Nuru got excited. "You were a stowaway? Where'd you hide? You would've froze to death in a wheel-well where they store landing gear. Did somebody sneak you in?"

"No." Trouble felt indignant. "I paid to be shipped."

Nuru's eyes got wide. "Shipped?" he asked in amazement. "Like a package?"

"Yeah. Air cargo."

"You gotta be kidding. What's the real story?"

"Air cargo," Trouble repeated.

"Yeah, like someone overnighted you to Nepal. I'm sure."

"Bleerio overnighted me, to be exact. I don't have a credit card to buy a plane ticket, but my parents have an account to ship large crates by air cargo service, so I used it. Sometimes it pays to have parents in the antique business. People expect you to ship crates all over the world.

Room for a backpack, bottled water, some Power bars. Gets cold, though. Cargo planes aren't heated like passenger jets."

"You're serious, aren't you?" Nuru pulled off the wool cap and ran fingers through his thick black hair like a comb. He stared at Trouble in disbelief. "Really serious?"

"Very."

It was Nuru's turn to say, "Wow." He cocked his head. "How old are you anyway?"

"Thirteen last week," Trouble answered.

"Yeah. Well, I was thirteen a month ago," Nuru bragged. "What's your name, huh?"

"I'm Trouble."

"I know that, but what's your name?"

"Trouble – really."

"Uh, like, what's it short for? You know, what's your real name?"

"That's it. My name is Trouble. My parents had this uneasy feeling about me, right from the beginning."

"Yeah, well, so why aren't your parents with you, Trouble? You didn't come to the Himalayas all alone."

Trouble countered, "Where are *your* parents? You didn't come to the Khumbu Cybercafé alone, did you?"

"Hey, it's my country. I just traveled a few days by yak. What's your excuse? I mean, you came here from New York City. Visiting Namche Bazaar isn't exactly like taking the subway to Greenwich Village. So, why aren't you with your parents?"

"You sure want to know a lot." Trouble acted evasive. He twirled a grungy spoon in his hand and realized the place setting probably never got washed, just wiped with a rag. He dropped the spoon and it clanked on the table.

Nuru rolled his eyes. "How are we gonna be friends if we don't get to know each other?"

"Who says we're friends?"

"Ouch." The Sherpa teen recoiled from the comment, shoving his chair away from the table as though he were going to get up and leave.

Trouble apologized. "Sorry. That was rude. I've been through a lot. What'd you wanna know again?"

"Kids don't go to foreign countries alone. Why aren't you with your parents?"

"Because I haven't seen them for two years." Trouble made a quarter-turn in his chair, facing away from Nuru. Talking about this was hard for him, but he felt his friend deserved an explanation. “My parents are archeologists. My dad went on an expedition and didn’t return.”

“What about your mom?”

“My mother went looking for Dad. She hasn’t come home either.”

“Have you heard from them?”

Nervous, Trouble crimped the bill on the New York Yankees cap he was wearing.

Nuru grimaced at having his favorite baseball cap deformed.

“Oops. Sorry.”

Nuru sighed, “Oh well, nothing you can do about it now.” He cocked an accusing eye, cranking on the guilt. “About your parents?”

“Haven’t heard from them, no phone call or anything. Last correspondence I got from Mom was postmarked here. That’s why I came to the Himalayas looking for her. I can’t just sit around.”

“Did both your parents come to Nepal?”

“I don’t know if my father came here. But mom sent me a package from this area. I thought that was kind of weird. She usually sends things from Siberia.”

“Siberia? Like in Russia?” Nuru removed the yak hair cap he’d gotten from Trouble. The wool itched his scalp.

Trouble nodded. "Mom is always on a dig in Siberia. She specializes in uncovering kurgans, Scythian burial mounds."

"Oh, well, that's good. Um, what's a Scythian?"

"Mom told me Scythians were savage warriors. They scraped all the flesh from their victims' skulls and used them as drinking cups." Trouble knew that image would gross out Nuru.

"Yuk," was his reaction to drinking from a dead human's head. "How'd your parents meet if your mother was always in Siberia, digging up old skulls?"

"My parents met in Siberia. Mom was working a tomb and robbers attacked her, trying to steal gold artifacts she'd collected. My dad's also an archeologist. He was digging nearby and helped scare off the robbers."

"What do your parents do with all the gold they find?"

"Most of it goes to the Russian government, for display in museums. They get to keep a few of the artifacts, as payment for their help in finding kurgans and digging up treasures. What my parents keep goes to our antique store in New York, for sale to private collectors. We have all kinds of stuff they've found over the years, on their expeditions."

"Bizarre. If I found gold, I wouldn't put it in a store. I'd trade it at the Namche Bazaar for cool discs and DVD's, get me some really hot shoes and the latest trekking jacket."

The owner interrupted them, slopping drinks on the table, a pair of glasses with tapioca marbles jumbled at the bottom of Chinese tea. The purple and white drinks looked thick as smoothies, but had a pungent odor, as if sprinkled with untold spices. "You want something to eat?" the owner grunted. "Got a special tonight on alu acchar and gundruk. Fresh and hot."

"Gundruk?" Nuru complained. "Who'd want that? The stuff's four days old. You were serving it when I first got here, last week. By now, it smells like the inside of a shoe."

"You don't like what I serve? Then pay your bill and leave. You can't pay? I'll take your computer." The owner put a massive hand on the laptop display and squeezed, distorting the screen.

Nuru started to panic and his face twisted in fear. "Ah, no, don't hurt my laptop."

"Oh?" The owner smiled and squeezed the computer a little harder. "You have money to pay me this time?"

"Sure, um, just let me explain …" But Nuru didn't get a chance to finish his appeal.

The café's back door slammed open with a crash. Men in camo fatigues and heavy boots stood in the doorway, poking automatic rifles into the room. They radiated impatience and hostility. Trouble felt the heat of ugly stares on the back of his head and saw their images reflected in the tea glasses. Their sinewy bodies seemed taut as bungee cords stretched to the point of snapping. Pairs of restless eyes darted around the room, searching, watching for danger like rats daring a nighttime food hunt. Instantly, every PC was slapped shut and went mute. All conversation died. It felt quiet as a church.

2

An officer wearing starched green khaki elbowed his soldiers aside, squeezing between them. He took a quick step inside the café and halted. The captain put hands on his equipment belt, fingers caressing automatic pistols slung on both hips like a Western gunfighter, daring anyone to move. Without warning, he bellowed at them, snapping orders. “One of you must have seen an American boy, about thirteen years old, carrying a backpack. He’s wanted for questioning.” The captain snarled, “I warn you. It’s illegal to harbor a fugitive.”

The café owner glowered, his watery green eyes peering through heavy lids. “You bring problems into my café,” he whispered to Trouble. “It’s the end of you.”

“What did you say?” the officer demanded.

“I told them their double order of alu acchar and gundruk would be ready soon, most honorable captain.” The owner’s smile would have greased the axle on a yak cart.

“I’m hungry myself,” the captain moaned. “Come on,” he told his men. “We have to search this village before we get any dinner.” He gave the café owner and his guests an envious look, then kicked open the alley door with a boot. The soldiers followed, leaving the door open to the dark night. Cold air wafted into the room. A kid at the closest table slammed the door shut and every PC flipped open, roaring back to life like nothing ever happened.

Trouble exhaled. “Thank you,” he whispered to the owner.

“Your double order of alu acchar and gundruk will be here in moments. I expect a generous tip,” was his answer. “Oh, and it’s not on special anymore. Full price, yes?”

“Yes,” Trouble agreed.

“Gouger,” Nuru complained, after the owner left.

“He saved my life.”

“Wait ’til you’ve eaten his cooking. You may change your mind. His food smells like your socks after days on a long trek – and the flavor’s even worse.”

"It doesn't matter what the food tastes like. I need a lot of calories."

"Why? You trying to get fat? Guess you're gonna become a Sumo wrestler, huh?" Nuru puffed his cheeks like a balloon.

"Very funny." Trouble smiled and shook his head in amazement. "I'm a little small for Sumo wrestling."

"Yeah. So why do you need the calories, smarty?"

Trouble shrugged. "To climb Everest."

"Climb Everest?" Nuru looked astonished. "I thought you were searching for your parents."

"I am," Trouble assured him. "My mother's letter talked about finding a Yeti cave on Everest. I have to explore that cave. It's the only clue I have."

"Trouble," Nuru moaned. "People don't just hike up the world's tallest mountain. You need porters and equipment, not to mention permits. It takes weeks to mount an expedition. You aren't just going to a skateboard store to admire the latest planks."

"No kidding. Look, I'm not climbing Everest's summit. I'm just scaling the West Ridge. I'm not even going to the ridge's crestline."

The owner slid metal plates heaped with steaming food on their little table, almost knocking off the notebook PC. Nuru caught his laptop computer and scowled at the proprietor.

The owner grunted, "Gundruk and alu acchar, double portions. Goes on your bill, Nuru. Pay up tonight before you leave or don't come back."

"Right," Nuru sighed. "Paying's easier than climbing the West Ridge. You really are crazy, Trouble. Did you know that?"

"Um, burgood," he mumbled, stuffing his face.

"Huh?"

Trouble gulped down the food so he could speak. "This is good." He poked a steaming pile of cabbage, flecked with spices and chopped vegetables. "Gundruk is like sauerkraut. Alu acchar reminds me of pickled potatoes. Spicy and I love hot foods."

"Great. Put some in your backpack. Maybe it'll keep you warm on Everest."

"You're such a pessimist, Nuru."

"No, I'm a realist. Everest's West Ridge is on the border with China. It's bad news to go there. The Chinese aren't nice to people who cross their border without permission. People tell stories about hearing gunfire and seeing bullets kicking up snow. A lot of climbers die in avalanches. Some guides say the avalanches were caused by Chinese artillery. There aren't soldiers that high, but somehow they monitor by satellite or something."

"Good to know. But I'm not crossing into China. I'm looking for a Yeti cave on the West Ridge."

Nuru fidgeted. He leaned over the table and whispered. "I don't tell this to just anyone. I know where the Yeti cave is located. It's on the Chinese side."

Trouble laughed. "You really have to win this argument, don't you?"

Nuru blushed with anger. "I'm not making this up. I was born with a birth defect. I couldn't walk like other kids. My legs were all twisted. It got worse as I grew. My dad went to the monastery and prayed. One night, a Yeti stole me from my bed and took me to his cave. He cured me."

"You look serious, like you're telling the truth."

"I'm not lying," Nuru huffed.

"Sorry. Look, I believe you. Were you frightened when the Yeti grabbed you?"

"I was only scared for an instant. Then I felt his warmth, like he was going inside me, telling me I was safe. Once I got to his cave, I wasn't in pain anymore. I felt very tired and fell asleep. When I woke up, a lot of days must have passed. I was outside on a snow ledge. The Yeti took my hand and pulled me to my feet. I started walking with him. I thought it was just a dream I was having, something I imagined. So I didn't want to wake up, even when my dad rushed from the village and hugged me. I don't remember what happened in the cave but I know it's on the Chinese side of West Ridge."

"Cool." Trouble beamed. "You can lead me right to the Yeti's home. Let's go."

"Er, not so fast. You have to apply for a visa. My dad knows how to get visas for entering China. He's led several expeditions on Everest. Dad's a Sardar, a foreman for the Sherpa guides assisting climbers. The Sherpas have to carry supplies to all nine camps along the route. A hundred fifty yaks are used to provision the base camp alone. From there, Sherpa porters haul everything on their backs. It takes weeks to prepare for an ascent."

"I can't wait around for weeks. I don't have enough money for a long stay."

"No problem. You can live with us. We've got an extra room."

"Sorry, I can't stay that long. I have to get home soon. The antique shop … Bleerio means well, but he can't deal with customers.

When I'm gone, there's no sales. No sales, no money. You know what I mean?"

He nodded. "Look at it this way. You want to climb the West Ridge, right?"

"Yeah," Trouble agreed.

"We live near the base of Everest, where you begin the ascent. It's not far from our home to the West Ridge. You've got nothing to lose by staying with us. It gets you close to your goal, doesn't it?"

"What about your parents? How will they feel about having me stay with them?"

"No problem. Mom loves visitors."

"You ought to ask your mom first," Trouble suggested. "It's only polite – especially since she's standing in the front door." Trouble pointed at a woman in the doorway, framed by soft glow from the sunset. She was wearing a traditional Sherpa angee-style dress, emerald green with billowing sleeves. Her chest was covered in a thick vest, made of modern Polartec fabric. The light blue vest had a pattern dappled with red Canadian maple leaves. Heavy gold rings dangled from her pierced ears. The woman's head was covered by a tightly wound handkerchief, anchored with a ribbon tied across the top. Her face looked pretty, yet weathered from the harshness of living at such a high elevation. The oval face seemed friendly despite harsh lines at the corners of the eyes, making her appear older.

Nuru turned around and forced a smile. "Hi, mom," he said weakly.

Sensing a problem, Trouble put Nuru's Yankee baseball cap back on his head and reclaimed the wool trekking hat.

"It's not the hat," Nuru whispered. "It's my café tab. The owner –" He jabbed a thumb at the scowling proprietor. The man was edging through the crowd, intent on giving Nuru's mother a bill for his food and gaming.

Trouble rolled off his stool and slid around tables packed with jabbering, waving kids. He grabbed the bill from the owner before the tab got to Nuru's mother. "Do you take American dollars?"

The owner glared. "This isn't your bill. It's Nu –"

"New to me, yes," Trouble interrupted. "I don't travel much. Currency exchange is new to me." He pulled out twenty dollar bills and gave them to the proprietor. "Enough, right?"

"No," he grunted.

"OK. I'll take the dollars back and pay in rupees." Trouble looked at the bill. "Let's see. The dollar's fallen against the euro and the yen, but not against the Nepalese rupee. The exchange rate is a hundred dollars for seven thousand four hundred rupees. That'd be …"

"Dollars are fine." The owner stuffed bills in his apron pocket. "Currency exchange isn't that new to you, boy."

"Oh? I'm just getting started." Trouble smiled like he was trying to get his dad to sign a school absence form.

"Glad I met you now, before you get more started," the owner mumbled, then walked away.

Trouble spun around and ran into Nuru's mother.

"That was very nice of you. Nuru will work in my booth at the Namche Bazaar until he earns the money back. I'll send it to you in the mail. My name is Dooli." They shook hands.

Nuru joined them. "Oh, hi Mom." He looked sheepish. "Trouble was hungry and I ordered some food."

"Trouble?" Dooli asked, curious about the name.

"Yeah. That's my name. Actually, I try to stay out of trouble."

Nuru snickered. "Yeah, right. That's why I had to rescue you from Maoist guerrillas."

"Guerrillas? Here in Namche, with all the soldiers around?" Dooli was astonished.

"Yeah," Nuru boasted. "They wanted to kidnap Trouble and hold him for ransom. So I pulled Trouble inside the café. We swapped caps to hide him in the crowd."

"I'm glad you explained the hats. You still owe me half the price of that baseball cap. Pay me back before you trade it for something else, Nuru."

"Ah, sure Mom. Look, Trouble needs our help."

Dooli acted skeptical. "Where are your parents?"

"That's why he needs our help." Nuru played with the zipper on his North Face pullover. "See, Trouble came here to find his parents. They're lost … or something."

"Oh, they'll turn up. Namche isn't that big. There's only one luxury hotel and a hostel. Your parents aren't going to sleep in a tent like us … are they?" Dooli stared at Trouble.

Uneasy under the stare, Trouble hesitated. "Well … my parents have been missing for two years. But last month, I got a package from my mother, sent from a village near Mount Everest. I came looking for her."

"Yeah, and I told Trouble he could stay with us while he looks around. Can he?"

"Of course you can stay. Hospitality is a Sherpa tradition. We have a room at the top of our house, private and warm. It's yours as long as you need it."

"I'll pay," Trouble rushed to offer.

"You've already paid – too much." Dooli scowled at Nuru. "We leave for home first thing in the morning, at daybreak. Nuru and I will strike the tent before dawn. Then we'll get you. Where are you staying? In the hostel?"

"In the hostel, sure," Trouble lied.

"I thought so," Dooli said calmly. "We have an extra bed roll. It's warm in our tent and you'll learn how to live as we do. You'll have to stay in our tent on the journey anyway. It's five days riding on yaks to our village." Dooli put a firm grip on Nuru's arm. "Come, before you run another tab, gambling you can be the top at *World of Warcraft* or *Sims 2*."

"How did you hear about that?" Nuru winced.

"Mothers talk." Dooli gave Trouble a knowing smile. "Come on. Nuru needs to help me load supplies on the yaks. There won't be time in the morning." Dooli headed for the door.

"You do live near Mount Everest?" Trouble asked Nuru.

"Right at the base. Near the Khumbu glacier."

"Great." Trouble shouldered his backpack.

"You won't think it's great after riding a yak," Nuru muttered.

"Oh, I rode horseback on a three day camping trip. It wasn't bad," Trouble countered.

"We don't have saddles," Nuru warned. "And there'll be no toilets or showers. We can't have fires at night because of the guerrillas. The higher we go, the colder it gets. Wait 'til you wake in the morning with snot frozen to your lips."

3

The journey proved to be even worse than Nuru warned. Meals sat in Trouble's stomach like icy rocks. Breakfast was a cold gruel called "saltoo," made of ground amaranth seeds, tasting like stale oatmeal. Snacks were limited to dried fruit, tasteless chunks of apple or icky sweet apricot leather. The main course of every meal was always the same – buffalo jerky, tough as a belt and taking forever to chew, exhausting jaw muscles. Forget sodas or energy drinks – they had no time to heat water for tea. A few sips from a frozen canteen became the only beverage each day, leaving them dehydrated, aching to soothe their parched lips. Trading for warm food and drinks wasn't possible. Each sunset, they camped next to a tiny hamlet, but the villagers had nothing to spare.

With no running water, a hot shower seemed nothing more than a phantom dream. A toilet became squatting against a frozen boulder, trying not to soil your pants, racing frostbite to complete your poop. Sub-zero cold always surrounded them, chilling Trouble, stealing energy and depressing his mood. By midnight, their tent felt like a meat locker, making sleep impossible. Each breath crystallized to frost and snot did indeed freeze on his lips. Trouble's stomach turned into a lump, hard and small like a baseball.

The final day was the worst, pushing to make it home without spending another night in the frigid tent, its canvas slapping in the moaning wind, icy drafts billowing under the edges. Hungry and exhausted, Trouble clung to the neck of his yak, a small buffalo with long, sharp horns. The animal didn't like carrying a restless teenage boy and found new ways of showing its displeasure all the time. Trouble had to be vigilant to avoid getting bitten, gored, kicked or dumped. The yak brayed like a donkey every time he got prodded to move ahead, rather than pausing to scour lichen off rocks with his rough tongue.

The trail wove along the mountain's sheer limestone face, at times becoming so narrow even his yak had difficulty staying on the dangerous path. Often the animal walked on a narrow ledge with its hooves sliding like ice skating. Rocks were coated in black ice, invisible in the dim moonlight.

After sunset, Trouble peered into the night, hoping to see lights in the distance, marking their destination. Finally, the moon escaped storm clouds and became a golden volleyball balanced on the world's highest peak. Moonlight painted glow on the base of Mount Everest, where a village lay chiseled into the granite mountain like the steps of a ladder. The settlement's terraced hillsides were packed with narrow homes and tiny crop patches. Tile roofs reflected stars like twinkling pinpricks of light. With so little air at that altitude, Trouble saw a thousand times more stars than the clearest night in New York.

Yet Trouble found no solace in the dazzling view. In front of him, a steep walkway plummeted to a flooded crop terrace. His yak balanced on spongy planks, walking across a narrow pool of water. They traveled at the edge of a steep cliff, plunging to a canyon below. Their yaks crawled along the dangerous trail for an hour to reach homes built into the mountainside. The short caravan of riders halted after days of exhausting travel.

Nuru gestured at the closest house. "Dad leads expeditions as a Sardar, so we own one of the largest homes in the village." His voice swelled with pride. "Our house is four stories tall."

"Yeah, great place." Trouble replied without really looking. Sitting that close to Nuru, he could only see the back of his friend's parka. Trouble was afraid to have his yak step backwards for fear he'd tumble off the ledge.

"Stay here," Nuru ordered. "I'll wake Dad and explain we have a guest."

Dooli put a restraining hand on Nuru. "I'll talk with Ang Dawa. You can give the yaks some food. Drop their saddle bags on the ground. We'll unpack in the morning."

She looked at Trouble. "I'll only be gone a moment. You won't have to wait long in the cold." Dooli yanked a rope latch on the door and vanished inside the house. A bulb flickered and light glimmered through cracks in the door.

With Nuru out of his way, Trouble could survey the house. The home was shaped like a drooping stack of pancakes, slumped against the mountain for support. The layers grew shorter until the top floor held only a cramped attic. The small windows on each level were different sizes and shapes. Still, the home looked cozy and warm. In fact, the longer he waited in the bitter cold, the more inviting the house felt.

Finally the door opened. Dooli said warmly, "Come in."

"Um, thanks." Trouble stepped inside. "I won't be staying long."

"You may stay as long as you need." Dooli pushed a squat, four-legged stool at Trouble. "Sit down. Make yourself comfortable. I'll stoke the fire. We leave the stove dormant at night, when we're asleep. Uses less fuel." Dooli prodded open the cast iron door on a potbellied stove. She reached in a modern plastic bin, like the kind used for curbside recycling. Dooli pulled out a pair of bricks, dark brown in color. "Yak dung. Dried in the sun. Burns very hot. We use everything our yak produces, even its droppings." Dooli gave Trouble a knowing smile. "You'll be telling your friends about the yak dung, no doubt."

"Oh, no. Makes perfect sense, burning yak dung."

Trouble heard Ang Dawa snort a quick laugh. He was sitting in a corner, drinking rice wine, sipping it from a leather-bound shepherd's flask. Dooli shot him a scolding look, but it had no effect.

"Yak crap, burn it all the time at Harvard, eh what?" he muttered. Ang Dawa took another swig from his flask.

"Ignore him, Trouble," Dooli advised. "My husband is upset. Tomorrow, he will feel better and help you find your mother."

"Not tomorrow," Ang Dawa slurred. "Chomolungma is only nice to those who wait. She is cruel to fools who rush."

"Chomolungma?" Trouble asked.

"Chomolungma means Goddess Mother of the World," replied Dooli. "It is our name for Mount Everest. Ang Dawa's had too much rice wine and thinks you mean to scale Everest. He dreams of another expedition there, but it's only a dream. He wants the money to build another room on our house, and where he could put it, I don't know. We can't go up and we can't go out, yet that doesn't stop him from dreaming when he's drunk too much wine." Dooli prodded the stove's fire to life and slammed its door with a clank. "I'll go upstairs now to fix your room. You'll sleep at the top, where it's warmest. You are our honored guest."

"Please, don't make a fuss. I can sleep down here." But it was too late. Dooli ascended ladder-like stairs and her head vanished inside a dark hatch in the ceiling.

All Trouble could do was sit there in silence, studying the room. It resembled nothing he'd seen at home. The floor was made of rough planks about the size of roofing shingles. Tar caulked the seams between boards to prevent cold drafts. A light bulb dangled over the kitchen area, crowded by a potbellied stove and a well-used prep table. Carving knives were stuck tip-first in the table's scarred wood. The scrubbed tabletop looked clean, yet was tinted with vivid stains from chopped herbs and peppers. In one corner, they'd stacked shrink-wrapped cartons of bottled water against ceramic water jugs with wooden lids and rope handles – the modern world shoving aside ancient ways.

Across the room, a tapestry of red and gold silk hung on a stand, a Buddhist weaving for prayer and meditation. Near the religious art was a small television set and DVD player. Alongside the TV stood a modest collection of movies in frayed packaging, indicating the discs had passed through many owners. A bundle of DVDs waited by the door, tied with string. It looked like that stack would be traded with friends, swapped for movies Nuru's family hadn't seen yet.

Trouble heard a rattling of stairs above his head. He looked toward a hatch in the ceiling, where Dooli strained the old ladder with her descent.

Dooli went to the kitchen and loaded more fuel in the cast iron stove, unlatching the door with a kindling stick and shoveling more yak dung on the bed of red cinders. The new bricks hissed and instantly burst into flames, causing Dooli to slap the iron gate shut in a hurry. "Off to bed, both of you. Nuru, you have school tomorrow. Don't stay up all night talking with Trouble."

"Sure, Mom." He began climbing the ladder, bending its spongy rungs under his heavy feet. The wood protested with squeaks and groans.

Trouble hesitated to get on the fragile stairs, concerned about the ancient timbers. The old staircase was trembling from Nuru's rapid ascent and Trouble stalled by watching Dooli wrap a blanket around her husband. Ang Dawa was snoring in a corner, drunk from his rice wine.

Dooli talked gently, "He is a good man. Just afraid now. Business has been slow. Political troubles keep people away. But Ang Dawa will help you search for your mother."

"Sure." Trouble nodded. "Well, to bed …" He started up the ladder, adding a final, "Goodnight."

At the top of the stairs, the attic bedroom seemed tiny, more like a walk-in closet than a room. The peaked roof's exposed beams formed a wooden rib-cage above Trouble's head. A tiny oil lamp hung from one rafter beam, swaying like a lantern on a sailing ship as it rolled on ocean waves. The miniature lamp provided barely the illumination of a lit match.

Weak light from the oil lamp allowed Trouble to see a small religious painting, a Buddhist Thangka, tacked on the wall as a sort of headboard. The outline of Buddha was royal blue against a shimmering gold background, with a red halo around his head. Underneath the Thangka, there was no bed, just a woven mat lying on the floor. Everyone in the house slept that way. Trouble lay down on the mat and curled into a ball, pulling a yak hair blanket over his shoulders. He tugged at the blanket and its coarse weave chaffed his neck. The rug-like cover smelled of dust and unwashed dogs, even though the material felt clean and looked new.

He couldn't help feeling a twinge of homesickness. He missed his own room, with its musty smell and litter of favorite toys and books competing for space on narrow shelves. By comparison, this place felt naked, barren as the plastic hollow inside an abandoned refrigerator. Loneliness and cold underscored his downbeat mood. Sleep that felt so overpowering and beckoning on his journey flew away like a jet lifting off a runway, leaving him behind. His eyes teared with exhaustion, yet his restless mind wouldn't quit its worrying.

Attempting to quiet his brain, Trouble stared at a window-pane pattern stenciled by moonlight on the bare floor. That pale cross seemed a gateway to something important, ideas that danced hypnotically in his mind, always staying just beyond reach. The harder he tried to catch the thoughts, the more Trouble's mind went to his problems, stuck on all the issues he didn't know how to solve. He couldn't stay for weeks, waiting for Ang Dawa to decide the weather was perfect. Every day's delay left Trouble's mom and dad in jeopardy.

After a few minutes of worrying, he heard a light snore, meaning Nuru was asleep. Maybe Trouble should leave now and explore Everest's West Ridge a bit, see if he could do the climb by himself. First he had to get out of the house. There was no way to descend the inside stairs without waking the whole family.

Fortunately, he'd seen a ladder outside the window for use in a fire, its top rung peeking over the window sill. The fire escape beckoned as a way to leave without being seen. They'd never hear him go, if he was careful. Trouble flipped the window latch and it opened without a sound. There was a whispered creak of hinges and bitter night air rushed inside, its cold breath freezing Trouble's skin. He closed the window and waited for the first hint of morning, when there'd be sunlight to heat the frigid air as he walked.

Finally, pink dawn outlined the mountain and frost began misting off the rooftop. It was time to leave the house and try to find his parents. In only a few seconds, Trouble moved outside, sliding along the roof and climbing down the ladder. An easy descent on the fixed ladder gave him a false sense of confidence. He'd climbed Mount McKinley in Alaska with his parents one summer. McKinley formed the tallest peak in North America. He wanted to believe the West Ridge of Mount Everest wouldn't be much harder, even when he knew it wasn't true. The world's tallest peak was legendary for its hostile environment, merciless to those who trespassed on its slopes.

4

After leaving Nuru's home, Trouble found a village trail going West and followed the narrow footpath of bare earth edged by frozen tundra. Arctic cold dried his eyes and stung his ears like needles. The trail ended at an icy wasteland, where his footsteps crunched on a thin layer of packed snow, then sank into cold mush. Pulling his feet out of deep snow was hard work and soon Trouble felt exhausted. He paused to eat a snack, taking off his blue nylon backpack and sitting on it, using the bag as insulation from cold ground.

Even a tasteless energy bar seemed delicious after missing dinner last night. Trouble took another bite of the stale peanut butter granola snack and chewed the dry food without enjoyment. His eyes scanned the valley where Nuru's village clung to a steep gorge, frosted rooftops sparkling like jewelry in the morning sunlight, a lovely image. Closer to Trouble, however, was a disturbing sight.

Nearby, two people bobbed and weaved, dropping from sight when they fell in a pit of deep snow. Someone was navigating the difficult area Trouble just crossed, heading straight at him. The pair struggling across the white expanse of crusted snow might be Ang Dawa and Dooli, his wife. They were chasing Trouble to bring him back, force him to wait until Ang Dawa felt safe to make an ascent. Trouble assumed the Sherpa guide thought his guest wanted to climb Mount Everest, scale the peak at 29,035 feet. It wasn't true. Trouble only wanted to find a Yeti cave on the West Ridge, at a much lower elevation than the dangerous summit of Everest.

Trouble doubted he could outrace Ang Dawa, an experienced mountaineer, yet he had to try. The Sherpa would want Trouble to mount a formal expedition in search of his mother and father. He couldn't afford expensive permits, visas and climbing gear, much less a host of porters. Once Ang Dawa knew Trouble didn't have any money, he'd have to go home and never find his parents.

Trouble jammed his half-eaten snack in a pocket on the backpack and slung the heavy rig over his shoulders. In front of him, the West Ridge's sharp crags were outlined by a rising sun, its warm light steaming vapors off the icy rock. He got up and ran, trying to open a gap between himself and his pursuers. Trouble charged toward the West Ridge, plowing through deep snow. A few minutes of labored effort left him out of breath, standing at the edge of a vast glacier sliding down Mount Everest. He'd reached the fringe of a dangerous area known as the Khumbu Ice Falls.

Even though he wasn't trying to ascend Everest's summit, Trouble still had to cross a glacier where climbers sometimes fell to their death. Mountaineers walked across what seemed packed snow, only to find they were stepping on thin ice. The brittle crust broke and a climber tumbled hundreds of feet, falling into a hidden ice canyon. This deep hole is called a "crevasse."

The Khumbu Ice Falls was notorious for these invisible death-traps, waiting for someone to walk into them. The treacherous ground forced Trouble to move carefully, probing with the long handle of his ice axe for hidden crevasses. He was looking down, intent on making progress, and didn't notice terrible winds hitting the West Ridge with hurricane-like fury. Far above Trouble, flurries of snow whipped across the sky like sheets snapping on a clothesline. The air around him changed and became charged with static electricity, prickling the fine hair on his arms.

Suddenly a noise like a giant explosion shocked Trouble and he fell backwards, tumbling into a deep pocket of snow. High above, a long piece of the ridge crest tore loose, setting off a chain reaction. One section of the crest pulled down the next. A block-long chain of rock plowed into the snow below, triggering an enormous avalanche.

Snow boulders the size of homes bounced down the ridge, gathering more snow and growing larger. Some of the huge globes tumbled into crevasses and disappeared. Other snow boulders hit the glacier and rolled toward Trouble, making a terrifying ripping noise, shredding everything in their way.

The violent shocks sent a blast wave of air rushing toward him, stinging Trouble's face with needles of ice. He struggled to protect himself from the assault, using his backpack as a shield. Trouble closed his eyes and curled into a ball, letting his thick bag take the fury of the ice storm.

When the wind blast stopped, an even more terrifying thing happened. The ground under him began to shift. The ice became a living thing, quivering like a giant animal waking up, angry at Trouble for being on its skin. The glacier was reacting to the tremendous pressure of the avalanche, tons of rock and ice hastening the glacier's perpetual slide down the mountain, causing an earthquake. All he could do was wait, sit there hoping for the best until the tremors subsided.

After a few seconds, Trouble opened his eyes and blinked, trying to focus his vision. The people chasing him were approaching with alarming speed. The earthquake hadn't slowed them because they weren't walking on the Khumbu Ice Falls. They were crossing firm ground in front of the glacier and making fast progress. Trouble had to move.

With difficulty, he got to his feet inside the deep snow pit. Wearing a heavy backpack made the struggle even tougher. Trouble pushed hard against the mushy snow bank and one side of his body came loose, while the other remained stuck. The result was a clumsy, off-balance spin. Trouble kicked a foot out to brace himself. In horror, he saw that his boot touched nothing and there was only cold air under his shoe. The shifting glacier had formed a new crevasse. Bits of snow were falling into the bottomless hole, spiraling down the pit's translucent blue sides, making beautiful patterns of spinning white flakes. Soon Trouble would follow the tumbling snow, whirling into the center of the earth, never to be seen again.

His arms flapped as he tilted backwards, but the effort seemed useless. He tried leaping to the other side, using his momentum to hop across the gap before it was too late. The jump was a brave attempt, yet he knew it was doomed from the beginning. Trouble hit the other side hard, knocking most of the air from his lungs, leaving him gasping for breath. Then he began sliding into the hole.

Skating down the surface, he clawed at slick ice with gloved fingers and found no grip. His falling picked up speed and blue ice flew past his face until Trouble became convinced it was the last thing he'd ever see. Suddenly his boots collided with a ledge, his fall broken by a thick pile of snow. Trouble looked up and realized he lay only a few feet below the top. Better yet, gouges in the ice could be used as stairs to walk out.

There was not a moment to lose. The crevasse began to close, threatening to crush him with tons of pressure. Trouble started climbing the steps, fighting against slick ice shuddering and moaning under his boots. Going up the ice staircase seemed to take an eternity. Every effort happened in slow motion, with Trouble fighting to clear the hole before it slammed shut, flattening him.

Gasping, he made the top and yanked his feet away from the opening. A moment later, the crack snapped shut. The sealed crevasse groaned and creaked, its sides working like monster jaws grinding food into the earth's stomach. When the ice quit moving, the surface welded into a perfect seam and it looked like nothing ever happened.

He panted, trying to recover his breath. Trouble stared at the clean snow in disbelief. One second there was a tear in the earth so deep it looked bottomless and the next moment the crevasse vanished. Only the fear in his stomach made the episode seem real.

After a few moments, he came back to normal. A shadow blanketed Trouble's face and he realized someone was standing over him. Nuru's familiar voice joked, "Having fun?"

5

Trouble looked up, expecting to see Nuru and his father, Ang Dawa. He felt relieved that Nuru was with a friend, a leggy teenage girl. Her skin looked paler than Nuru and her lips were badly chapped from wind burn. The teen wore a snug-fitting snowboarder's parka with racing stripes down her arms, its modern look contrasting with her traditional Sherpa trekking cap. The hat's long flaps wrapped around the girl's cheeks and were tied under her chin. The purple ear flaps made her head look like a huge grape. She stared at Trouble and circled around him in bobbing steps like a street performer. Her break dancing motion flowed in a rapper's tango, stopping over the vanished hole.

"Don't stand there," Trouble warned the girl. "Move away from that crevasse." He pointed where a hole was located only seconds earlier.

Nuru squinted a concerned look. "Trouble, there's only flat ground here, no crevasses. You've become delusional from lack of air to breathe. It's the high altitude." He bent over and shoved a mask in Trouble's face. "We brought you an oxygen bottle. I knew you'd need it. A whiff of this and you'll feel better."

Trouble pushed away the mask. "I don't need oxygen." He stared at Nuru's friend, dressed in bright colors. Besides the purple cap, she wore an orange parka over turquoise hiking pants.

"My name's Tattoo." She pulled back a sleeve to show pictures drawn on her arm with colored pens. "I don't just draw tattoos. I paint dZi beads also. You know what they are?"

Trouble shook his head. "What's a dizzy bead?"

"A dZi bead is an ancient rock with great spiritual power. They keep you safe." Tattoo reached in her pocket and pulled out a collection of polished rocks. She gestured at a pebble. "This one's an original, real old. Lots of people have worn it. You have to be experienced before you carry around something like this. Old spirits can screw you up real bad."

She poked another small pebble. "This rock is OK for beginners. Makes you feel warm and thirsty. Couple of days wearing it and fat people lose weight. But you aren't fat. This other bead's got an evil eye painted on it, so you can put the hex on your enemies. You ever fly on planes?"

"Sure, that's how I got here." Trouble felt amused by her enthusiasm for superstitious items.

She picked out a big rock with eyes painted all over it. "Take this one, then. It's a nine-eye dZi bead, natural agate found in Tibet. It's just like the one Mr. Chen wore. He was on a China Airline plane when it crashed in Nagoya, Japan. Mr. Chen was the only survivor."

Nuru rolled his eyes. "Chen sat near an exit door, so he got out before the plane caught fire. That had more to do with Chen's living than wearing a dZi bead. And Mr. Chen wasn't the only survivor. Another man also lived."

Tattoo countered, "Other guy probably carried one of these, the best dZi bead you can ever have. Very rare. Thirteen eyes." She dragged out a rock striped in brown and yellow layers. Eyes were painted all over its surface. "Wear this and you can get anything you want. Gives you top spiritual power." She held the pebble with reverence.

Trouble stared at the rock. "How much you want for it?" He was hoping the dZi bead would help find his parents. That was what he wanted most of all.

Nuru interrupted. "Trouble, pay no attention to what Tattoo says about these things. She paints rocks for her father to sell at the Namche Bazaar. Tourists buy them, not the locals. Next thing you know, Tattoo will show you her singing bowls, fill your luggage with useless stuff to take home on the plane."

"They're not useless," Tattoo huffed. "And I make the best singing bowls in Nepal, from all seven metals. Gold for the sun, silver for the moon, copper for
Venus …"

Nuru stopped her. "We got the idea. Cut the sales pitch, Tattoo. Save it for when you work the family booth."

Tattoo fell silent. From her edgy looks, it was clear Tattoo felt uncomfortable when she wasn't talking. She stared at Trouble for a bit. "Nuru said you came to find your parents." She pressed her treasured thirteen-eyed dZi into Trouble's hand. "You keep this while you're here, but I want it back when you leave, OK?"

"Sure," he agreed. "It's a deal – and thanks."

She nodded. "Your mom found a Yeti cave. I want to meet a Yeti. That's why I came along. Where's the cave?" Tattoo craned her neck and swept the ridgeline with her eyes.

Nuru sighed in disgust. "Tattoo, I told you. We aren't here to find that cave." Nuru shifted his gaze to Trouble. "We're here to bring you back, Trouble. You have to wait until my dad says it's safe. We won't climb for another month."

"I can't wait that long. I have to get back to New York, so I can manage my parents' antique shop. Bleerio works hard, but his approach to people is, well, a bit crude. I've got to be there or customers don't buy anything. No sales, no money."

"So go home and come back when the weather gets better." Nuru picked up the oxygen bottle.

"I can't." Trouble fidgeted. When his parents were gone, the antique shop made only enough money for him to eat. It wasn't going to pay for another trip to the Himalayas.

Nuru frowned. "Look, you have to wait. You can't climb now."

"Says who?" Trouble felt defiant.

"Says the mountain," Nuru shot back. "You can't do it alone. See those crevasses? How are you going to cross those huge cracks in the ice?"

"Same way you did after the Yeti cured you." Trouble put a smug look on his face, but it didn't last.

Nuru became sarcastic. "Oh yeah. You gonna ride on a Yeti's back while he leaps across the giant crevasses? That's real good. Guess you better call the Yeti on your cell phone. He'll carry you. You don't need us crummy old Sherpas. We'll be going." Nuru jammed the oxygen bottle in a jacket pocket. He angrily zipped his parka. "Bye."

"I'll just have to find a way around the Ice Falls," Trouble bluffed. He knew better. Falling in the crevasse taught him it was impossible to do everything himself.

"Can't go around the Ice Falls," Nuru told him.

"Right," he mocked back.

Nuru gave Trouble a smug look. "We use aluminum ladders to bridge crevasses. You need a ton of equipment, like special sunglasses to keep from going blind in the ultraviolet rays. Best of all, the West Ridge has overhangs so you gotta have rocket-fired anchors to hold the rope. Plus lots of rope. Where you gonna get these things, huh?" He stared at Trouble with a triumphant smile.

The longer he stared, the angrier Trouble got. He wanted in the worst way to win the argument, yet he didn't have any answers. "Well, I don't know. I'm gonna try anyhow. I've got to. This is my last chance to find my mother and father."

There was a long silence, broken only by the sound of their breathing. After a while, Tattoo spoke. "The 1982 Russian expedition scaled West Ridge. They left a ton of stuff behind. We could use their equipment."

Nuru didn't believe her. "There's no discarded equipment this low. People abandon stuff when they're exhausted. The junkyard is there." His arm swept an arc up the mountain, outlining the area above Khumbu Ice Falls. "Climbers only dump equipment at base camps four and up. My dad says there's a ton of stuff all the way to camp nine, just below the crest. There's nothing down here. Anything this low was resold."

"You're wrong," Tattoo insisted.

Nuru sneered. "The Russians came here twenty years ago. The glacier eats gear, dumps it in crevasses. Their equipment's gone, history, buried under tons of ice. Nobody could find it."

"Oh, yeah," Tattoo glowered.

"Yeah," Nuru glowered back.

Tattoo moved so close to Nuru their noses touched. "You don't know everything, Nuru. The glacier vomited back the Russian stuff. Their equipment got shoved downhill by an avalanche and popped out. I know where the stuff is. I've seen the gear. I can take Trouble to it."

Nuru recoiled, backing up a step. "You never told me this. How come you know where the Russian stuff is?"

"Because I come out here on my own." Tattoo felt proud of herself.

"Why?" Trouble asked. "It's dangerous to be here alone. What were you doing on these Ice Falls by yourself?"

"Same as you," Tattoo replied, looking even prouder of herself. "Nuru told me a Yeti lived here and I wanted to find him."

"Great." Trouble got excited. "Then we're partners. Where's this Russian equipment?"

Tattoo pointed. "Over there. I'll show you."

They started walking and Nuru called after them. "It isn't safe."

"So go home and wait for us," Tattoo jabbed at him. "If you're chicken."

"I'm not chicken," Nuru told them.

"Prove it," Trouble taunted him.

"Yeah," Tattoo joined in. "You're always telling me how your dad taught you to climb. Afraid to show us, are you?"

"You guys are crazy," Nuru muttered. But he went with them, trudging over the difficult terrain. Every time he glanced at the vertical ridge in the distance, a shiver raced along Nuru's spine. The idea of trying to climb Everest's West Ridge scared him. He wasn't alone in being afraid of the area. None of the recent expeditions followed that route.

When they took a rest break, Nuru said, "You know guys, after the Russians, no mountaineering team tried a West Ridge ascent. It's too dangerous."

Trouble pulled out a notepad and flipped pages. He glanced at his notes. "I did some homework before I came here. Correct me if I'm wrong, Nuru. I believe only the 1979 Yugoslavian team did an entire ascent on the West Ridge. The 1982 Russian expedition went up Everest's Southwest Face for most of their climb. They reserved West Ridge for their final push to the summit."

Nuru and Tattoo exchanged glances of amazement. "Um, sure," Tattoo mumbled. "That's what I meant. Maybe the Yugoslavs got their equipment from the Russians. That's why there's funny writing on it, in the ceramic alphabet."

Nuru laughed.

Tattoo's cheeks flushed. "What?" she asked in an irritated voice.

"The Russian alphabet is called 'Cyrillic' not ceramic, dummy. You should listen in class instead of drawing pictures on your arms."

"OK, so I didn't know what their alphabet was called." Tattoo sulked. "It doesn't matter whose stuff it is. It's good junk and it'll get us up the ridge."

Impatient, Trouble rose to his feet and started walking across the slushy ground. Tattoo and Nuru followed him, weaving around Trouble like agitated bees. Their motives for being with Trouble were exact opposites. Tattoo felt excited to go on an adventure and Nuru was anxious to end their march, return home.

In a short distance, Tattoo halted and pointed at a shallow crevasse. Within easy reach lay a jumble of climbing equipment, from sunglasses to rocket-propelled anchors. She grinned. "See, exactly as I said. A ton of gear."

Tattoo slid in the hole and began pawing through equipment, tossing items to Nuru and Trouble. She found plastic tubs filled with metal clips and played with them like a nimble, restless monkey. Her fingers snapped clips open and shut, tumbled the pieces in her hands and clipped them into chains. "I love the hot colors – metallic red and chrome blue. These guys know how to make puzzle pieces."

Nuru groaned. "They're called carabineers, Tattoo."

"Carabineers?" she echoed, looking embarrassed.

"Climbing gear, used with ropes," Trouble explained. He grabbed a blue one with a complicated pulley arrangement and held it up. "This one's used for ascending, going upward. The little saw-teeth grip the cord so it doesn't slip."

"Yeah," Nuru agreed, sounding confident so he could be the expert. He picked up a different type of clip. "This kind is for sliding down a rope. The shape creates drag, slowing your fall. It's for when we descend, after you realize how stupid it is to climb Mount Everest by yourself." Nuru shoved the clip in Tattoo's face.

She recoiled from having a piece of gear poked at her eyes. "We aren't doing it by ourselves, Nuru. You're always the expert and you're with us. Remember?"

Trouble stifled a laugh. To break the tension, he pointed at a nylon tote. "What's in the duffle bag?"

"I dunno." Tattoo ripped open Velcro flaps and gear tumbled out on the snow. "Weird." She held up a helmet that looked like it belonged in a coal mine or a cave exploration.

Trouble took it from her. "The headlamp's to help you do camp chores at night, so you don't have to keep a flashlight in one hand. Let's you use both hands to cook and clean."

"Sure." Nuru snatched the helmet out of Trouble's hands and turned the protective gear upside down, exposing its lining. "See the felt? It's insulation, to keep you from getting frostbite. Doesn't always work." Nuru tossed the helmet away, spinning it like a Frisbee. "You can still lose your nose, lips, even an ear. Sure you want to go?"

They ignored his attitude. Trouble helped Tattoo pry open a wooden crate. "Cool," Tattoo announced, holding up an ice axe. "Now I have something to protect myself from Nuru. I just have to take off this dumb leash. It gets in the way."

"Whoa," Trouble stopped her. "That leash keeps you from losing the axe if it slips out of your grip. Put your hand through that loop and twist to wrap the leash around your wrist. There, you got it."

Tattoo made a few practice swings with the axe, giving Nuru a menacing smirk. "How come these things are so light? I thought axes were heavy."

"They aren't made for chopping wood, dummy." Nuru picked up his own weapon and held it at arms length, blade pointed at Tattoo's head. "The metal's some exotic stuff, like they use in airplanes. That's why it's light." He made his own practice swing.

Trouble pushed Nuru's arm in another direction, so the sharp point of the ice axe didn't threaten Tattoo. "Enough cave man, you guys. We gotta work together."

"Sure," Tattoo grunted, stabbing her axe in the ground and wriggling her hand out of the leash. "Help me free up some backpacks for us to use. They're stuck in the ice still."

"There's no point wasting energy on all of the packs. Choose one that looks like it fits you and we'll chip it free." Trouble jumped in the hole with Tattoo and grabbed an axe to use in carving out a pack. "Which one do you want?" he asked her.

"The yellow one. I love yellow."

"You choose by size, not color, Tattoo." Nuru shook his head in disgust.

"Well, it'll fit me."

"And a gorilla," Nuru sniped.

"The orange one's closer and easier to get out," Trouble suggested. He began chipping away at the ice.

Tattoo shrugged. "Orange is OK." She looked disappointed.

"You'll be a lot happier with orange, after an hour of climbing," Trouble assured her.

Nuru worked on freeing his own pack, a dull gray one but it had lots of pockets.

Ever curious, Tattoo soon lost interest in the excavation. She moved away from the guys and opened a cardboard shoe box, expecting it would hold crampons, the slip-on metal teeth used to add grip to a climber's boots. She grunted a sad, "Oh." Then she put the box on a ledge and paused for a moment.

"What is it?" Trouble asked, concerned about her.

"Uh, I found a journal kept by the Yugoslav climbers and some old photographs. Pictures of Ang Phu mainly. I guess we leave it here and pick up the box on the way back. Give the photos to his family. They may want them."

"Ang Phu, the Sherpa who died on the way down after making the top of Everest?" Trouble asked.

"Yeah," Tattoo confirmed, shaking her head. "Ang Phu was good, a top guide. Some called him another Tenzing Norgay, the Sherpa who went with Sir Edmund Hillary on the first successful ascent. West Ridge climbs are tough. Seven deaths on that team. Only five made the top. One of those was Ang Phu and he fell on the way down, died. It's why people don't try West Ridge anymore."

Trouble sighed. "That's probably why Yetis live on the West Ridge. People have a hard time getting up there."

"Great," Nuru muttered. "This is crazy. How are the three of us going to succeed where a team of ninety people almost failed to reach the crest?"

"Because," Trouble explained, "we aren't going for the crest. We're stopping much lower."

"In the Himalayas," Nuru reminded him, "you start where other people finish. The highest peaks in Europe and America are lower than where we are now – and we've got to climb another two thousand feet before we look for this cave."

They glared at Nuru.

"OK, I'm grabbing a ladder," he said. It's all right, he told himself. He just had to wait. They were sure to quit. Nuru would be home before nightfall, eating a warm meal, watching his favorite DVD. Wouldn't he?

6

Tattoo held a ladder straight up and pulled a cord, extending the ladder's reach, high as the roof of a two story building. She dropped the aluminum ladder over a wide crevasse and the metal clanged against rock-hard ice, forming a bridge across a deep chasm. Underneath the extension ladder lay a bottomless hole, its glassy sides twinkling in sunlight. Sapphire blue ice made the hollow look like a giant Christmas ornament. Lovely as it seemed, this pit could be a death trap, where you fell and kept falling – until you hit bottom and felt nothing ever again.

Tattoo eyed Nuru to see if he still wanted to play the role of expert climber after gazing into that crevasse, knowing they had to walk across a slick, wobbly ladder.

Nuru tried to look confident, but there was a catch in his voice when he talked. "I'll go first, show you how it's done." He handed a braided nylon rope to each of them. "You wrap the cord around your waist. The other end is attached to me."

"These are safety lines, right?" Trouble confirmed.

"Yeah. The ropes are in case I fall. You limit my drop." Nuru rolled his shoulders to release tension.

"It won't be easy pulling you out of that hole." Tattoo pointed at the chasm.

Feeling nervous, Nuru played with the slack in the ropes, jiggling the braided cords in his mittens for reassurance. "You don't have to lift me. I'll climb out using my ice axe and the metal teeth strapped on my boots. You got it?"

Trouble looked at iron spikes clamped on Nuru's shoes. The thick needles were shaped like alligator teeth, pointy and sharp. Cold frost was turning to ice on the nasty looking grippers, known as crampons. "Those metal spikes make it slick walking the ladder. Wouldn't you be better off without them?"

"A bit safer," Nuru admitted. "But what happens if I fall? I'm stuck in a pit with icy sides and no traction. It's hard to climb out unless you can push against the wall with your legs."

"All right," Trouble agreed. But he was still worried his friend would tumble into the hole.

Nuru shouldered his long backpack, almost as tall as the Sherpa and loaded with heavy equipment.

"Hey, maybe you should try crossing without that pack," Tattoo suggested. "The backpack makes you top-heavy. It's hard to keep your balance."

"I have to bring the pack across sometime. I might as well do it now." Nuru swaggered to the ladder. Then his courage evaporated. Nuru stalled by fidgeting with his ice axe and adjusting his trousers.

Trouble checked to make sure the rope felt tight around him and dug his feet into the snow. When he glanced at Nuru, he had a foot on the first ladder rung. The aluminum creaked from his weight and sank deeper in the snow. The shifting ladder unbalanced Nuru and he teetered for a moment, then caught his balance.

In careful movements, Nuru stepped over the chasm. He made it to the other side and shot his fists in the air. Triumphant, Nuru turned around, a beaming smile on his face. He bragged, "Come on. It's easy."

Tattoo managed to walk the ladder without a mistake, carefully placing each step of her green snow boots on the slick aluminum rungs. Nuru and Trouble held ropes across the gorge like handrails, steadying

Tattoo, helping her stay balanced. The first and last person crossing were most at risk.

When Trouble finished, they lifted the ladder and moved to the next bottomless hole in the ice. So it went, right to the final crevasse. There, Nuru and Trouble got across and waited for Tattoo to join them. She'd almost reached their side when Nuru made a mistake, teasing her. "Bet you're scared, huh?"

"Nah." Tattoo held out her arms and bragged. "Nothing to it."

At that moment, her foot slipped and she tumbled forward, falling hard on the ladder. Frozen aluminum rang like a gong from Tattoo's impact. The extension ladder dug into the snow, making gouges. The ladder slanted, angling Tattoo downward. Something fell from her pocket.

"My Nintendo!" she yelped. Tattoo shot out an arm, trying to snare the falling toy.

"No," Trouble shouted, but it was too late.

The ladder twisted. Then it flipped upside-down. Tattoo was hanging from one rung, her legs kicking at empty air.

Nuru yelled advice. "Swing a leg up and hook it over the ladder. Do it now, before your hands get tired."

Tattoo didn't listen. She became rigid with tension and couldn't hear the advice screamed at her.

"I'm going out there to help her," Trouble insisted.

Nuru shook his head. "I can't hold a safety line for both of you."

"I'll go without a safety line. Tattoo can't hang on for long."

"Fall and you both die. You shouldn't go out there," Nuru warned.

"I've got to. She can't make it without help." Trouble shed his backpack. He lay down on the ladder and slid toward the dangling Tattoo, feeling cold metal eat through the parka's warmth. He paused to catch his breath and the ladder welded to his jacket in a frozen streak. He had to tear himself loose to edge forward, ripping the jacket's nylon skin from the ladder, making a sound like pulling a Velcro strip.

"Be careful," Nuru shouted.

"No kidding," Trouble grumbled in sarcasm. Inch by inch, he moved over Tattoo, keeping his eyes on her face. She was holding tight, fixated on the dark pit underneath her body. He tried to get her attention. "Tattoo, I'm here. Look at me."

She acted too worried to recognize his voice. Trouble reached down and tugged on her grape trekking cap. "Give me your foot," he instructed her. "Swing your leg up and I'll grab your boot."

"Why?" Tattoo wondered.

"I'll hook your foot over the ladder, so your hands don't have to carry all your weight."

"What good will that do?" Tattoo complained.

Trouble explained, "Then you can crawl to the other side. You'll be upside-down, but you'll make it."

"I'll try," she agreed.

"Swing your leg," Trouble urged her.

"It hurts to swing. My hands feel so much pressure. I'm afraid I'll let go." Tattoo made an attempt to bring her legs up and couldn't get her feet higher than her waist.

Trouble's arms couldn't quite reach her legs. He stretched his body, daring to bend over the ladder's edge. He felt the metal structure twisting under him, threatening to dump him into the chasm. Every movement, however slight, resulted in audible creaking and groaning, the ladder protesting any shift in his weight. "Bring your knees up. I'll grab your pants and do the rest."

Tattoo brought her knees up and they were still too low.

"Higher."

He heard a grunt below him and Trouble's fingers closed on Tattoo's nylon pants. He grabbed the turquoise fabric and, brittle from the cold, it made a sound like dry cereal being crunched. "Now bring your feet up." He waited a long, terrible moment before she obeyed. Finally, Trouble had one of her ankles curled around the ladder. Then he got the other boot up, its bottom crusted with snow. Trouble's gloves snagged in the teeth of her crampons and he wriggled his fingers loose. He took a jackknife from his coat pocket and opened the blade.

"What are you doing?" Tattoo asked in a worried voice.

"I'm going to cut your pack straps. Without the heavy backpack, it's a lot easier for you."

"No." Tattoo shook her head. "My pack has the rockets. We can't get up the ridge without them. You cut off my pack and all this was for nothing."

"Tattoo, you're more important than this climb. I'm cutting your pack loose." Trouble was firm.

"No." She brushed away his arm, knocking the knife from his hand. The blade spiraled down the ice canyon, clattering against its sides. "See? I can hang with one hand. I'm slipping this pack off and handing it to you."

"OK." Trouble agreed with reluctance. He undid the belt strap going around Tattoo's waist. She carefully removed an arm and handed the strap to him.

Trouble grabbed her pack and its weight unbalanced the aluminum ladder. The extension ladder wobbled, threatening to flip again, leaving him dangling on the bottom. He slid his legs over the side, balancing himself like a tightrope walker. The ladder stabilized and Trouble wormed backwards to firm ground, holding the backpack.

Without her pack, Tattoo followed with surprising ease. "There," she announced, kneeling on the ledge. "We make a good team."

"Oh, absolutely," Nuru deadpanned. "There's just one thing, though."

"What's that?" Tattoo asked, seeming unfazed by her brush with death.

"This is the easy part." Nuru pointed at the steep cliff. "That is the hard part."

"Yeah, well. What we just did was pretty hard, Nuru." Tattoo glared at him.

He ignored her stare and coiled some rope. "Suit yourself." He shrugged, trying to look casual. "You realize we've no guarantee of finding the cave. We could do all that climbing for nothing."

Tattoo stomped her foot in anger. "You told me and a lot of kids that a Yeti took you to his cave. You said it was up there." Tattoo jabbed a finger at the West Ridge. "You bragged about knowing where the cave was. You saying it was a lie, after we've come all this way?"

Nuru talked with amazing calm. "I wasn't lying, Tattoo. Give me a break. It's been a lot of years since I was there. I was just a little kid. Things will look different now. The mountain shifts. Pieces of the ridge fall off, like the avalanche we saw today."

Tattoo wasn't satisfied. Nuru's backpack was lying on the ground and she gave the pack a fierce kick.

Nuru shoved Tattoo away from the pack and they squared off, like they were going to punch each other.

Trouble spoke in a calming voice. "It's OK. You don't have to worry. I can find the cave. I have a compass."

Nuru snorted. He kept his glaring eyes on Tattoo. "Compasses are worthless here, Trouble. They get jerked around by Everest's magnetic field. Put your compass away. It's useless."

"Not this compass. It doesn't point North. It only points at the spot where a Yeti was born, inside that cave." Trouble held out an ancient stone, a beautiful cobalt blue egg made of rare lapis lazuli. Gold inlays decorated the egg, writings in the Yeti language that were supposed to give the stone mystical powers. Around the egg's equator, a pattern of rare gems formed a wreath of edelweiss, star-shaped alpine flowers. The stone felt heavy in his hand, like a can of cola.

Tattoo stared at the egg like she was hypnotized. "Wow. That's even better than my dZi beads. Where'd you get it?"

"My mom included this egg with her letter. She said it's a Yeti compass. Instead of pointing North, it points to their home, the place where they were born. Watch." Trouble held the birth egg in the palm of his hand. The stone twisted, pointing at a spot on the West Ridge. No matter where he moved, the blue egg always pointed at the same place, a cleft in the rocks high above them. Trouble zipped the precious stone in his parka. "Do you want to see a Yeti or not?"

"Sure," Tattoo agreed in amazement.

Nuru looked disgusted, but he couldn't back out. "OK, grab your gear. Let's go," he announced without enthusiasm.

7

Trouble, Nuru and Tattoo climbed for several hours. They found no trail leading from the glacier's edge, no steps carved in the mountain. The trio were forced to do a vertical ascent on the cliff face, hauling themselves up, crag to crag. Hundreds of pin-shaped rocks lay below, like a bed of nails. The wind-sharpened spikes waited to pierce them like swords if they fell. Above, a steel-gray cliff rose out of sight, dwarfing their bodies, shrinking the trio to ants crawling up a refrigerator. The hard work of climbing wore them out, and a lot more effort remained before reaching their goal. Exhausted, they paused on a narrow ledge, panting. The dry, icy air turned their breath to chimney smoke. They sat in silence, resting weary backs against the cold mountain, dangling their legs off the rocky shelf.

Tattoo put her head down like she might throw up. "I feel sick."

"We all do," Nuru sighed. "Our bodies are low on water. We're dehydrated. On Mount Everest, you exhale a gallon of water a day just resting. You lose even more when you climb."

Trouble scraped his glove across the cliff and wadded loose snow into a lump. He handed the white tennis ball to Tattoo. "Try putting this in your mouth. Maybe the moisture will settle your stomach."

Nuru shook his head. "She hasn't drunk water for hours. It'd take two buckets of snow to fill her up. She has to eat ice." Nuru broke off an icicle.

Trouble cautioned him, "No, don't do that. An icicle here isn't like a popsicle in the freezer. It's much colder on Everest than inside a refrigerator. Icicles this cold weld to your tongue. Pulling away the ice tears off skin. It really hurts."

"Oh, thanks." Tattoo dropped the icicle.

Nuru volunteered, "I'll drag my pack up here. We'll melt the icicles. I've got a hiking stove inside, from that junk pile Tattoo found."

"Junk pile," Tattoo grumbled. "We wouldn't be this high if I hadn't found the climbing gear."

Nuru teased her. "Oh, you're to blame for us being here, huh?"

Tattoo was in no mood for a joke. She pushed Nuru hard, shoving him closer to the shelf's edge. Nuru raised a fist to retaliate.

Trouble hurried to stop them. "No rough stuff. It's too dangerous. Help me drag the packs up with that energy. Huh?"

"Yeah, all right," Nuru sulked. He shot Tattoo an angry glare.

"I thought you were friends," Trouble said.

"We are," Tattoo laughed. "But he gets on my nerves."

"Sure. How about helping me?" Trouble grunted, heaving on a thick yellow rope. His backpack was dangling a hundred feet below. It was too dangerous to wear backpacks while climbing.

Once their gear got to the ledge, they filled a pot with icicles and assembled the lightweight stove. Wearing gloves made it a clumsy project, piecing together a small metal frame and insert a butane cylinder. The hiking stove's thin blue flame had a sulfurous odor that added to their queasiness. The weak burner was too anemic for quick progress, taking forever to heat water.

Thirsty and restless, they held gloved hands under their arms or rubbed frozen noses, trying to ignore cold shadows sliding over them. Their butts felt frozen, the arctic ground sucking away warmth through layers of thermal underwear and Gortex pants. They tried to ignore the deep chill and stare at brittle chunks in the tin pot, willing the clear ice to melt. Their combined psychic power had even less effect than a tiny butane flame. Finally, the ice dissolved in a tantalizing puddle. Nuru added a packet of energy boost and filled three dented cups with liquid. The brew had a strange coloring from the energy boost powder. They drank it just the same, despite a salty lemonade taste.

Tattoo gulped her cup and wanted more. "Good. But not enough."

"OK. We'll melt another pot." Nuru dumped icicles in the pan and ignited the flame. An hour later, they cooled the stove by pushing it in snow, then broke down the apparatus and jammed it in a crowded backpack.

Tattoo edged around them to scout the climb. It was her turn to lead. She craned her neck, looking for the best place to resume their ascent. Tattoo frowned. "We're stuck under an overhang like the eave of a roof. We can't climb higher unless we do a human fly trick, crawl upside-down on the ceiling."

Trouble looked at Tattoo. "How do we become human flies?"

"Rocket-fired anchors are used on overhangs like this. We fire at the underside of the rock. Assuming the anchor holds, we pull ourselves up."

"Great, we've got a solution." He looked in Tattoo's pack for rockets, opening the main compartment, tightly packed with metal cylinders, red safety tags dangling from their tips.

"Using rocket-fired anchors isn't that easy," Nuru muttered. He didn't look happy. "This is the worst part of the climb."

"Why?" Trouble asked, pulling out a missile.

"You'll see." Tattoo sighed, taking the rocket from Trouble. She moved to one end of their ledge and took aim with the rocket, bracing herself against a boulder. She triggered the device and they heard a loud pop, like a rifle crack. A dart shot forward, trailing thin wire behind. A muffled thud indicated the dart hit the overhanging ledge. On impact, the projectile spread barbed prongs inside the rock, giving it holding power. A wire dangled from the dart back to Tattoo's launcher.

"That light wire will hold us?" Trouble felt skeptical.

"No," Nuru answered. "It's only leader string, for feeding a rope. Tattoo pulls on the leader wire and it tugs a rope upward. The cord goes through a pulley on the anchor and the rope follows. With luck, the rope goes through without sticking."

Tattoo flattened herself against the ledge. "Avalanche – look out."

A basketball-size rock shot past her with the ripping sound of a chain saw. The rocket-propelled anchor was pinned in the stone basketball. White leader wire trailed like spaghetti behind the falling rock. The leader wire ripped the launcher from Tattoo's hands with a terrific jerk, burning a scar across her gloves. The launcher followed the stone, bouncing off the mountain in giant leaps, gathering speed. Ice and snow stuck to the falling boulder, growing it to the size of a car. They heard a loud crash when the rock hit bottom, gouging an impact crater like a meteor hitting earth.

"That," Nuru commented, "is the first problem with these rocket-propelled anchors."

"And the second?" Trouble asked.

"The other problem," Nuru answered, "is worse. The only way to check if a dart holds is trying it. And if the dart doesn't hold, you follow that boulder."

Tattoo stared at the impact crater a thousand feet below, a cone like the hollow top of a volcano.

"Not reassuring, is it?" Trouble hoped an ironic joke would take away the tension.

"No, it isn't." Tattoo looked stressed.

"Anything else I should know before we get started?" Trouble asked.

"Yeah," Tattoo laughed. "I hate hanging upside-down." In a few minutes, she did exactly that, dangling upside-down on a cliff outcropping. Tattoo was giving their first successful rocket-fired anchor a real test, letting it hold her full weight.

Nuru and Trouble held safety lines clipped to Tattoo's harness. The safety lines wouldn't do her much good if an anchor pulled loose. Tattoo would fall and hit the mountain so hard she was certain to be injured, if not killed.

The leader on each new overhang took a grave risk, so they rotated going first, testing the anchor. Trouble led on the next one, then Nuru. Finally it was Tattoo's turn again.

"How many more of these things?" Tattoo sounded irritated. None of them liked hanging upside-down from a little clamp.

"This should be the last one." Nuru pulled on the anchor's white cord, feeding rope through a pulley high above them.

Trouble was hauling their backpacks to the ledge where they were standing. "I'll lead again," he volunteered.

Tattoo shook her head. "No, me. I should go."

"We could flip coins for it. Odd person out." Trouble pulled three pennies from his coat. They juggled a coin in their hands and held out their fists. He counted, "One, two, three. Open."

Tattoo's coin showed tails and theirs came up heads. She was still the leader. She laughed, but they saw fear in her eyes.

Nuru gave the rope a vicious tug, then yanked again. The anchor held and Tattoo started up the cliff. The safe part of her climb passed all too quickly. In a moment, she reached the critical point, dangling upside-down from the rocket-fired anchor, blood rushing to her head, making her giddy and disoriented. Tattoo grunted as she drove a metal piton into the overhang with her ice axe, basically hammering a giant nail into a granite wall. A second later, she clamped her rope through that piton and heaved a sigh of relief. "I'm safe. You're up, Nuru," she challenged him.

Nuru sighed and tried to look brave. He followed and soon his body dangled in air, hung from the anchor. Like Tattoo, he clipped his rope through the piton above and felt much better. In his moment of relief, Nuru failed to notice rock fragments sifting down his parka. The rocket-fired anchor wobbled when Nuru left the metal clamp, moving to the ledge above. "OK, Trouble," he called out.

"Going." Trouble moved up the cliff face, thinking the anchor remained in sound condition. Above him, Nuru and Tattoo braced themselves and kept the slack in his safety lines to a minimum. He let go of the last handhold and dangled from the underside of the cliff, held by the rocket-propelled anchor.

Tugged by his weight, the anchor pulled loose a half inch, then caught again. He felt a momentary jerk and Trouble thought his grip had slipped on the icy rock. He inched forward, pulling himself toward the piton, the metal clamp that meant true safety for him. He was almost there when the rocket-fired anchor gave way, tearing out of the rock with a fierce ripping sound.

At first, he only felt the sting of gravel hitting his face. Then he fell. The ledge that seemed so close now vanished. His mind couldn't grasp what was really happening. It had to be a nightmare. He'd wake up in his bed, sweating but all right. Yet safety ropes clamped to his waist smoked from burning through his harness loops.

Above him, Nuru and Tattoo braced themselves for the moment when the slack played out and Trouble's weight snapped the ropes tight. Nothing could have prepared them for how it really felt. The jerk felt so violent and the pull so extreme that both of them were ripped from their footholds. They slid toward the precipice. Their boots scrambled to catch on solid rock, but every foothold crumbled under the force dragging them downward. A spray of rubble flew over the edge and fell toward Trouble.

His luck held. The volley of rocks shot past without harming him, like a blast of shotgun pellets missing a bird. Falling and twisting, the world swirled around Trouble in a dizzying pattern. One moment the cliff face raced past him and the next he saw nothing but clouds and sky.

Suddenly, he jerked to a halt. The quick stop bent him backward like a bow pulled taut to launch an arrow. He thought his spine was going to break from the pressure on his body.

None of them knew how it happened, but somehow Nuru's feet lodged behind a small boulder and stayed there. He grinned a silly smile but it vanished as he watched Tattoo fall over the edge of the precipice, dragged by Trouble's safety line. Nuru knew he couldn't hold both of them. He'd have to release their ropes to save his own life, letting them die. His fingers touched the release lever when the cord twanged. The blow knocked his hand away and almost yanked Nuru from his perch. He strained to get his fingers back on the release lever. Though sweat clouded his vision, Nuru thought he saw a hand wagging just beyond his boots.

"I snagged the piton," Tattoo gasped. "I'm OK. Just resting a second."

Nuru pushed the release lever back and slid the safety catch in place. "Can you see Trouble? Is he all right?"

Tattoo looked down. "Yeah, I think so. He didn't hit anything. He's swinging around like crazy."

"Then get your lazy butt up here," Nuru laughed. "I need your help."

"Yeah, like I'm dangling here for fun, on vacation. Well, in spite of your personality, Nuru, I'll help you."

"Now would be a good time." There was no response to Nuru's latest sarcasm, but gloved hands appeared on the rim, followed by Tattoo's purple hat. A minute later, Trouble felt a tug on his rope, pulling him upward.

8

Nuru moaned. "This was a mistake. We should never have climbed." He kicked a rock over the ledge and the pebble skipped down the cliff, making chipping sounds. "We can't go on. It's too dangerous. There's only an hour of daylight left. We've got to climb down while it's light. At the bottom, we wait for the moon to rise. Then we cross the glacier. We won't need our backpacks, so it'll be safe on the ladder, walking over crevasses. It's a good plan, right, Tattoo?" Nuru stared at his friend.

Tattoo had her eyes closed and was sucking air from an oxygen bottle. She lifted the oxygen mask off her face and laid her head against the rocks. "I dunno," she mumbled. "We came all this way. Now we're givin' up. It doesn't make sense."

Nuru acted disgusted. "I'll be grounded for months if I don't get home before dark. So will you, Tattoo. No movies. No Cybercafé. Nothing but homework. You want that?"

"Maybe it's worth it, if we see a Yeti."

Nuru kicked another pebble off the ledge. "Dad will go searching for me, soon as it gets dark. He'll find I wasn't in school today. Trouble's gone and so are we. He's not stupid. He'll know we tried climbing the West Ridge. At dawn, everyone in the village will be looking for us. They'll be so mad, they'll kill us. We gotta get home."

Tattoo looked at Trouble. "What do you think?"

"You should head home, like Nuru said. Maybe use one of the tents we found and spend the night at the glacier's edge. It's risky walking a ladder in the dark, even by moonlight." Trouble tried to stand and found getting up was hard work. His leg muscles felt stiff from climbing. He bent over and began reeling his backpack upward. The heavy pack sat on a ledge below them, a vivid blue lump parked on a snow field.

"What are you doing?" Nuru demanded.

"I'm going on. I don't blame you guys for …" He almost said "quitting," but caught himself. "… for returning home. Makes sense."

"Then why are you going on?" Nuru was shocked.

Trouble shrugged. "It's different for me. This might be my last chance to find my parents. It's only a few minutes to the Yeti cave."

"Don't you realize what happens on Everest after dark? Nighttime temperatures can kill you. We're lucky there's no wind chill yet." Nuru looked at a plastic thermometer clipped to his parka. "It's below freezing now. You can't last overnight without shelter."

Tattoo glanced at Nuru. "We should go with him, make sure he gets to the cave. Trouble can spend the night inside the cavern, where it's warmer."

"I don't know," Nuru hesitated. "A few minutes delay could leave us stranded on a ledge, exposed. Frostbite is no joke. You can loose fingers, even your nose."

"OK, then. You start down and I'll catch up with you." Tattoo put her boot in a foothold and climbed after Trouble.

"This is stupid," Nuru mumbled. He followed Tattoo anyway, anxious because it was so late in the day. Every time he paused, Nuru checked the sun's progress toward the horizon. The brilliant orb seemed to accelerate, racing toward the world's edge. Orange fingers spread across clouds, creating an illusion the sky was melting, yet the air became colder each moment. Nuru felt his muscles become rigid, like he was meat in a freezer turning into a stiff block. Dryness pierced his nose and throat with sharp needles, making it difficult to breathe.

Each cleft in the rock face, every boulder, forced exertion from tired muscles and demanded lungs swallow thin air, screaming for more oxygen. Nuru poked his head over the final obstacle and gasped, "Do you see the cave?"

"No," Trouble answered in a sad voice.

Nuru grabbed Trouble's elbow. "Come on. Let's go home. Be reasonable. You've had your look. There's nothing here."

Trouble yanked his arm free. "Let me think."

Tattoo unclipped her safety rope and walked to them. They were standing in a hollow, a deep "V" made by a giant boulder splitting in half. "Maybe a landslide buried the cave entrance," Tattoo offered.

"It's possible," Trouble agreed.

Nuru sulked. "So there's no way to enter the cave. We should go home."

"Go ahead, if you want." Trouble walked around the cleft, touching the blue stone in his pocket. "I'm convinced there's a Yeti dwelling here. We just can't see it."

Nuru was impatient. "It's getting dark. Let's go."

Trouble shook his head. “I know there’s a cave here. That blue stone is supposed to jiggle when it’s near a Yeti home. The rock is jumping with excitement. It’s practically leaping out of my pocket. The stone gets more excited at the back of the ridge.” He walked over and peered down.

Nuru warned him. “That’s the China side of Everest. It’s dangerous. I told you about it in the Cybercafé. The Chinese shoot at people if they see them up here without a permit.”

Trouble ignored the cautions. “I can’t see anything. It’s too dark. Why don’t you guys hold my ankles and I’ll lean over. Maybe the cave opening is under this ledge.”

“This is the last thing we do, Trouble. Then we leave. You agree?” Nuru insisted.

Trouble agreed with reluctance. “Yeah. We go home if I don’t see the cave.”

Tattoo and Nuru held his ankles and Trouble wormed over the cliff edge. He felt blood rushing to his head. Their tight grip on his legs hurt, pinching his ankles like wearing snowboarding boots that were too small.

“You see anything?” Tattoo asked.

"The cliff is smashed-in, like a wrecked car. It's real dark. I need a flashlight. Pull me up, will you?"

He got no response.

"Hey guys, pull me up. Will you please?" Trouble waited. Nothing happened, except their grip tightened on his ankles.

"Ouch. You're hurting me. Pull me up." They still didn't respond. "What's going on?"

There was a slight pause before Nuru answered. "We got trouble."

"Yeah, I'm here. Now pull me up." He thought Nuru meant his name when he said "trouble."

"No," Nuru corrected him. "We don't have your kind of trouble. We have big problems."

"Like what?"

"Cats," was Tattoo's hissed reply. "We got a cat."

Blood pounded in Trouble's head from hanging upside-down. He shouted, "You need oxygen. You're getting delirious from the thin air up here."

"No, she isn't," Nuru whispered. "There is a cat. We have to keep very still. We can't help you. You're going to have to push yourself up, Trouble."

"How am I supposed to do that?" He felt irritated by their lack of help.

"I don't know. Just do it fast." Nuru sounded disturbed, more upset than Trouble had ever heard him.

He was hanging by his ankles over a sheer cliff. Lifting his body felt like doing an upside-down push-up. The exertion left him panting. By the time he got on the ledge, his eyesight was blurry and sweat dripped off his forehead, making it hard to see. But in that pure, clear air, Trouble smelled a pungent odor of feline scent glands and damp fur, as though he stood in the Bronx Zoo, peering in the lion cage.

When his vision returned, Trouble was looking into a pair of greedy yellow eyes. Below the hungry eyes, saliva dripped off sharp fangs as a huge cat stared at tonight's meal. It seemed to be wondering which of them would taste best.

"Snow leopard," Nuru whispered. "They're fast and cunning. Snow leopards hunt in a pack, as a family. One male, many females. They've never been seen this high. I have no idea how a leopard got up here."

Trouble offered an explanation. "My father once told me snow leopards are Yeti watchdogs, their burglar alarm. The Yetis found some way to tame the cats, as a way of protecting themselves from people. It means we're close to the Yeti cave. The snow leopard must live there."

"It isn't alone. There must be more leopards in the cave," Nuru pointed out. "Remember, they hunt as a family. I heard they like meat fresh and bloody, so they kill people slowly, ripping off their limbs. The screams carry for miles. It happened in our village. An old man went alone to visit his grandchildren. The snow leopards had nothing to eat for months, so they lost their fear of people."

Trouble bent down, groping for his ice axe. He moved in slow motion, keeping his eyes on the leopard. His gloved fingers had difficulty feeling the weapon. He risked a quick glance to find the ice axe and snatched its orange handle. When his eyes went back to the leopard, the cat had inched closer. "It has such a long, furry tail. I've never seen a leopard in a zoo with a tail that long and thick."

Nuru explained, "They use their tail like a blanket, wrap it around themselves at night. It's also a weapon. Snow leopards club you with their tail. They try to break your legs so you can't escape."

"Oh, great," Tattoo moaned.

The cat sniffed the air, twitching its nostrils, confused by the smells it inhaled. The cat fixed its yellow eyes on Trouble. The leopard's stare drilled into him, showing a mixture of resentment and fear.

"Trouble, I think it smells that Yeti stone," Tattoo suggested. "Maybe your pebble will keep the leopard from attacking you, like a dZi bead."

"What about us?" Nuru complained.

"Maybe the rock will protect all of us," Trouble offered. He reached in his pocket and removed the blue stone. He unwrapped it from a soft gray cloth and held the polished gem so the leopard could see the pebble.

The animal cocked its head, puzzled by the presence of a Yeti artifact. The snow leopard paced in a tight circle, keeping its stare on the beautiful stone. Hesitating, the cat lay on the ground, looking confused.

Tattoo exhaled in relief. "That was close."

"It's still close." Nuru whispered, afraid of the leopard. "The cat is blocking our path off the mountain. Look at the sun." He pointed at long shadows jutting from every peak. The shadows seemed like dark fingers pulling the blanket of night toward them. He shrugged. "All we can do is wait and hope the cat leaves – soon."

9

Icy wind flowed through the hollow where Trouble, Nuru and Tattoo stood, adding chill to an already cold twilight. The gusting wind blew ice off the mountain, stinging their eyes and skin with frozen slivers. Their eyelashes and caps became frosted with ice crystals, numbing their scalps and faces. Trapped by the snow leopard, there was no way to escape the bitter wind and they were all freezing, including the cat.

Yet the snow leopard didn't leave. The cat wrapped its furry tail around itself for warmth. The sleek carnivore sank to the ground, but kept its body poised to leap in an instant. Ice covered the leopard and its white-on-black markings blended into the snow-covered rock. With that camouflage, the cat vanished like a ghost, except for the yellow eyes, their surreal intensity painted on a blank canvas of white snow. Seldom blinking, the cat never took its piercing gaze off Trouble, Nuru and Tattoo. There seemed to be a frightening amount of intelligence behind those golden eyes, isolated globes of color in an albino snowscape.

Tattoo broke the silence. "It's got to sleep, right?"

Nuru was scornful. "You going to walk around the leopard after it goes to sleep?"

"No," Tattoo admitted. "I'd just feel safer if it was asleep. I don't like the way it looks at us."

Trouble spoke. "The cat's guarded us for an hour. The leopard isn't going away and we're freezing to death. We should try for shelter before it gets darker."

"I'm game," Tattoo agreed, shivering. "I can't stay out here much longer."

Nuru doubted there was a solution to their problems. "What are you proposing?"

Trouble suggested, "We'll try the cliff behind us. Maybe we'll find shelter over the side."

Nuru risked a glance over his shoulder. "How're we going to get down there? It's already dark on that side of the mountain. We can't climb down, even if that leopard would let us."

"Ropes. I'm going to kneel and drive three pitons in the ground. Then we slide down the ropes."

Nuru sneered. "And that cat will wait around for you to do that?"

"I don't know what it will do," Trouble allowed. "Do you see another option, something else we can try?"

"No," Nuru admitted. He paused, thinking it over. "OK, get on with it."

Trouble knelt down, giving the snow leopard a wary glance He placed a metal spike on the rock and hit the piton a gentle blow with his ice axe. Even that soft blow rang like a bell. The snow leopard tensed, lifting its head.

He dared another hammer blow and the sleek carnivore sprang to its feet. Trouble struck the piton again and again. The cat growled, complaining about the noise. Fortunately, it didn't attack.

Trouble grabbed another spike from the bag clipped to his pants leg and drove the last piton home with ringing blows. The cat gave a series of yelps and bared its fangs, a pair of dirty ivory slices contrasting against the crystalline snow. The carnivore hissed and spat in displeasure, contorting its face to an ugly mask of snarling flesh.

"Hurry," Tattoo urged.

"There," Trouble announced. "I've got three pitons anchored in the rock."

Nuru tossed coils of rope at Trouble, landing at his feet in puff clouds.

He clipped ropes to pitons and tossed the stiff coils over the cliff, letting them unfurl down the mountainside with loud slapping noises. "You both know how to rappel?"

"Yeah," Nuru answered. "You wrap a rope around your back, so the friction slows your fall. Then you jump off the cliff."

Trouble felt concerned about their safety. "The cat hesitates to attack me 'cause I'm carrying the Yeti stone. You go first and I'll follow."

Nuru and Tattoo wrapped a rope around themselves. Trouble stayed in front, trying to act as their shield. It didn't work. The cat became aggressive, determined to prevent them from leaving. The carnivore slinked toward them with a dancer's balance, stopping right in front of Trouble. The snow leopard's growling sounded like a chain saw ripping limbs off a tree. Nuru and Tattoo remained frozen to the spot, hypnotized by the cat's menacing eyes.

"Get going. You can't wait any longer," Trouble urged them.

The leopard sank on its haunches, coiled for an attack.

Trouble shouted, "We'll go together, on the count of three. One –" He didn't get any farther in his count. The leopard sprang and they had to jump off the cliff, falling into thin air.

They looked up and saw a pair of furious yellow eyes above them, getting smaller and smaller as they fell. The trio sank blindly in the dark, unable to see even their hands clutching the rope. They expected to smash against rocks any moment. Their hearts pounded from anxiety and it felt like their veins would explode. The whole world became just one thing – falling, falling and more falling.

10

The trio dropped in free-fall until their ropes snapped tight. The violent jerking pulled the ropes off their hips and they slid down the braided cords, their gloves smoking from friction. Heat melted the gloves and burned their hands. In the dark, they couldn't see where they were going. They could feel themselves swinging outward, arcing away from the solid rock. At one point, their swing halted and they were dangling in space. Each of them was a pendulum frozen at the end of its arc, motionless for a brief second. Then gravity swept them toward the cliff. Wind rushed at their faces and they collided with the mountain in a torrent of grunts and thuds. It felt painful, yet hitting the stone ledge stopped their fall and saved their lives.

The shock of his collision with the mountain wore off. Trouble checked the condition of his friends. "You OK? Did you break anything?"

"My leg hurts, but I don't think it's broken." Tattoo sounded dazed.

Nuru moaned. "I twisted my ankle when I landed. There's no way to know how bad it is. I don't dare stand up. I might fall off the ledge."

Trouble attempted to comfort Nuru. "Once the moon rises, we'll be able to see. Try extending your leg out straight. See how that feels."

Nuru straightened his leg, making a scuffling noise. "Yeah, that feels better. You have any idea where we are?"

Trouble shook his head. "No. I couldn't see anything in the dark. We fell for a long time. I guess we passed the Yeti cave and didn't see it."

Nuru felt depressed. "Great. We dropped into China. Nobody will look for us here. Without a visa, Sherpas won't go on the Chinese side of Everest. They're afraid of being shot. We have no food. We can't move around to stay warm. It's a race. Do we freeze or starve?"

"We can climb by moonlight, using the ropes," Trouble insisted.

Nuru wasn't convinced. "And face that snow leopard?"

They heard scratching above them, followed by a gnawing sound.

Tattoo offered an explanation for the noise. "Maybe the snow leopard's eating. I read that lions sleep after they eat. Snow leopards might do the same. It's possible we could sneak past the cat when it falls asleep."

Trouble listened to the gnawing sound again. "I wonder what the leopard is eating? That cat might be chewing on our ropes."

Trouble discovered his guess was right. A hundred-foot length of braided nylon slapped Tattoo on the head, whipping her shoulders and arms. "Ouch," she yelped. For a moment, she felt angry enough to fight the leopard.

Like Tattoo and Nuru, Trouble fought to get free from the rope coil, tangled around him like an octopus. He threw off a twisted mess of nylon cord and peered into the darkness.

The leopard's yellow eyes stared back, shining like glass marbles. The cat was thinking, deciding what to do next.

"I've got a bad feeling about this," Trouble warned them. The gnawing sound resumed. "We'd better get out of the way."

They pressed themselves against the mountain, flattening their bodies against the cliff, but found no protection on the exposed ledge. The cat chewed through Nuru's line and the heavy cord fell. The wet rope slapped them, stinging their tired bodies.

Tattoo raged at the cat. "I'd like to whip you with this rope."

"That," Nuru observed, "isn't a bad idea. Maybe we have some defense against the leopard after all." He took out a pocketknife and cut a length of nylon to use as a whip, like an old-fashioned lion-tamer. He finished in seconds and pressed his body against the icy slope, hoping to avoid the sting of the last rope when it fell.

But Trouble's cord wasn't cut. It hung there, a straight line running up the mountain. The nylon braid tantalized them, promising a way back to their equipment and safety. "Why didn't the leopard chew through my rope?" he wondered.

Tattoo offered an explanation. "It's confused by something. I don't know why."

Cautiously, Trouble moved forward and looked for the cat. The feline was there, staring at him in hatred. The leopard's twin, glowing marbles formed the only lights in that icy darkness.

"I wouldn't press your luck by going up there," Nuru advised. "You got some tolerance from that animal with a Yeti stone, but that's all."

Trouble licked his dry lips. "I'll wait. Maybe the cat will leave in a few hours."

"We'll freeze by then." Nuru rubbed his arms and shivered. His jacket's nylon shell made crinkling noises in the frosty night air.

"We'll take turns sitting in the middle where it's warmest." Trouble slid around Nuru, putting him in the center. Trouble looked at the glowing dial on his sports watch, the numbers shimmering in fluorescent green. "In half an hour, Tattoo can be in the middle."

"OK," Nuru muttered.

Thirty minutes later, they rotated places and checked for the leopard. It was still there, pacing in tight circles, prowling the ledge above in restless agitation. Each time they looked, the cat was watching them, waiting to attack, its body poised like a tightly wound spring.

In two hours, they felt like statues left in a barren park for winter, bronze figures covered in a dusting of light snow. The only thing proving they were alive was the growling of hungry bellies, demanding calories that could be turned into body heat. The cold rock around them acted like a vacuum cleaner, sucking all warmth from them.

Nuru's teeth chattered as he talked. "I'm not going to make it until morning."

"I feel the same way," Tattoo whispered. She couldn't speak any louder. She didn't have the energy.

"Hang on guys," Trouble urged them.

Nuru sighed. "I can't move. I just want to sleep."

Trouble nudged him. "You've got to stay awake." But Nuru's head leaned on Tattoo's shoulder and they both fell asleep. Trouble could hear their shallow breathing. He knew how dangerous it was for them to sleep in the cold. Their circulation would slow and they'd suffer frostbite, then death. Trouble made an attempt to wake them, rocking their shoulders and tapping their heads. It seemed useless. Nuru and Tattoo only stayed awake for a few minutes before slipping away again.

Trouble heard no sound of the leopard's restless pacing. He waited, listening for the click of sharp claws on hard rock or the muffled crinkle of cat feet on thin ice. Trouble decided to climb up and grab a backpack with its vital supplies. He needed food and water to revive his companions. Better would be finding shelter for them, discovering a small cave where they could huddle for warmth.

Trouble put his arms out and groped for the last rope. Twice he felt the coarse nylon braid yet failed to grab the cord. When he had it in his grasp, he tugged on the rope and it held, giving him confidence it would support his weight.

Trouble willed himself to move, pulling on the rope for lift, navigating by feel, not by sight. In that inky night, there seemed no difference between opening his eyes and shutting them. He felt blind either way, sightless in the dark. The blackness worked against Trouble, slowing every move to a crawl and disorienting him.

One more cautious step upward and then another, each movement bought with pain and fear. It was impossible to tell how much progress he'd made. Trouble had no idea how many steps remained before he reached the cleft, where a leopard may be laying in ambush for him.

Squinting through the darkness, Trouble saw a light flickering in the distance and his heart jumped in fright. Did that glimmer come from the snow leopard's yellow eyes? Trouble recoiled in fear and the light disappeared, letting him feel safe for a moment. He returned to the higher position and the light was still there, smoldering like blue smoke. The illumination seemed to ooze from pores in the mountainside. Reflection of moonlight, he wondered?

Trouble looked at the night sky and it was filled with millions of stars, masked by a creamy gauze of clouds. No moon burned through the haze, not even a crescent lunar wedge. Somehow the diffuse light came from within the rocks, where dim glow outlined the jagged shape of loose stones. Trouble realized there'd been a small landslide, a pile of tumbled rocks covering a tunnel opening. Was this the Yeti cave? No, it seemed too small.

He brushed aside a gravel of tiny pebbles and they fell, making a slight clicking noise when they tumbled against frozen ice. The exertion caused him to pant and his breath coated his cheeks in white frost. His lips went numb, but he couldn't stop. They needed shelter too badly. He kept working, moving rocks by lifting them aside, exposing more eerie blue light. Why he found dim light inside the hole puzzled him, but there seemed no point in worrying about it now.

Soon, he had enough clearance to squirm in the hole and check out the burrow. The tunnel seemed to be a shaft like an air duct in a building. A slight draft of warm air drifted along the tunnel, making it cozy. They could spend the night here, in relative comfort, avoiding a fight with the snow leopard. Trouble still had to make a frightening descent in pitch blackness and somehow get his exhausted friends to follow him. They could be safe for a few hours, but that was all the time he could buy them. Every problem, every threat would still be there when they woke up, waiting to claim their lives.

11

Tattoo stretched and rubbed her groggy eyes. She looked around and saw weak light painting glow on the tight confines of a hole. She rubbed the walls and found them smooth, polished as jewelry stones sold at the Namche Bazaar. It almost seemed that she'd fallen into a well. Feeling confused, she asked, "Where are we?" Her voice echoed along the confined space, softly repeating her last syllable.

Nuru's throat was so dry it was hard to speak. He ran his tongue over cracked lips. "We're in a small tunnel. Trouble found the hole last night and dragged us inside for shelter. We've got to get some water," he croaked.

Trouble sighed. "Yeah, I know. I'll check for the leopard. If the cat's gone, I'll go for the backpack so we can get the stove and melt ice."

He crawled toward the tunnel opening, every movement painful from stiff muscles and thermal underwear so gritty with caked sweat it rubbed his skin like sandpaper. The noise of his motions became echoes chasing him along the tube until he reached the tunnel's mouth.

He looked outside and discovered China's side of the West Ridge was dark despite morning sunlight bending over Everest's summit. The rock face above lay wrapped in black, dark as a slinking Ninja. Trouble glanced upward, squinting through heavy shadows, scanning the cliff for a snow leopard. He saw no cat, but also discovered no rope dangling from the ledge. Overnight, the leopard chewed through his rope and it fell in a tangled heap with the other safety cords. The rope was now a pile of yellow spaghetti on the ledge below. "Blast," Trouble snapped. "I can't climb up and get the stove to melt ice. We need water desperately."

Tattoo hobbled along the shaft, coming up behind Trouble, hunched in a squat. "I'll explore the tunnel. Maybe there's a place where melted ice pooled and we can drink the water."

"I'll go with you." Trouble followed her. The narrow tunnel was so cramped he could only get to his knees. When he talked, his voice echoed along the tunnel, drilled straight into the mountain. "Whatever cut this hole made a flawless tube. The sides are glassy smooth. It's weird how this hole can be so perfect."

"Yeah," Tattoo whispered. "The perfection scares me. It feels like we crawled into a trap."

"I hope not." Creeping through the burrow felt like crawling inside a sewer pipe, dangerous and claustrophobic. The hole seemed a cylindrical coffin, with little air to breathe.

After a while, the tunnel widened and they could walk bent over, half standing. A hundred crouched steps brought them to a junction where several passages met. In this chamber, they found room to stand and Trouble felt happy to stretch his body, straighten his aching back.

Tattoo lifted her arms, pointing at dim glow on the walls. "All these tunnels are filled with soft light, like a bedroom nightlight. Where does the glow come from? It can't be sunlight. We're too far from the tunnel opening."

Trouble pointed behind them. "The glow comes from that moss covering the floor. The plants shine, the way sea organisms fluoresce in the wake of a ship. Look at those dark footprints marking our trail. Every step crushed plants and they don't glow anymore." Behind him, black steps marked their path through a field of shimmering moss. The trampled moss gave off a strange odor, like pine needles mixed with wet dog fur, a good smell blended with a bad one.

"Too bad for the moss. Sorry we had to step on it. Well," Tattoo consoled herself, "there was nowhere else to walk. Besides, the plants will grow back."

Nuru's uneven movements echoed along the tunnel. He was following them and had to favor his damaged ankle. His scrunched form soon became visible. "Ah," he gasped in relief, straightening himself at the junction. "My back is killing me. I'll stand here for a while."

"Good idea. You rest and we'll split up, do a little exploring," Trouble said. "Tattoo and I will go different ways. We'll come back here to report."

Tattoo shrugged. "Which tunnels should we try?" There were many holes fanning from the junction.

"Use Trouble's stone," Nuru suggested. "Maybe it'll point to the Yeti cave."

Trouble removed the blue gem and held it in the palm of his hand. The polished stone quivered, pointing first at one tunnel and then another. "The egg can't make up its mind," he concluded. Trouble wrapped the antiquity in cloth and returned it to his pocket. "Doesn't seem to matter which way I go." He picked the closest opening. "I'll try this passage."

He'd only taken one step when growling echoed along the tunnel. Somewhere inside that shaft was a leopard. "Uh oh. It does matter which path we take. I'll try this other tunnel." Trouble bent over and walked into the cramped shaft.

"We'd better stick together. I'll go with you." Tattoo followed him into the hole.

Nuru called after them. "I changed my mind. I don't want to wait here. The leopard might find me." Nuru hobbled after them.

They only walked for a few minutes before the burrow sloped downhill. The farther they went, the more the shaft bent downward. Soon, they had to brace themselves to keep from sliding, pushing stiff arms against the walls. Every step on the glowing moss squeezed out vegetable oil, making the floor slick. With an injured ankle, Nuru had difficulty keeping his balance on greasy slope.

The floor tilted more with each step. Finally, the shaft angled downward like a ski slope. Here, Nuru's injured ankle gave way and he fell, slipping on the greased floor. Nuru rolled downhill, a bowling ball shooting toward pins at the end of a lane. Trouble and Tattoo were the pins. When Nuru hit them, they tumbled on each other with a collective grunt and began a frightening slide.

Out of control, they flew down the shaft, lubricated by slimy plant growth. The farther they slid in the greasy hole, the quicker they went. There was no traction and no handhold when they grabbed at the tunnel's sides. They tried to use their boots like brakes, but found no grip. Soon, they didn't even try to stop themselves. They were moving too fast, flying along the tunnel like they were on a toboggan in the Olympics, trying for a world record. Their bodies shook and vibrated from the extreme speed, teeth chattering as their heads shook like bobble-head dolls. The shaft tilted until the slope became almost vertical. At the end of the tunnel, the floor disappeared. With nothing under them, they shot into empty space, arcing downward for the longest second.

"Oh, no," Nuru screamed. "We're gonna crash."

They hit bottom with a splat and it hurt like being spanked with a board. Trouble collided with the ground in a stinging thud that brought tears of pain to his eyes. Finally, the pain dimmed and Trouble shook his head to clear his mind. He looked at their curious environment, hoping to get some orientation. They'd landed in a frozen arena, round and smooth like an ice rink.

Trouble struggled to rise on the slick ice, spinning his legs before twisting up like a fallen ice skater. Using his boots for skates, he glided around the rink. After a little practice skating, he headed for a low wall bounding the area. He wanted to see beyond the rink. In a few strides, Trouble reached the edge and halted, leaning against the wall. He was surprised to realize they'd slid down the tunnel and dropped on some kind of observation deck.

He looked out, expecting to see the sky, and discovered they'd landed inside an enormous cavern. The dome was covered with beautiful minerals and looked like the interior of a geode, a hollow rock lined with crystals. Across the roof, purple amethyst mixed with glittering quartz. Those minerals blended with blue agate to form dazzling stalactites, thick needles dripping from the ceiling like huge icicles.

The cavern's lighting system was a tangle of vines wrapped around the "icicles." Like the tunnel moss, these vines were light-giving plants, their leaves blossoming in a rainbow of glowing colors. Moisture ran down stalactites and fed the vines with minerals and water. The dripping moisture resonated across the vast cavern, sounding like wind chimes ringing, adding musical harmony to the visual beauty of the hanging garden.

"Wow," Tattoo said. "I had no idea Everest was hollow."

"Me neither." Trouble felt equally surprised at discovering the world's highest mountain wasn't solid inside. Instead, the interior of

Mount Everest formed a vast cavern. "Do you remember the Yeti cave looking this way, Nuru?"

"Um, well," Nuru hedged. "Actually, I'm kinda fuzzy on the cave part. I just remember waking up outside, on a snow ledge."

"The cavern isn't all beautiful." Trouble pointed downward, where an ugly hill rose almost to their viewing platform. The mound was soot black with red stains on the sides.

"Euuw. What do you suppose that ugly lump is?" Tattoo scrunched her face like she was smelling a foul odor.

"My dad once took me to a steel mill. They had a pile of iron ore that looked like this hill." Trouble stared at the horizon. "There's a glow on the other side of the heap. Something's over there. Maybe that's where Yetis live."

Nuru was curious what they were talking about, but his ankle hurt too much for him to stand up without assistance. He slid to them on his butt and they helped him to his feet. To brace himself, Nuru leaned on the platform's short railing. By accident, his hand touched a peculiar symbol etched into the quartz wall. The ice rink shuddered like there'd been an earthquake, vibrating like a spinning blender. They twisted in a spiral, spinning and descending at the same time.

"What's going on?" Nuru asked, afraid they were going to be hurt again.

Trouble peered over the edge to see what was happening. "This thing's an elevator and you hit the down button by accident." He pointed to the hieroglyph under Nuru's fingers. The drawing glowed, black lines highlighted on a yellow background.

Nuru jerked his hand from the bright hieroglyph, but the elevator's turning movement continued anyway. They kept spinning and sinking, twisting and falling at the same time. It was like being on a centrifuge ride in a theme park, back pressed against your chair, stomach tumbling. The scary motion left them feeling dizzy.

"If this is an elevator, why is it spinning?" Tattoo felt nauseous and wished the twisting would stop.

"This lift works like a bolt. To descend, the bolt screws into the ground and gets shorter." Trouble struggled to keep his stomach calm.

Finally, the elevator quit spinning. They paused for a moment and let their sense of balance return.

Tattoo craned her neck to look around. "We're at the bottom."

"I guess this is where we get out." Trouble rolled over the wall of smooth crystal, clear as glass. He reached across the low barrier and helped Nuru raise his sprained ankle. "Let's explore. We certainly can't go back the way we came. There's no way to climb up that greasy hole. We're trapped here, unless we find another path out." He stared bleakly at the giant mound in front of them, blocking their way.

12

The black hill rose in front of them like a huge sand dune, cresting a hundred feet in the air. They looked both ways and the dune seemed to roll on forever, like a giant ocean wave. The monotonous charcoal landscape loomed over them, featureless yet menacing. Exhausted from yesterday's exercise and sore from tumbling hard on the ice rink elevator, Trouble spoke without enthusiasm. "I guess we have to climb over this mound."

"I don't think my ankle can take it." Nuru rubbed his leg.

Tattoo volunteered to try climbing the powdery hill. "I'll scramble up, see how hard it is." She jogged up the dune, kicking sprays of black dust in the air. "This is worse than running in sand. You can't get any traction." A few yards up the hill, she quit, exhausted. Tattoo plowed downward, her feet punching cone-shaped holes in the slope. She hit bottom and looked at the mound in disgust.

Tattoo grabbed a handful of the black powder and licked it with her tongue. She made an ugly face at the flavor. "Tastes like metal. It's probably iron. The powder rusts soon as it touches moisture. See?" She held out her palm to show how the black dust turned red on contact with her saliva.

Trouble looked at rusty powder coating her hand. "That explains red streaks all over the hill. They're rust marks. But why is such a large pile of iron dust inside this cavern?"

"Who cares?" Nuru complained. "We don't need to know why there's metal here. We just need to get around the hill so we can find a way out and go home."

Tattoo threw the handful of black dust back on the pile. "Sure. We can't climb over it. Which way do you want to go, left or right?" She glanced at Trouble.

"Both ways look the same to me. Nuru picks. He's got the injured ankle."

"We'll go that way." Nuru began hobbling along the iron pile, hoping to find a shortcut.

With a few minutes of walking, they came to an area where the finely granulated powder changed to pebbles the size of charcoal briquettes used in a backyard grill. In a few more yards, the pebbles grew larger and jagged, becoming shale, looking like chunks of coal. The air smelled sour and it hurt their lungs to breathe.

Tattoo volunteered, "I'll try climbing here. See if it's any easier." She got about ten feet up the hill and stopped, captivated by something she'd discovered. Tattoo bent over and poked a hand into the dune.

"Why'd you quit?" Nuru complained, irritated by Tattoo's sudden halt.

"Found something," Tattoo chimed back.

"What'd you discover?" Trouble asked.

"A yellow bottle. Could be an old oxygen cylinder." After a moment Tattoo yelled, "Hey, there's two bottles, on a wooden frame."

"I thought we were trying to get out of here." Nuru acted impatient.

"Yeah, well that's what this guy was trying to do, get out of the cavern." Tattoo straightened her posture.

Trouble was astonished. "You found a body?"

"Yeah," Tattoo confirmed. "I guess he was a climber and got hurt. Found his way inside the cavern, wanted to spend the night."

Tattoo held up a small diary. The leather-bound book seemed tiny, about the size of a wristwatch dial, with just enough room for one thought to be noted on a page. She flipped through the small diary.

Trouble called out, "What's it say?"

Tattoo read the diary entry aloud. "Caught in freak snowstorm. Blizzard came out of nowhere. George fell. Rope between us broke. Couldn't help him. Lost my ice axe when he tumbled." Tattoo flipped more pages. "Goes on to say this climber was stalked by a pack of leopards. 'One of them clawed my leg. Fought off cats with oxygen bottles. Lucky I didn't throw bottles away when the gas ran out. Found hole in mountain. Crawled inside. Discovered Everest is hollow.' "

"Is there a date written in the journal?" Trouble asked.

"The last entry was June 8th 1924," Tattoo responded.

"What's it say on that page?" Trouble hoped for a clue on how to exit the cavern.

"It just says 'Leg infected. Feels like it's on fire. Swelling. Had to take boot off. Can't walk anymore. Doesn't matter. Trapped here. No way out.' "

"No way out?" Nuru repeated, frightened by the journal entry.

"Yeah, that's what he wrote." Now even Tattoo looked depressed.

"Well, I still believe there's an exit." Trouble said. "This climber got injured and couldn't move around. 'Cause he didn't find a way out doesn't mean we can't leave."

"Sure," Nuru mumbled.

"Any name on the diary?" Trouble asked her.

"No, just the initials A.I."

"A.I." Trouble repeated. Looking stunned, he muttered a quote from a famous mountain climber. "Because it's there …"

Tattoo shrugged. "Huh?"

"George Mallory was once asked by a reporter why he kept trying to climb Mount Everest. He gave his famous answer – 'because it's there.' Mallory made the highest progress on Everest until Sir Edmund Hillary and Tenzing Norgay reached the peak."

Nuru was amazed. "George Mallory died in 1924, trying to reach the top. His body was found recently, after decades of searching, but they never found his companion. Maybe A.I. is Mallory's lost climbing partner – Andy Irvine."

"Could be." Trouble nodded. "You find any other items?" he asked Tattoo.

"Old tube of zinc oxide, used for sunscreen. Empty tin of beef jerky and a broken altimeter. I can look for more." Tattoo burrowed into the dune, scraping away shale. She tossed out an old boot with hobnails screwed in the leather sole for traction, primitive gear compared to modern climbing equipment.

"Hey," Nuru shouted, "You going to spend all day on this project? I thought we were trying to get out of this cavern and go home."

Tattoo ignored the remark and kept digging.

Nuru tried a different approach, knowing Tattoo was superstitious. "That climber's ghost is going to haunt you, Tattoo, for robbing his grave."

Tattoo straightened up. She was holding an antique film camera with the brand name Kodak printed above the lens. "I'm not robbing a grave," Tattoo said without conviction. "The man just died here. He isn't buried."

"What's the difference? Those are his possessions. You're disturbing his spirit." Nuru acted smug now. He knew Tattoo was rattled.

"OK, I'll put his stuff back." Tattoo threw the small items in the hole. She felt tempted to keep the camera, but a smirk from Nuru changed Tattoo's mind. She tossed the Kodak down and the camera sprang open. A small film canister tumbled out and rolled down the slag heap, catching behind a rock. Photos that might prove Mallory reached the top of Everest before Hillary lay only yards from Tattoo's boots.

Many expeditions had searched in vain for Andy Irvine's missing camera and its film that might prove Mallory reached Everest's summit before anyone else.

She moved toward the film canister but Nuru called out, "Leave it. Let's get going."

Tattoo hesitated for a moment, then slid down the iron dune. By the time she reached bottom, her clothes were covered in black dust. She looked like a chimney sweep after a hard day of work, knocking ash out of flues.

Nuru smirked at the dirt.

Tattoo glared back. "Oh yeah, smart guy. What are you gonna look like after you get to the top and slide down the other side?"

"Let's get started," Trouble suggested, hoping to avoid a useless fight. "I'll climb alongside Nuru. I can help in case his ankle gives out."

"Thanks," he muttered. Nuru limped to the base of the dune and began hiking up the soft dirt, scuttling like a crab. Trouble shadowed Nuru, remaining at his side. They kept going past the long-sought film canister, hunted by so many expeditions.

When they got to the dead climber's burrow, Trouble paused for a moment and looked inside. The diary had fallen into A.I.'s skeletal hand, as though he were holding the book out to show them something.

The open page held a frightening message. It read – "No way out of cavern. Looked everywhere. Left rust trails all over this dune from my sweat and blood. This is where I'll die."

13

The trio fought their way up the steep dune, leaving behind them a black cloud of choking dust. Shale crumbled under their hiking boots, making each step spongy, doubling the effort needed to ascend the hill. Their lungs ached from inhaling iron filings, yet they couldn't stop to catch their breath. They were afraid of getting enveloped by the dirty cloud trailing them. Black grime coated their faces like oily ink, slipping into their pores and invading their ears. Covered in soot, they looked like razers, the workers who strip fire-damaged buildings prior to renovation.

Sweating all the time, perspiration dripped off their foreheads and painted rust on the iron dune. Streaks of rust marked their trail to the crest of the black mound. Reaching the top, they were too exhausted to notice what lay ahead of them. They stood around, trying to catch their breath, panting. When the trio finally lifted their heads and looked, they made a startling discovery. They stood at the edge of a city crowded with bizarre structures.

Office towers in this lost civilization were round, not square. They saw low buildings shaped like hockey pucks and drooping twenty-story tubes. Once in a while, a hundred-story monster jutted from the middle of shorter pipes. The building windows were round, like bullet holes. Drilled randomly across the structures, the windows appeared to be damage inflicted by a gang drive-by, spraying bullets from a machine gun, knocking holes in walls. At higher levels of a building, the window glass became dull, looking like cataracts on an elderly person's eyes.

When they walked into the city, it felt like exploring a bad neighborhood in Manhattan at night, when no one's on the streets and it seems a ghost town. The trio moved in dark canyons formed by skyscrapers, yet they found no cars, no steam vents, no lights in windows from early risers, no rumble of a subway beneath their feet. The silence in this deserted city was frightening, leaving them concerned an unseen enemy was hiding in one of the abandoned shops. They halted, straining their ears for sounds of life and heard none. There were no cell phones, taxi horns, screeching brakes, roaring buses – not even the drip of water.

The city had no pattern to its streets. There wasn't an obvious grid where Fifth Avenue met 42nd Street, followed by 43rd. Here, the alleys curved, meeting at strange angles, snaking around buildings in a confusing tangle. They found no sidewalks and most of the streets seemed just wide gutters. They felt like small insects crawling through a field of toadstools, hoping they weren't eaten by a spider.

They discovered monuments shaped like cemetery headstones, but they couldn't read the inscriptions. Building signs were written in a strange language none of them could translate. The obscure hieroglyphics gave no insight into this vanished culture. Large clocks were embedded in a building wall. The clocks had stopped at different times and none of them showed a date when the timepieces quit working.

They walked in a city designed for a million occupants, yet the trio felt all alone. The more they walked, the more eerie it seemed not to see anyone. They looked in trash bins, hoping to discover fresh garbage, indicating the city was still occupied. The only trash was food that dried out long ago, becoming a shrunken-head version of itself. They continued exploring, trying to find clues. A few buildings had courtyards with decaying patio sets, built for oversized creatures. An average person would feel like a dwarf sitting in them.

In a playground, rusted chairs curved in rows facing a puppet stage. A dusty marionette lay sprawled across the stage, a corpse smothered by a rotted curtain. Stage drapes had fallen off their rod and formed a blanket over the puppet, as though he'd died and someone covered his body. The vacant stage was littered with dusty props, living room furniture and a spiral staircase leading to a faux balcony.

The faded green puppet theater was surrounded by struggling flowers, dried arctic poppies forming an orange spicing on withered purple saxifrage. Down one block, blue gentians dotted a scraggly carpet of snowy edelweiss. Nearby, a few Himalayan orchids persisted, survivors fighting off neglect. Their flowerbed was overgrown with weeds, threatening to crowd out the red orchids.

After so much decay, they were relieved to discover a park with a cracked fountain burbling water. "At last, we can drink," Nuru groaned.

For a few minutes, they quenched their terrible thirst, guzzling water from the fountain and rinsing iron grit off their faces. Their throats no longer itched, dry and sticky from the black powder coating their mouths.

Tattoo looked around, searching the park area surrounding them. "We're been in the city for an hour and haven't seen anyone. Where are all the Yetis?"

"I think they're dead," Trouble answered sadly.

Tattoo frowned. "How'd they die?"

Trouble shrugged. "Not sure. Maybe for the same reason a lot of species vanish – pollution, loss of natural habitat, global warming."

"I can't believe they're all gone." Tattoo said. She pointed to water spraying from a brass sphere and rolling into a pool below. "The fountain's a map. It's the top half of a globe, the Northern Hemisphere. Maybe it shows where they went."

Nuru sniped, "Didn't think you knew about hemispheres, north or south."

"I know geography better than you do." Tattoo slapped her hand in the water, splashing Nuru, drenching his coat.

"Hey, you shouldn't do that. It's too cold to get wet."

Tattoo shrugged. "What are you complaining about? You're sitting near the equator, in the tropics." She poked her finger through the spouting water and touched the globe. "There's America, Trouble's home … and Nepal, where we live."

Trouble walked closer to the map. "There's a dashed line across the globe. The line begins in Svalbard Island, near the Arctic. Svalbard is mainly a place tourists visit to photograph Polar Bears."

"Why do you look shocked?" Tattoo wondered.

"Because this Svalbard Island thing is really bizarre. The line on this map runs through the same places where my parents made archaeological digs. They started excavating in Svalbard, above the Arctic Circle, and worked their way across western Siberia, into the Tibetan Plateau and the Himalayas."

Tattoo's eyes tracked the dashed line across the brass globe. "Trouble, your parents work awfully hard to find old treasures. Why bother?"

"I don't know. We rarely sell artifacts my parents find on their digs. Our shop makes money from curiosities they buy at estate auctions."

"What kind of things do you sell in the shop?" Tattoo asked.

"We have a collection of knight's armor. Rich people love having a knight in shining armor standing in their entry hall. We also sell fossilized eggs from extinct birds, like the Dodo."

Nuru scoffed, "That's it? No wonder you can't make a lot of money."

"No, we've also got original architectural drawings for famous New York landmarks. A blueprint set for the Empire State Building sold just before my parents disappeared. That money kept me alive. The drawings were purchased by an architect for conference room decoration."

"You ever sell anything interesting?" Nuru sniped.

"Yeah. Old telephones and radios with big knobs and dials. There's even a Nazi radar set in the basement. Somebody called about it the other day. So these digs never made sense to me. My parents spend all their money traveling half the year and never take me along. Bummer."

Nuru finally agreed with something. "Yeah, that sucks. Guess I'm lucky Mom takes me to Namche Bazaar. I hate staying home, even if I have to spend five days on a yak." Nuru slipped off a boot and soaked his sprained ankle in the fountain, hoping cold water would reduce the swelling. He took his eyes off the injured leg and looked at Trouble. "I'm starved," he complained. Nuru scanned the park. "All these buildings and no food."

"I'm hungry too," Tattoo said. "Why don't we explore some more? See if we can find something to eat."

Nuru put his boot on and they walked for a few minutes, curving along the streets. There was no sign of life anywhere. Everything was quiet, like watching a silent movie, a metropolis without honking taxis, screeching buses dragging on their brakes to stop, cell phones bleeping ring tones, timers buzzing in fast food places or distant sirens wailing on fire engines.

"Depressing," Trouble commented. "A huge city, only nobody lives here." He gazed into a shop window littered with dead flowers. Bouquets had become clay-like lumps in the bottom of dirty vases. Wreaths of dried herbs had crumbled to multi-colored powder. Shriveled bonsai trees looked like withered claws.

Tattoo tried to break the sad mood. She went inside a hardware shop and came out with doorknobs shaped as Platonic solids – three, four, five and six-sided figures. The doorknobs were made from heavy quartz. "Hey, look at me," she yelled. She tossed doorknobs in the air, showing off her juggling skills. Tattoo acted like a circus clown, sticking out her tongue and contorting her body to catch doorknobs behind her back. She wanted to perk up her friends. After Nuru and Trouble scowled, she gave up and put the doorknobs back in the display window. Tattoo ran across the street. "What's this place?"

"Looks like an abandoned newspaper office." Nuru limped inside and picked up a thick bundle of sheets, printed in cryptic symbols, arranged in columns with a headline in larger font.

Trouble bent over a machine filled with a long roller. Symbols were embossed along the rim. The roller looked like an ancient pillar toppled on its side, as if an Egyptian column in Luxor fell over. Ink pads waited for an operator to push the right buttons so printing could begin.

Trouble pressed on the typewriter-like keyboard. Gears creaked and clanked. The roller turned in a slow grind and was met by a dry ink pad. Then the roller shifted forward to press against old, yellowed paper. No matter how many times he tapped keys, no symbols appeared on the paper. The ink pads looked like dried mud, with no fresh color to print hieroglyphs on a page.

Tattoo scratched her head. "Where's the ink? I'm gonna leave them a note, in case anyone comes back."

"There's some ink on the shelf, I think," Trouble replied. "But maybe you should learn their language first, before trying to write them a letter."

"Oh, yeah," Tattoo said, her face reddening. "Um, what do you suppose they called this machine?" she asked, changing the subject.

"A broken typewriter." Trouble replaced the lid on a tin of red ink. The crimson liquid had become hard cake and seemed useless.

Hunger made Nuru impatient. "I thought we were looking for a place to eat," he grouched.

"Yeah, OK," Trouble agreed. He put down the newspaper and moved outside the office, looking along the street. He spotted hieroglyphs carved in the side of a nearby building. "You know what? I may understand that sign." He began walking faster, waving for them to follow. "Come on." In a block, he stopped and looked puzzled. "I don't get it. I must have missed the sign for it."

"Missed what sign?" Nuru asked in irritation.

"There should be a café near here," Trouble informed him.

"It doesn't matter if you find a café," Nuru complained, with his typical pessimism. "The cookies are old, hard enough to use for building stones. Nobody's eaten in this city for years. We should get outta here. Go home."

Trouble ignored his attitude and backtracked along the street, checking hieroglyphs for a familiar pattern of squiggles. In a few doorways, he stopped and peered at symbols above a threshold, a mix of squares, triangles, birds, snakes and eyes. "Well, that hieroglyph's not quite the same. I don't know why they changed the symbol, but this might be a café. Problem is, I don't know how to get in." He pressed on a cathedral door, at least twelve feet tall, a gray barrier pocked with circles of white frost. The panel seemed rigid, so unbending it could have been steel. Its surface felt smooth and flat as a sheet of plastic, and there were no hinges or latches. Getting inside remained a mystery.

Tattoo pushed on the door various ways and it didn't budge. She felt no movement. "Hmm," she thought aloud, "if I lived here, how would I get in?"

"Maybe I'd go through this door instead." Nuru acted smug. He was standing in an open doorway next to them. They were so preoccupied they hadn't noticed him open another door.

"How'd you do it?" Tattoo asked with suspicion.

"A little science, some geometry, careful thought. Four years of study would allow you to do the same," Nuru taunted.

Trouble gave Nuru a skeptical look. "In other words," he said, "you leaned against the door and it opened."

Nuru shrugged. "I'm not giving away my secrets, but you could be right. Why don't you check it out?"

Trouble stepped through the door and was shocked by what he saw. He barely had the presence of mind to move aside, making room for Nuru and Tattoo.

14

Trouble saw colored snakes crawling out of holes in the café walls and wriggling on the floor. A braid of snakes coiled around the restaurant, twisting themselves into a single giant serpent. In the middle of the dining room, the bloated python slithered down a hole, an opening large enough to be a storm drain. Without that hole, Trouble couldn't have entered the café. The endless serpent would have filled the room, crushed the door down and squeezed along the street, making a block-long snake that kept growing, twisting along the avenue. Instead, the serpent escaped by wriggling into the storm drain, making a dangerous sucking noise, though it had no venomous head and no rattles on its tail.

The snake's bizarre slurp wasn't the only weird sound in the café. Odd slapping came from glass cabinets built into the walls. The smacking noise was made by thick batter dropping on platters. In moments, each blob of dough congealed, looking like a cow's meadow muffin.

Nuru looked disgusted. "Gross. I wouldn't eat this stuff. It's yucky."

"Yeah? Well, I bet you're wrong. They smell good. I think this snake is ice cream. It smells like ice cream." Tattoo stuck her thumb in a yellow serpent and licked her fingertip. "Good, if you enjoy strawberry ice cream. Me, I prefer chocolate."

Trouble got busy trying different colors. "The violet snake tastes like chocolate. It ought to be brown. I don't know why it isn't."

"For the same reason vanilla is blue." Tattoo shrugged. "Who knows?"

Trouble looked at Nuru. Despite his words, Nuru was busy eating cookies. "What's your favorite flavor?"

Nuru had stuffed his mouth with a waffle-sized cookie and his cheeks puffed out. He tried to talk and couldn't. "Er wrm. Ats i er en de glaz."

Tattoo snickered. "He does that at school when he eats lunch."

Nuru didn't stop eating, but he glowered at Tattoo.

She continued, "I think I can translate for Nuru. He meant to say 'They're warm. That why they're in the glass.' He's saying the glass cabinets keep the cookies warm."

Nuru surfaced from his chewing. "I feel sick from binging on sweets. Maybe I should check the other room for something healthy to eat." He went in the back and returned in seconds, looking even worse.

"What's wrong?" Trouble gave him a concerned look.

Nuru bent over like he was going to be sick, vomit back the cookies he'd eaten. "Don't go in there. You don't want to know."

Trouble and Tattoo to rushed in the back. They had to admit Nuru was right – they would've felt much better without knowing what the ice cream and cookies really were – vomit and excrement.

The weird ice cream snakes came from a process that looked like sick kids, vomiting up their lunch. A bundle of quivering throats made retching sounds, like people fighting the urge to throw up and then vomiting. After the gagging noise, a piece of snake slid through billowing lips. The throats gave an "Ahhh" of relief and the retching process began again. The throats worked in unison, gurgling like a bizarre choir.

The cookie-making process was even more disgusting. Steaming brown lumps dropped from the rear end of a dog-shaped plant. It was exactly like a pet squatting in a park to relieve itself during a walk with its owner. The effect was complete with a soft plopping noise and a troublesome odor. Both the smell and the shape changed when the lumps dried, becoming cookies. The knowledge they'd put such things in their mouth, chewed and swallowed them wasn't comforting.

"Well, at least they're organic," Trouble said, trying to focus on the positive.

Tattoo's reaction was closer to Nuru's. "Euuw," Tattoo said in disgust. "I didn't eat these things. Tell me I didn't eat them. Please …"

Nuru joined them. "I warned you."

"Yeah, you did," Trouble admitted.

They stood there, watching a dog's rear end push out one hot, steaming mess after another. They felt grossed-out and fascinated, observing excrement change shape and smell, turning into cookies. Both the dog butts and the ice cream throats were made from giant sponges. Ice cream snakes had the same color as the sponge that made them. One bundle of throats held sponges colored yellow, violet, blue and blood red.

The dog butts, however, were all the same brown hue but different shapes. The shape of the canine rear-end determined what type of cookie got made. Like the ice cream throats, the dog butts worked in unison and sprouted from a common root. In both cases, this large root sank into the floor and vanished, implying another subterranean level existed below.

Fascinated by the sponges, Trouble barely heard the café door open. A chime rang in the front room, announcing a new customer. Trouble came out of his trance, startled by the surprise entrance of another creature in a deserted city. He spun and in quick steps reached the doorway separating machinery from the customer area. His eyes scanned the dining room and spotted the intruder bending over a violet ice cream snake. He put a finger to his lips, warning Nuru and Tattoo to be quiet. They all stared in shock at the animal.

"Is it dangerous?" Tattoo whispered.

"I don't know ..." Nuru muttered.

15

In the café's entry room, a tall penguin with a long, sharp beak examined squirming ice cream snakes. He moved in cautious steps, staying close to the door. The nervous bird scanned the restaurant, suspicious that he wasn't alone. The penguin felt anxious as he filled a wooden mixing bowl with his flippers. The flippers were fin-like arms, paddles big enough to row a boat.

His web feet were dirty yellow, with claw-like toes. Short legs led to a white chest wrapped in a tuxedo coat of black fur. Mustard-colored hairs grew under his chin and formed a bowtie for his tuxedo. A band of fuzz swirled across his head, looking like a jogger's ear band for running in icy wind. The penguin's long beak was dull and worn. His fur had known better years and was spattered with gray, showing his age. The impression of old age seemed reinforced by his pinched eyes, carrying a hint of pain.

Bewildered, Trouble stared at the tuxedo bird. "What's a penguin doing here?"

"I don't know. Maybe he could help us." Tattoo started to move forward but Nuru stopped her.

Nuru put a finger to his lips, indicating they ought to be silent and observe. "You might scare the penguin and he'd scream. Leopards will find us if he makes a racket. Wait 'til he leaves. We'll follow him and see where he goes."

But the penguin overheard their whispers and moved in their direction, investigating the sounds. Too late, they made an effort to hide in the machinery. The penguin stepped in the back room and saw them huddled behind sponges oozing ice cream. The look on the bird's face turned from loneliness to horror. He dropped his bowl in shock and his beak hung open. Quickly, he recovered, scooping up the bowl and dashing from the café. Racing into the street, the tuxedo bird chirped with all his might, an off-key soprano yelping in obvious distress.

Nuru limped behind Trouble and Tattoo, chasing the penguin. They shouted, "Stop yelling. You'll bring the leopards to us."

The penguin didn't slow at all. The aged tuxedo bird ran along the street with a speed that defied his years. Tattoo ran after the bird. Nuru and Trouble decided to join the chase. The penguin darted into a narrow lane between a pair of low-rise buildings shaped like hockey pucks. At the end of the alley, he ducked through a small hole in a fence, forcing his pursuers to crawl on hands and knees, delaying them. But after a while, old age caught up with the penguin. The bird slowed and his web feet slapped the pavement in exhaustion. He acted out of breath from running fast and screaming alarms at the same time. The penguin bent over with his chest heaving so violently it threatened to dump all the ice cream from his bowl.

They almost caught him when the tuxedo bird did a strange thing. He put his web feet in a pair of metal slippers. Trouble had seen these devices lining city streets and mistaken them for curb markers. He was about to have that false impression corrected by the penguin.

The bird used a flipper to tap a series of Roman numerals on the side of a building. The penguin seemed to be entering a Personal Identification Number, the way people enter their PIN to get cash from an ATM (Automated Teller Machine). When he finished, the metal slippers glowed with neon light. The shoes lifted off the pavement, floating the penguin along the street. He accelerated, racing away from them.

"Blast," Tattoo complained. "He's escaped."

"No he hasn't." Trouble felt excited. "Put your feet in a pair of slippers. I'll enter the penguin's ID number. I memorized his code as he punched it in." He looked at Nuru and urged, "You too."

Trouble keyed in a sequence of numbers. Nuru's and Tattoo's slippers glowed neon bright, floating down the street. Trouble moved to another pair of metal shoes and put his boots inside. The slippers were designed to fit huge feet, so Trouble's large hiking boots seemed lost inside the metal shoes. Quickly, Trouble punched in the code so he could follow Nuru and Tattoo. The chase was on. The three of them accelerated, shooting along the avenue faster than a sprinter running the hundred meter dash.

A gap of almost a city block separated the penguin and Tattoo, the closest pursuer. As a result, the king penguin didn't realize he was being chased. He calmed down and softened his alarm chirps, sagging in exhaustion from the excitement. Then some instinct caused him to look over his shoulder and a shocked expression returned to his face. The bird resumed chirping, in the loudest bellows he could manage. Any snow leopards in the vicinity would surely hear the racket and investigate.

In spite of the danger, Trouble was fascinated by his ride. Although the city felt decayed, the streets looked perfect, with no potholes. The paving had an off-white hue, almost beige, the color of beach sand. A slight texture to the surface didn't bother the gliding slippers since they flew above the ground, not touching anything.

Trouble once experienced such a floating effect riding a "Bullet" train in Japan. High-speed trains like that don't run on wheels. They float on a magnetic field created by the train's own motion, allowing the massive train to hover, gliding above the metal rails. Flying along this street felt very similar to riding in a bullet train.

The penguin chase lasted for several blocks. Then the tuxedo bird leaned over and touched his shoes. Gradually, he slowed and pulled to the side. Tattoo and Nuru flew past the penguin and realized they also had to touch their slippers so they could stop. Lagging behind, Trouble had a chance to learn from their mistake. He bent down, touching the cold metal slippers with his fingertips. A tingling sensation went up his arm, like an electrical shock. His gliders slowed and curved to the side, right to the spot where the penguin left his shoes.

He jumped off the slippers and chased the penguin, talking in a soft voice, asking him not to be afraid. In a few minutes, the bird slowed in exhaustion, wheezing from the strain. At his age, this was too much exercise. Trouble was only a few steps from the king penguin when the bird ran toward an unusual structure, a large bubble made of plastic. The plastic tent looked like a balloon, stretched tight, inflated with warm air to keep the bubble from collapsing. The warm air once protected plants from cold temperatures. Now the plants were dead, a tangle of dried-out creepers hanging from a skeletal tree. The once-lovely park looked like the set for a Halloween fright-night movie.

When the penguin dashed inside the thick plastic bubble, Trouble jumped through the doorway before a sliding panel could close, delaying him. They ran along an overgrown path, thorn bushes forcing them to hurdle low branches filled with treacherous barbed needles. Around them, dead foliage assumed demonic shapes, its scaly roots reaching for their ankles like grasping claws. Despite the obstacles, Trouble gained on the penguin, touching the bird's shabby tuxedo coat, but he got away. Suddenly, the bird paused at the shore of a murky lake that lay hidden from view by all the dense brush.

Trouble almost collided with the tuxedo bird, barely managing to stop before he injured the elderly penguin. Trouble attempted to reassure the nervous creature. "Hey, we're both alone here. Won't you help me?"

The penguin ignored Trouble and sat in the water with a sleek motion. He balanced his ice cream dish on his stomach and did a quick backstroke across the scummy pond. The tuxedo form shot through dirty green water, driven by the power of his enormous flippers. The penguin swam so fast he cut a wake like a motor boat, a black Vee rippling in the slimy green algae.

"Hey," Trouble yelled, feeling helpless.

Tattoo arrived, panting from the chase. She offered, "Let's run around the lake, in case the penguin gets out. Nuru can stay here. It'll be easier on his ankle. He'll keep the penguin from doubling back here."

"OK," Nuru agreed.

Tattoo dashed in one direction and Trouble ran the other way, circling the lake. Trouble stayed focused on the bird and failed to notice danger ahead. He collided with the plastic bubble in a screech and was flung backwards, tumbling to the ground. Trouble picked himself up, but it was too late. He watched the penguin swim under the bubble's edge and keep going. The lake extended for quite a way outside the tent, where steam misted from the warm lake as it met the city's cold, dry air.

"Why you …" Trouble stamped a boot in frustration. "You pulled a trick, luring us into the park. You knew how to escape the bubble and leave us inside." He jogged back and rejoined his friends, Nuru and Tattoo. Trouble felt discouraged. "We'll never find that penguin." He looked at his friends for sympathy and was irritated by Nuru's smug look. "You think it's fine the penguin escaped."

Nuru acted cocky. "I told you the bird would panic if he saw us. I also warned you he'd bring snow leopards down on us with his screaming. We have to get out of here before the leopards come."

"But it's warm inside this bubble," Tattoo complained.

Nuru was firm. "We gotta leave. It isn't safe here."

Tattoo sulked. "We could wander for days, starving. We need to find someone to help us."

For once, Nuru agreed with Tattoo. "I have an idea on how we can do both, get out of here fast and find some help."

Tattoo moaned in skepticism. "Your last 'good' idea was eating those cookies."

Trouble wanted to hear Nuru's plan. "Go on," he urged.

"The penguin's escape was improvised. He thought it up on the fly. The bird wanted to go somewhere else. Then he realized we were chasing him and ran in this park, so he could ditch us by swimming the lake."

Trouble felt confused. "So?"

"I'm guessing the bird was heading home. Remember he punched in a bunch of numbers when he used the metal slippers."

Trouble gave Nuru a puzzled look. "I thought those numbers were the bird's PIN."

"So did I," Nuru agreed. "But it's possible the bird entered his home address, not an authorization code for using gliding shoes."

Trouble got excited. "You want us to hop in the gliders and see where they take us. Maybe we'll go to the penguin's home, where he lives. Right?"

Nuru smiled. "Let's get out of here before the leopards show up."

They walked out of the park and rode the "slippers" again, flying along curving streets at high speed. The longer they rode, the faster they went. Wind stung their faces and made their eyes weep. Seldom did they see a bright color. When they did, it seemed just a vivid streak. The disorienting ride felt like being inside a video game. Scenery zipped past while they stood still, doing nothing. After minutes of flying, the gliders slowed to a halt, stopping in the middle of a skyscraper complex like Rockefeller Center in New York. There was a giant building at the core, surrounded by high-rise structures.

Nuru looked around. "OK, the penguin stopped here. He probably entered one of these towers."

Trouble was discouraged. "There's a lot of buildings here. To find this penguin, we have to search …"

"Let me figure it out," Tattoo interrupted. "I like word problems. I'm good at them. Let's see … There's fifteen structures. Most have fifty floors. The central skyscraper has about a hundred stories. I'd guess each floor has twenty apartments. Um."

Nuru smirked and rolled his eyes.

Tattoo hated being mocked in this way. She tried to ignore Nuru's attitude. "It's only a hundred seventy apartments to check. We can do it," Tattoo said, trying to be the group's cheerleader.

Nuru sniggered, making it even more embarrassing for Tattoo.

"Well, your math is close," Trouble consoled Tattoo. "You got the correct digits. It's only the decimal point that's off."

"Yeah," Nuru sneered. "A lot off."

"Big deal," Tattoo grunted.

Nuru complained, "This penguin is history. There's 17,000 apartments in those buildings. We're done looking for him. The numbers are against us."

"It's all against us," Tattoo complained. Even the optimistic Tattoo acted depressed. "We're trapped without food. There's no chance anyone will look for us inside Everest. The exit is guarded by snow leopards. Of course, that doesn't matter since we're clueless where the exit is."

Trouble hoped to perk up Tattoo. "We can find a way home, even if we're alone here."

But Trouble was wrong. They weren't alone. At that moment, they were watched by three pairs of eyes. One set of eyes felt happy that humans were inside the city, delighted to have some company, even from a different species. Another pair of eyes showed distrust and resentment, irritated by these unwanted visitors. And the last pair gleamed in hatred. That creature seemed determined to kill the humans at the first possible instant.

16

Trouble, Nuru and Tattoo sat on a bench for a long time, worrying about their problems. It was early evening and a dank, woodsy smell filled their noses. The odor of rotting vegetation seemed extra intense in the pure alpine atmosphere. A slight breeze carried the pungent scent on frigid air. Cold sliced through their insulated parkas, piercing the skin. Sweat from running froze on their bodies, coating arms and legs in a thin layer of ice. Shivering in the frigid temperature added to their downbeat mood. Trouble pushed stiff legs off the bench, rubbing his arms in a vain attempt to feel warmer. "Let's try that park again, where the penguin escaped."

"Why?" Nuru grouched. "There wasn't any food."

"True. But it's warm inside the plastic bubble."

"He's got a point," Tattoo agreed.

"All right. I give in." Nuru slid off the high bench, careful not to re-injure his ankle. "By now, the leopards have left the park. It's a long walk, though. We don't know its address, so we can't use slippers to glide there."

"Walking keeps us warm," Trouble encouraged him.

They were leaving when Trouble heard a high-pitched shriek. He turned in the direction of the cry, startled to discover the same penguin they'd chased to exhaustion. He was standing in an entryway, framed by massive doors. His slight body looked like a splinter wedged between giant redwoods.

The tuxedo bird squawked without enthusiasm. He shrugged, as if saying, "Well, I tried and they weren't interested." The bird's flippers lifted briefly and dropped to his sides. He stared at them through hooded eyes, filled with mistrust. The tuxedo bird gave them only a moment to follow him. When they didn't respond, he turned around and shuffled inside the skyscraper.

"Whoa, wait," Trouble yelled. He ran after the penguin, with Nuru and Tattoo close behind.

The king penguin looked afraid of them, yet the bird stood his ground. He waited for the trio to get close, then wobbled inside the building, glancing over his shoulder. He acted anxious, yet determined to make certain they were following him. It seemed weird behavior, especially since he'd fled from them only minutes ago.

Tattoo almost grabbed the penguin when Trouble stopped her. "Touching frightens him. Let's see where he goes. He seems to be leading us somewhere."

"All right." Tattoo pulled her hand back.

"I don't like this," Nuru complained, yet he kept walking behind the penguin.

The woodsy, dank odor became more concentrated inside the building, like a mildewed basement. Compensating for the bad smell was a feeling of warmth radiating from the walls. The icy film on their skin thawed and its moisture disappeared, wicked away by thermal underwear. Their muscles became more fluid in the heat and it felt easier to walk in normal strides.

Soon they reached an elevator similar to the one they rode into the cavern, a bolt that spun around, rising by threading itself out of the ground. Like the first elevator, this lift had a low wall of fine crystal. With a bit of a struggle, the elderly king penguin jumped the barrier. He skated across the floor, skidding to a halt before a long string of symbols.

The trio boarded the elevator and the penguin touched a hieroglyph with his flipper. They felt a sudden jerk, like a slight earthquake. Nuru leaned against the wall for support and the penguin chirped in a scolding tone, waving his flippers, urging Nuru to move away from the barrier.

Suddenly, the elevator wall spun and Nuru twisted, falling to the icy floor. Trouble skated to Nuru and offered him help to stand up. Nuru grabbed him and they both fell, skidding across the ice. They collided with Tattoo and then all three of them lay flat on the ground, slipping every time they tried to stand. With the bolt twisting upward, it felt very unpleasant to lie on the floor, spinning on the ice. The penguin didn't try to help them. He rolled his eyes in disgust and scolded them in high-pitched chirps.

Trouble gave up trying to stand and sat there, watching the elevator twist up the building's interior. Each level in the skyscraper had the empty look of a vacant warehouse. He couldn't see any doors or interior walls. It seemed no one had ever lived on the floors they were passing. Trouble saw no abandoned possessions, no furniture and there weren't even marks on the walls from someone moving out.

He watched the elevator blur past floors and finally it slowed, nearing the top of the high-rise. Trouble felt light shining on him and looked up to see a transparent roof, tinted blue-green. Though old and cracked, the broken glass dome painted their elevator with the aquamarine tones of an ocean lagoon. The visual effect made Trouble feel submerged, like he was underwater and fighting his way to the surface to get a breath of air.

Trouble was relieved when the elevator stopped at the building's top floor, halting in front of an unusual balcony. Astonished, he found himself looking at a terrace filled with sand like a tropical beach, as if they were shipwrecked on an island. Tile mosaics covered the balcony's walls. Perfect at one time, the tiles had shattered and become splintered with cracks.

The sandy balcony led to another surprise, a spiraling ramp coiled like a nautilus shell. The curving slope reminded Trouble of the Guggenheim Museum in New York City. The museum's interior follows a winding curve, twisting upward through galleries. Similar to the Guggenheim, paintings and tapestries hung on these walls, mixed with free-standing sculptures.

Sadly all the sculptures were lying on their side, damaged from falling off pedestals and hitting the floor. Dusty paintings and tapestries dangling at strange angles, tilted like a rollercoaster track. One jilted tapestry showed the Battle of Hastings, marking the Norman conquest of

England in 1066 A.D., a major landmark in British history. Competing armies of horsemen and archers clashed on a faded green battlefield. Other art works they passed were splashes of colors and shapes with no attempt to capture reality, like a Jackson Pollock painting.

At the top, the nautilus shell ramp ended in a huge apartment door in the shape of an oyster shell, like an open fan held by a Japanese Geisha. The penguin leaned against the pearlescent surface of the door and it pivoted open. The tuxedo bird led them through the oyster doorway into a huge loft, a single large room like the penthouse level of a renovated SoHo warehouse. Trouble's eyes swept across the soccer field size area and made a frightening discovery. In the center of the apartment reclined an enormous creature, lying on a couch.

The giant appeared old and in ill health. He made a labored attempt to stand and pain showed in his eyes. Still, the worn giant was a threatening sight. Even leaning over a cane, he was more than ten feet tall. Atop the immense body sat a regal face, very human in features. The handsome face was framed by a curly beard, bleached by time to match his neck-length silver hair. The gray of old age sprinkled through his black fur, though powerful muscles rippled in his arms. His body resembled a bear standing on its hind legs. The creature's feet looked huge, ending in sharp claws providing excellent traction on icy rock.

Likewise, the hands appeared gigantic. His long fingers had curving nails, talons that could easily tear a handhold in an icy slope – or rip open a person's throat.

Even more frightening was the snow leopard at the giant's side. The cat bared its fangs and snarled, poised to spring. Its powerful muscles quivered under the mottled white and black-spotted fur. The thought of being attacked by a huge creature and a vicious leopard caused the trio to shrink together. They formed a tight group and moved backwards, only to find the oyster shell door behind them was closed. They had nowhere to run when the giant moved toward them, using his cane as a walking stick. His long feet slapped the floor in drumbeats, echoing across the empty room.

It was almost beyond their courage to stand there as the huge beast approached. Trouble swallowed hard when the creature extended an arm in his direction. The giant's sharp claws moved slowly toward his face. At the last moment, the creature brought his hand up and touched Trouble's forehead with the soft pad of a palm. The massive hand made contact with Trouble's skin and warmth surged through his body, bringing a sense of calm. The giant rested his hand on Nuru and Tattoo in turn, closing his eyes when he made contact. They also seemed calmer.

The creature surprised them by talking. "Touching you, I learned that all of you speak English." He pointed to Nuru and Tattoo. "You also know the ancient Sherpa tongue, plus Nepalese. You understand a smattering of other languages, words learned from vendors at the Namche Bazaar. Am I right?"

Too stunned to reply, Nuru and Tattoo nodded their heads.

"And you, young man, are able to converse a bit in German and French, something you learned from your parents." He gave Trouble a wink. "I'm sorry I frightened you. There was no way for me to talk with you until I touched you and learned your language. Well, sit down. We've much to discuss. I haven't had visitors for a long time. I get very lonely, especially since I've been too ill to leave our city." The giant limped to his couch and reclined. He pointed to soft cushions nearby, indicating they should make themselves comfortable.

Trouble cleared his throat. "Uh, would it be possible …?" He pointed at the leopard. The snow leopard slinked forward. Its body language was the stalking motion of a carnivore getting ready to attack a cornered prey.

"Oh, yes. I forgot." The giant stared at the cat and talked in a strange language, a peculiar mixture of hissing and growling.

The bear-like creature explained his dialogue with the leopard. "I thanked Screecher for warning me about you and told him you mean no harm. I asked him to go home, leave the city."

It seemed clear the snow leopard didn't like what it was told. Screecher didn't budge. The leopard glared at the humans and snarled, raking the air with its claws.

The giant's next words weren't in English, but their tone made his message clear. The leopard was ordered to leave.

Screecher made a point of walking near Trouble. The cat sniffed at him, giving Trouble a scornful look. He tried very hard not to let his fear show.

The giant barked a command and Screecher's head swung around. An expression of contempt was in the leopard's eyes when it glared at the giant. The cat drifted toward the ramp, in no hurry to leave. Without warning, the leopard whipped its tail at Trouble's legs. He jumped to avoid a broken bone.

The giant smashed the floor with his cane and thunder crashed across the room. His voice became an imperial command, booming at the cat.

The leopard's back twisted in a violent spasm. The carnivore whimpered in pain and fell. When it got to its feet, the cat sprinted down the ramp and jumped on the elevator with a loud thump. The elevator whirred, beginning its descent, and everyone relaxed.

The bear-like creature apologized. "I'm sorry. Snow leopards are forbidden to come into the city. This was a gross violation, unjustifiable. Screecher's explanation was that he came to warn me humans were here. He's been waiting for an excuse to trespass. He sensed for a long time that few of us are left. Now Screecher knows the truth, that I'm the last Yeti."

"You're the only one? I thought there were hundreds of you." Tattoo shook her head in amazement.

The giant shrugged. "Just me, I'm afraid. I haven't been able to contact other Yetis in more than a decade. Seems they've all vanished."

"I wish the leopards would disappear instead," Nuru moaned.

Trouble managed to talk despite astonishment. "Yeah. Thanks for saving us from the cats."

The Yeti waved a hand, dismissing the appreciation. "I would have sent Screecher on his way earlier, but I was afraid for your safety. I kept him here, hoping you would find me before other leopards found you. Several cats were looking for you, scouring the city." His voice trailed off.

"We're safe now 'cause you control the cats." Nervous, Tattoo bounced a little in one of her break dance moves.

The Yeti sighed. "Don't overestimate my powers. Unfortunately, Screecher has now seen how old I am. Only instinctive fear, passed down through many generations of leopards, allows me to control him. So long as I have power over Screecher, we're safe. He's the dominant male, their king, so to speak. It was lucky you rode our magnetic levitation system for a while. That threw the leopards off your scent, kept them from tracking you. Otherwise, I'm afraid … Well, anyway, things worked out for the best. You followed my friend, Albert, and he brought you here."

"We were shocked to find a penguin inside Everest. I thought they lived in Antarctica, near the South Pole." Afraid he'd been impolite, Trouble rushed to say, "He's very handsome."

The Yeti petted the tuxedo-marked penguin. "Albert is an old and faithful helper. You might call him my butler."

"How long have penguins lived inside Everest?" Tattoo felt very curious.

The giant smiled. "A long time. Members of Albert's family have been with us … well, since before I was born in the year one thousand. Give or take a few years, of course. Recordkeeping wasn't accurate back then."

"You're more than a thousand years old?" Nuru was shocked.

"Yes." The Yeti turned to face Trouble. "I can prove it, if you don't mind a bit of history."

"You can? Go ahead," Trouble urged.

"Well, for one thing, I remember the Battle of Hastings in 1066. I stood there on a hillside with my family, watching."

"What were you doing in England? I thought Yetis lived in the Himalayas," Tattoo insisted. "That's what they say in the Namche Bazaar."

"Sorry to disillusion you. My parents were visiting an old friend in Scotland. Yetis still lived in the Scottish Highlands in those days."

"OK, so you hung out in Scotland. What was the fighting like at the Battle of Hastings? Lots of swords and horses, right?" Nuru acted excited.

The Yeti frowned. "Yes, sadly there was a lot of bloodshed. When the battle ended, we moved among the wounded on both sides, healing them as best we could. Of course, there wasn't much that could be done under the circumstances. Victorious Normans roamed the area all night, making it unsafe to linger."

"It must have been scary." Trouble wanted to be sympathetic.

The tall creature nodded. "Yes, it was frightening. That day made a vivid impression on me as a child. I got a firsthand look at the dark side of human behavior, as well as the very noble human capacity for courage and sacrifice. Anyway, that's why there's a tapestry about the Battle of Hastings hanging in my art gallery. You may have seen that drapery on the way in."

"Yes, actually I did see the tapestry. Um, fine needlepoint work. But I never thought … I mean …" Trouble stopped, at a loss for words. He didn't want to say that he never thought anyone could be so old.

The Yeti laughed. "You needn't be afraid of offending me by mentioning my age. Many centuries ago, I got used to the idea that I was … how shall I say it? Ah, yes. I got used to the idea that I'm a senior citizen's great, great grandfather."

The penguin interrupted his Yeti master. The tuxedo-marked bird made a questioning chirp.

"Albert wants to know if he is to serve refreshments," the Yeti explained. "Would you like some ice cream and cookies? Albert has brought them fresh from our local Coldery, an equivalent to your bakery."

Tattoo made a slight gagging noise at the thought of eating regurgitated ice cream or pooped cookies.

Trouble gave the Yeti an apologetic look. "We made the mistake of seeing how the cookies and ice cream were made."

The giant laughed, jiggling his gray beard. He rubbed a hand across his head, combing his silver hair. "Yes, it's a mistake to see how those items are created. Even Yeti children have trouble eating dessert afterwards." His eyes softened and became distant. "That is, when there were Yeti children in our city." He shook off the depression and again became the gracious host. "My name is Allyn. It sounds much like your Alan, does it not?"

"Yes." Trouble felt uncomfortable. "Are you King of the Yetis?" Perhaps he ought to bow to Allyn as a matter of protocol.

The giant smiled. "We've never had kings or emperors. I was the last elected leader of this Yeti colony, the largest. But to you, my guests, I'm just Allyn."

Nuru felt impatient. "I don't suppose, Sir Allyn –"

The Yeti interrupted. "I'm not a knight. You can just call me Allyn."

"Oh, sorry," Nuru apologized. "What I meant was, well …"

Tattoo barged into the conversation. "He means, Allyn, that he's hungry and wonders if there's anything else to eat besides ice cream and cookies from the Coldery."

"Well," Allyn hesitated. "You know, those items taste good, despite how they're made. And they are organic …"

Trouble smiled, recalling his comment in the Coldery.

The Yeti looked puzzled by Trouble's smile, but he continued anyway. "The cookies and ice cream are natural by-products made from the finest sponges. The whole system is environmentally sound."

"Huh?" Nuru acted suspicious. "Whaddya mean environmentally sound?"

"For one thing, uneaten vegetable waste is consumed by the sponges, who are by the way, very grateful for their role in our ecosystem. And the sponges are clean, despite their growing into rather peculiar shapes. I know those shapes are unpleasant to watch, but the ice cream and cookies meet our highest sanitary standards."

"Yes, I'm sure they do," Trouble assured him. "You mentioned vegetable waste. Where in the city do you grow vegetables? We'd be happy to cook some for you. And for Albert, of course."

"For Albert?" The Yeti seemed confused. "Albert only eats small fish. Well, he has acquired a taste for our ice cream. But a king penguin can't live on ice cream alone, anymore than a Yeti could."

"Sir Allyn – I mean, Allyn. Er, what do Yetis eat?" Nuru asked.

He laughed. "And can you have some?"

"Well, yes." Nuru acted shy.

"Other than the sponge byproducts we discussed, Yetis eat whole grains, berries, nuts and vegetables." Allyn shrugged. "Are you willing to eat such things?"

"Oh, definitely yes," Tattoo answered.

"And you also?" Allyn looked at Nuru first, then at Trouble.

"Sure," Nuru confirmed. Trouble nodded his approval.

"Hmm." Allyn looked a bit upset. "I've already eaten. Normally, I only visit the basement once a day. Well, there's no way around it. Come on, then. I warn you, the basement is a very unpleasant place. If you didn't care for sponges …" He took labored steps toward the ramp.

Trouble rushed to intercept him. "No, you sit down and rest. We'll take a short trip to the basement and be right back. There's no need for you to go along. In fact, we can bring you something for tomorrow's meal, if you like."

"You won't get lost?" Allyn looked more vulnerable than worried. It was obvious he missed having company very much and didn't want them to leave.

"Um, tell you what," Trouble volunteered. "Albert can go with Nuru and Tattoo, show them the way. I'll stay here."

Albert squealed at the idea of visiting the basement area. The penguin hopped up and down on his web feet, bouncing toward the exit ramp. Clearly his fish were kept downstairs and he intended to sneak an extra meal today.

Allyn thought it over. He rubbed the curly beard on his chin. "I don't like the idea of sending you down there without me. There may still be leopards in the city."

"Don't worry. We won't be in the city. We'll be in the basement." Nuru's hunger had overcome his fear of snow leopards.

"There are many paths into the world below this city. Every building has it's own basement area and they interconnect, like the catacombs under Paris." Allyn still felt concerned about their safety.

"Don't worry. We'll be careful." Tattoo and Nuru jogged down the ramp after the king penguin. The pull of hunger was stronger at that moment than any fear of what might happen. After all, Screecher was gone and he'd been told to leave the city. Soon they vanished out of sight, disappearing into the coiled nautilus shell ramp. There was a squeak of bodies sliding over the lift's crystal wall and a thump as Albert's flipper tapped the down button. Trouble heard a brief whir of the elevator descending and then silence.

17

After everyone left, the loft grew quiet, a vacuum without sounds. In the tense silence, Trouble felt anxious. He wondered if he'd been crazy to send the others away, leaving him alone with a Yeti, even though the creature spoke English and called himself "Allyn."

The elderly Yeti tried to put him at ease. "Why don't you have a seat on those cushions? I'm sure you have many questions. And I have a few for you." He tried to smile but pain seared his face. Allyn struggled to get comfortable on the couch, sinking into the red silk fabric. Once he felt better, Allyn's eyes resumed their vivid blue color, like wildflowers in spring. "Well, where do we start? You go first," he suggested.

"I don't know where to begin." Trouble struggled to find a safe topic and his eyes drifted to the museum-like entrance. "How did you get the art in your gallery?"

"I purchased most of it from artists in our city. I created the Battle of Hastings tapestry myself, when I was taking an art class through our university's extension program. I was a mere three hundred years old at the time." He smiled, knowing his age shocked Trouble. "I wove the 'canvas' from fine strands of bleached yak hair. Getting paints was the most difficult part. Yetis have never made ink or dye."

"Then how did you paint on your canvas?"

"I was fortunate to find a Yeti who traded with the Polo brothers, Niccolo and Matteo. Later, the Yeti traded with Niccolo's famous son, Marco Polo. Their caravans were loaded with vivid inks, obtained from artists at the court of Kublai Khan in Beijing."

"Yetis traded with people?"

Allyn nodded. "In the time of Marco Polo, we approached caravans when they made camp for the night, stopping at Lop Nur, a great lake north of Tibet. We offered jewelry in exchange for spices, paints and many things we couldn't make ourselves. We haven't dared trade with humans in recent years. It's become too risky."

"Then how did you build tall skyscrapers? You must have needed construction material from the outside world."

"We don't need anything from the outside to create our homes. You see, we don't build skyscrapers. We grow them."

"You grow them?" Trouble was amazed. "What kind of plant are they?"

"They're close relatives of the mushroom family. That's why the buildings appear in clusters, the way toadstools grow in a forest. This high-rise was the original mushroom in a cluster, so it's the tallest, and its descendents grow in rings around the building."

"How can you live inside a plant when it's growing all the time?"

"The plant only burps up a new floor every ten years. It's quite an event. The mushroom is kind enough to notify us it's growing. There's a strong aura pervading the building. The feeling is quite unmistakable. I've gotten too old to move everything. So my art collection got damaged the last time a new floor appeared."

"What about the windows? Do you poke holes in the plant so you can see out?"

Allyn shook his head. "The round holes are defects in the plant's living wall, although they're obviously useful flaws. Everyone likes windows."

"Your apartment walls are so bright. They don't look like a plant. Do you paint them?"

"No, we can't paint the walls. It would poison the mushroom. The walls look clean because the plant's old cells slough off. It keeps Albert quite busy once a month, sweeping up the molting skin."

"And the elevators?" he asked. "Are they part of the mushroom, too?"

"The elevators are inside a living plant, just as we are. But the lifts don't sprout from the mushroom, like a limb sprouts on a tree." Allyn felt uncomfortable and shifted on the couch. "The bolt-shaped elevators are actually crystals, mostly quartz."

"Where do you find the crystals? I saw that the cavern's dome looked like it was formed of minerals. Do you climb up there?"

"No. We don't have to harvest the crystals. This type of mushroom sweats quartz the way humans perspire salty water. We're lucky the toadstool concentrates that mineral. We provide the plant with a seed crystal in the right shape. New quartz forms around the seed, making the bolt larger as the building grows taller."

"I know when the elevator descends, it spins like a bolt threading into a socket. What causes the elevator to spin?"

Allyn coughed. "My throat is dry. Could you hand me some water?"

"Sure." Trouble poured water from a narrow pitcher into a goblet carved from ruby crystal, weighing as much as a daypack full of books. He brought it to the Yeti.

"Thank you." Allyn took a long drink from the glass, his meaty fingers delicately pinching the goblet's stem. "That's much better. You want to know how the lifts work. It happens like this. One elevator goes up and another elevator in a different building goes down, like a teeter-totter in a playground. Both elevators are the same weight, so they balance each other. When you came in my building, your elevator was lifted by a companion sinking."

"OK. One elevator canceled out the other. What about lifting the passengers?"

"We did need some additional power to raise you and your friends, plus Albert. Fortunately, lifting you a hundred floors in the air doesn't take as much energy as you might think."

"Where's the energy come from?"

"The power needed to lift you came from waterfalls in the city's basement. Melting snow creates waterfalls and we channel the flow through a hydraulic system. An underground waterwheel helps spin the elevator around. Channel water one way and you go up. Channel water on the other side and you go down. With nobody to maintain it, the system fell into disrepair over the years. I'm lucky our elevator still works. I'm too old to climb down the side of a hundred-story building."

"Um, thank you for the explanation. How many Yetis lived in these buildings? I mean, we estimated there's room in this skyscraper complex alone for 17,000 families. That's why we stopped chasing Albert. Finding him seemed hopeless."

"Oh, goodness. There's never been anything like 17,000 Yeti families in the entire city. Even in boom centuries, each family had its own building. I know that's excessive. It happened because we don't have the heart to stop the mushrooms from spawning little toadstools. After all, we had Yeti children. For the same reason, we didn't halt their growth. Of course, they do stop growing, when they get too old. After a certain age, they can't add more floors."

"What happens then?"

"The plant is sad for a time, but it adjusts. Personally, I was happy when my plant quit getting larger. It was a terrible chore to move all my furniture out until things settled down. This building failed to grow a new floor in the year 2000, by your calendar. The plant is still adjusting, but I was quite relieved."

"Sure, especially with your art gallery. You wouldn't want all those sculptures and murals damaged again. By the way, why did you decorate the entrance like an underwater coral reef?"

Allyn's eyes grew dreamy. "Those fish murals are beautiful, aren't they?" His mind drifted to a different time and place.

Trouble was reluctant to interrupt the Yeti's happy mood. In a few moments, he asked, "The sea is so far from Mount Everest. How did a Yeti get interested in oceans?"

Allyn's face became melancholy. "Oh, I wasn't always a stay-at-home. I went with other boys on an adventure once. We trekked to the ocean and found we could stay underwater for quite a while. Yetis have a lot of lung power from living at high altitudes. We can hold our breath for a long time." Allyn looked wistful. "I regret that I never got to the South Pacific. I've only seen pictures of it. I had a chance to go there once and I almost went. But going that far seemed risky."

"Wouldn't the tropical heat bother you?"

"I found a way to deal with hot weather." Allyn had a twinkle in his eyes. "Yetis are fond of tricks that let them get into mischief."

"What was the trick?"

"I'm afraid you'll be disappointed. My idea isn't all that clever. I stay underwater as long as I can, where it's cooler. My fur holds a lot of water, which lowers my temperature on land. When I dry off, I go in the water again."

Allyn took another drink from the goblet. "I did go to the Pacific Ocean once. Only it wasn't the South Pacific. Almost got to the Equator, but turned back. That's when I met Diana. I spotted her diving around a coral reef. She got a bit deep and her scuba gear quit working. She wasn't able to breathe. I couldn't let her drown. I popped from behind a giant clam and helped her. I startled Diana, especially when we got to the surface. Once Diana saw me clearly, she realized I wasn't something normally found in the ocean. We spent time together and fell in love, even though I'm a Yeti and Diana was human. It's happened before. I wasn't the first to choose a mate outside my race."

"Oh, wow. Now I know why you want the balcony decorated so it feels like being underwater."

"Yes, that was the thought. I miss Diana terribly. But I must confess something to you, Trouble." He looked sheepish.

"Yes?" He felt very curious to know what Allyn had to say.

"We, that is, Diana and I …" he stopped.

"Oh, it's all right. You mean you weren't married."

"Good heavens, no." Allyn flushed, which is a lot for a Yeti. "We had a beautiful ceremony, with friends on both sides. Of course, the people had to be hypnotized so they forgot everything, but that's unavoidable."

The Yeti stammered a bit. "Well, I'm afraid the next part is going to be a shock for you." Allyn hesitated. "Here goes. My Yeti name is nearly unpronounceable. It's Yergamegalorn Ergabish. The closest English translation of my name would be Allyn Jones." He paused. "Er, does that name sound familiar to you?"

"No," Trouble admitted. "Sorry."

"Your father never mentioned anyone with that name, Allyn Jones?" The Yeti looked disappointed.

"No, Dad never talked about an Allyn Jones." An idea was forming in Trouble's mind and it made him feel queasy. "You're …"

"Yes, I'm your grandfather. Diana was your grandmother. Your dad is our son – and I intend to scold him when I see him, for never telling you about me." His eyes didn't look angry, though. They were misty with tears.

"I don't get it." Trouble felt hurt. "Why didn't my parents tell me about you?"

"You were too young." He could see Trouble felt upset. "There's so much your parents didn't tell you. I should fill you in. Perhaps it will make you feel better."

Allyn struggled to his feet and paced with the help of his walking stick. The cane seemed large enough to be a tree limb. "Jones, by the way, is your grandmother's maiden name. I translated my Yeti last name into 'Jones' to honor your grandmother's memory. Diana passed away many years ago." A flicker of grief crossed his face.

He composed himself and went on. "Your father, as you know, is Indigo Jones. We called him 'Indigo' for a reason. Humans born to Yetis are the black sheep of their family. I named your father 'Indigo' because it represents a color of blue so dark it's almost black. I'm a rare exception among Yetis. I enjoy the company of humans. Most Yetis dislike people, even though we rescue them for humanitarian reasons. Diana never liked the name 'Indigo.' As a child, your grandmother loved spending summer in the Hamptons, her favorite place to visit. That's how your dad got his full name, Indigo Hampton Jones."

"I haven't seen my father in a long time. Do you know what happened to him?"

"Your mother told me Indigo went on one of his expeditions and didn't return. Julia looked for him in the usual places where he made archaeological digs, like cave dwellings in Norwegian fjords and Siberian Kurgans. Sadly, she found no evidence he'd visited any of their sites recently. Now your mother is also missing. I imagine you came looking for her."

"I did. Has something happened to my dad or mom? You have a good intuition."

"I'll meditate for a second. See if I come up with anything." Allyn closed his eyes and his face relaxed. He seemed to be falling asleep, the rhythm of his breathing slowing to a calm, deliberate pace. Yet a moment later, he awoke with a frightened expression, shaking his head like he was trying to chase away a nightmare. He bolted from the couch and hobbled toward the elevator. "Come on. I think we'd better check the basement. My intuition brought me a warning, about your friends, not your parents." He moved down the ramp in careful steps, putting most of his weight on the cane. Allyn's toenails clicked against the floor, marking the deliberate tread of his feet, the ramp shaking with his weight.

The strides were so long Trouble had difficulty keeping up with the Yeti and he was forced to jog. When they got to the lift, he asked Allyn, "Did you see an image of some kind?"

"Yes," the Yeti admitted. Allyn sat on the low elevator wall. Sitting made it easier to roll his legs over the barrier. Once inside the elevator, he tapped the Yeti hieroglyph for "basement."

Trouble prodded him. "What did you see?"

"I sensed fear among your friends and Albert. I hope we're not too late."

"The leopards?"

"Yes," Allyn nodded. "Snow leopards are in the city again – and that is a very bad sign."

18

The elevator ride seemed endless, carrying them downward from the 100th floor, spinning past the lobby into a buried world. The moment they sank below ground level, Trouble felt how different Yeti City was from its basement. Within seconds, the temperature grew warmer and he became uncomfortable in his parka. Trouble's discomfort was made worse by humid air, filled with ugly smells. Riding the elevator felt like standing in a damp bathtub overgrown by mildew.

The sickening atmosphere got even worse when they descended into the root of the gigantic mushroom. The plant's walls blackened, dripping mold. Pulsing cells quivered inside the walls, ingesting food and releasing obnoxious vapors. After a long stretch of trembling cells, the elevator ran through a fibrous area filled with collapsed growth.

"We're at the unfinished level, a new floor that never emerged," Allyn explained. "The plant was too old to grow another floor for the building."

"What will become of this unborn level?" Trouble asked.

"Eventually it will rot." Allyn looked sad. "We're about the same age, this mushroom and me. We're both a thousand years old, give or take a few. Invented at the same time, so to speak."

"Just yesterday," Trouble said, trying to improve the Yeti's mood. There was hardly enough light for Trouble to see Allyn's face. The plant's walls were very close, dragging against the elevator's sides, slowing its descent. The suction became audible in a squishing sound as the lift spun downward, forcing itself through the plant's tight grip. Suddenly, the elevator cleared the mushroom's narrow root base with a loud "plop." The lift jarred to a halt, threaded into its socket.

The whirring elevator motor stopped and everything grew quiet. Velvet darkness surrounded them, relieved slightly by light threading along a tunnel in the plant base. A humid breeze stirred in the tunnel, carrying unpleasant odors like a compost heap. Far away, tinkling water dripped into a pool.

Trouble felt uneasy in this strange environment. "Is this where we get off the elevator?"

"Yes." Allyn's speech was slurred and he seemed disoriented. He sat on the low elevator barrier, similar to the wall of an ice rink. "Help me get over the wall, will you? This heat drains my energy."

Trouble assisted Allyn, but holding his arm seemed like lifting a car. Trouble realized how muscular a Yeti was, even in old age. He felt relieved Allyn didn't need more assistance. Trouble jumped the low barrier and followed his grandfather into the tunnel. After a short walk, they exited the shaft and stood in a vast area filled with machinery used to move elevators up and down.

The elevator mechanisms resembled huge gears turning inside Big Ben, a massive clock tower in London. Everywhere Trouble looked, wheels spun and levers shifted. He followed Allyn through a maze of spinning gears and rope pulleys. Trouble was careful not to snag his clothing on a moving part and get caught in the dangerous machinery.

The farther they walked, the noisier it got. Troughs splashed water into streams that merged to become loud, pelting waterfalls. Unused water wheels creaked, rocking back and forth like abandoned windmills. Behind Trouble, the waterwheel for his grandfather's elevator screeched, raising the lift out of the hot basement. In reaction, another elevator began falling, balancing the weight of its rising partner. The spinning elevators blew soot in the air like helicopter blades stirring up dust when a chopper takes off.

With the gritty air and sticky heat, Trouble's grandfather wheezed, suffering a shortness of breath. Passing a gushing waterfall, Allyn signaled he needed a rest. He walked under the falls and stayed for almost a minute. After his fur got soaked, the Yeti stepped out and shook himself. He sprayed water the way a dog shakes after dipping in a lake. His thick salt and pepper fur smelled like a wet rug, pungent and musky.

"That's better," he announced. His eyes looked brighter and his wheezing disappeared. They resumed walking, pacing alongside a railroad track. The rails were spaced too close together for a real train. It seemed a narrow gauge system, the type of miniature railroad used to move ore in a mining operation.

In a few minutes, they came to a set of passenger cars, far smaller than modern double-decker rail carriages. Each of the little cars resembled a wooden crate, a box with small iron wheels for rolling along tracks. The passenger carriages weren't coupled together, making a long train. Instead, each cart moved by itself. The cars were lined up like a row of taxis, waiting to take you out of the station.

Allyn got inside the front carriage and water dripped from his fur, puddling on the wooden floor. He signaled Trouble to join him inside the miniature rail car. When he was settled, Allyn put his lips close to Trouble's ear, so he could hear his grandfather over the noise. "These basements were only visited by maintenance engineers. There's no magnetic levitation system to whisk you around. We'll have to use our muscles." The Yeti pointed to a teeter-totter bar in the center of the cart. "When I push down on my bar, your side goes up. Then you push down and my side comes up. Our pushing turns a crank, moving us along the tracks."

"Oh, I get it." Trouble waited his turn and gave his bar a push in rhythm to Allyn's efforts. They started moving, picking up speed each time they rocked the teeter-totter bar in the middle of their cart. Soon, they came to a switch in the rails and were shunted to another path. The track began descending, pitching downward at a steep angle. It was no longer necessary to pump the bar. The old cart raced downhill, flying around curves and popping over small hills. Every time they jumped a mound of brown earth, they experienced a sudden drop and Trouble's stomach lurched like it did on a rollercoaster, a very unpleasant feeling.

He clutched the sides of the cart as they clattered over a rickety bridge, a rough wooden skeleton of crude timbers. Trouble ventured a glance downward and wished he hadn't looked. He saw no bottom to the chasm under the bridge. The ride became even more frightening when they entered a narrow tunnel. Their speeding rail carriage clipped against limestone boulders on sharp turns.

Trouble wished the ride was over and had come to a safe conclusion. He definitely felt ready to have the car stop so he could get out. "Where are we going?"

"To the lowest basement, where food is grown. We needed a warm place to raise crops and the earth gets hotter as you go farther inside. We're descending to an old volcanic layer that once covered the entire globe. It's called the earth's mantle. When the mantle cooled, a crust formed. New York, for example, is built on top of that crust. But Yeti City is built inside the earth, with basements down to the mantle itself."

"Now I understand why it's so hot. How come it's also humid?" Trouble asked.

"The humidity comes from mineral springs. When an underground spring flows through a volcano, the water is boiled into steam. The steam becomes hot geysers, misting vapor like a tea kettle. Humidity from geysers helps the plants grow."

"But don't plants also need sunlight?"

Allyn nodded. "Our scientists invented a clever system to funnel sunlight down here. They bred a new species of giant earthworm. These worms look for sunlight by drilling through Mount Everest. At the surface, a worm traps light inside its body like a fiber-optics cable. Sunlight flows through the earthworm and a beam shines out the tail similar to a flashlight, bringing sunlight to our plants."

"How can these worms tunnel through a mountain like Everest, made of rock? I mean, normal earthworms only have to wriggle through dirt, not granite boulders."

"Acid," his grandfather answered. "These worms have an ability to ooze hydrochloric acid from pores in their body. When you entered Yeti City, did you notice the tunnel was perfectly round?"

"Sure. The sides of the ventilation shaft were smooth, like they were melted."

"Melted indeed, by concentrated hydrochloric acid," Allyn confirmed.

"What happens when the worm finishes its tunnel and gets to the surface? Can't it squirm out of the hole and escape?"

"No. The scientists caused a bulge to grow at the end of a worm's tail and it can't leave the tunnel. It's important the worm stays in the tunnel so sunlight can flow through the earthworm and shine on our plants, helping them grow. Your grandmother Diana improved the system. Diana ran worm light through crystals she invented. Her crystals amplify the light, letting the plants grow faster."

Allyn shook his head, anticipating the next question. "No, I don't know how Diana's light crystals work. It's too technical for me. All I know is that she used a type of laser, an intense light beam. Diana told me lasers resonate like a bell ringing when it's struck. Her crystals also ring when hit by sunlight, producing a laser."

Trouble frowned, wishing he understood more. He really only figured things out when he took them apart. Unfortunately, he was much better at taking things apart than he was at putting things together. Trouble learned it was best to know an expert who could reassemble gadgets after he dismantled them. That way his father didn't yell at him for destroying something valuable. Of course, the most valuable things in his life were his parents and friends. That thought filled his chest with anxiety. He hoped his parents were safe, along with Nuru, Tattoo and Albert.

"How long before we get to the agricultural basement?" he pressed his grandfather.

"Not long. Hold on tight. The last curves are sharp ones – and the stop is sudden," Allyn warned.

The Yeti wasn't kidding. They twisted through a set of tight curves at high speed and Trouble got slammed from side to side, barely able to keep from flying out of the box. He thought their antique cart would jump off the tracks, yet the old train car managed to grip the rails. He barely had time to recover from the sprain of those curves when the tracks ended. Their train carriage jetted from the tunnel and went flying into a large cavern. They fell in a sand pit, slamming against the push-bar mechanism. The blow knocked all the air from Trouble's lungs and he sat there in pain, rubbing his stomach.

Gradually, Trouble recovered and became aware of his surroundings. He was in a cave. It was too dark to know the cavern's size, though it seemed huge. Red glow flashed on the horizon and rumbling came to his ears from a vast distance. He remembered his grandfather mentioning that the cave held volcanoes. The volcanic eruption was followed by a soft earthquake, rolling the earth beneath their feet and shifting the horizon.

After the quake, violent geysers sprayed from holes in the cave walls. Blistering vapor jets appeared with a loud hiss, venting for a moment and then disappearing. One searing jet vanished only to have another geyser burst out. They never happened in the same place twice.

The cave walls were riddled with cracks and fissures, so there was no way to know where the next geyser would appear. Accidentally walking into a geyser would be fatal. Superheated steam could burn the skin off a person before they escaped. The cavern seemed to be Trouble's vision of hell, a place of eternal fear and darkness.

He saw only one point of brightness in the cave, where light beams sprayed from the cavern's roof. The spray of light came from a diamond-shaped crystal on the ceiling. The sparkling gem swung in a twitching motion, spasming to a rhythm of its own. Trouble realized the dancing crystal was attached to the tail of a fantastic creature, a huge worm.

The earthworm was shaped like a drill bit, with grooves spiraling around its skin. It had bored a hole through Mount Everest by oozing rock-melting acid. A bulging disk near the tail stopped the worm from crawling out the hole when it reached the surface. The fat tail disk sprouted antennas like a patch of wiry hair. Eye-like balls hung at the end of each antenna. The dangling eyeballs gyrated as the worm twitched. Sometimes antennas twisted around each other and then uncoiled violently, as though one eyeball couldn't stand touching another. The eyeballs blinked, recoiling from the brilliant light of the crystal laser, sparking on and off.

In that blinking light, objects appeared, then faded to blackness. Slowly, Trouble's eyesight adjusted to the flickering illumination. In the distance, he recognized the outlines of huge greenhouses, a dozen Victorian-style conservatories with elaborate domes. All the conservatories seemed in bad shape and vines had burst through cracked windows.

At one shattered greenhouse, a butterfly with wings the size of a stained glass window flitted through broken glass panes. In a tragic moment, the beautiful moth flew into a silver web and was caught by a spider the size of an octopus. Trouble watched a heartbreaking sight, but it wasn't the only tragedy happening in the greenhouses. A caterpillar large as a python devoured what few living plants remained inside a conservatory. An incomparable collection of rare specimens from ancient times was vanishing forever.

Trouble felt sad. "The plants must have been incredible."

"Yes, they were spectacular." His grandfather sounded upset. "Well, now you know why I don't come here often. The guilt feels terrible. I can't fix anything. It's hard enough just enduring the heat. Your mother used to keep things in better order, but Julia's been gone for a long time, as you know." He put an arm around Trouble and gave him a gentle hug.

"Mom will be back soon," Trouble reassured him, hoping it was true.

The Yeti sighed. "Well, we better look for Albert and your friends."

"Shall I call them?"

"No. There may be leopards here. I'm too old to handle more than one cat. Only instinctive fear kept them away. But that fear is vanishing, as you saw with Screecher. We'll have to quietly search the greenhouses for your friends."

"That'll take a while. These are pretty large buildings."

"Larger than you think. Distances are hard to judge in this light. The greenhouses are almost a half mile away."

"You're joking." Trouble was surprised.

"I wish I were kidding," Allyn said, and began hobbling toward the nearest conservatory building.

19

Walking in the cavernous basement, Allyn and Trouble became tiny specks in an oversize world. Everything seemed larger than life. Ahead of them, giant greenhouses loomed, an agricultural complex of block-long conservatories. With their elaborate domes, the Victorian conservatories resembled the Capitol building in Washington D.C. and its beautiful cupola. Each greenhouse appeared comparable in size to the Capitol, a huge structure housing the American Congress.

Overhead, dozens of massive earthworms dangled from the cavern's ceiling. Sadly, most of the worms seemed lifeless. The dead earthworms looked dried out and withered, faded to ashen skins. They dangled from the cavern's dome like deflated party balloons pinned on the ceiling with a thumbtack. Only one healthy worm remained, a highly animated insect wriggling like a beckoning finger. The earthworm's tail spun around, gyrating in a bizarre dance. At the end of the worm's tail, a crystal flipped bursts of light in the air, resembling a burning fireworks sparkler, hissing and crackling.

When he walked closer, Trouble realized the dangling crystal was broken, cracked in several places. The damaged lens pulsed like strobe lighting in a nightclub, splitting the darkness for a second, freezing all motion before everything vanished into shadows. With steam geysers blasting from the walls, walking in that fitful lighting felt like moving across a dangerous battlefield at night, lit only by explosions. It was a stressful, frightening experience.

In the flickering light, they took an hour to reach the nearest conservatory, a sprawling greenhouse covering a city block or more. The building's two-story front doors dangled from broken hinges, damaged by a falling worm. In contrast to the decaying building, a rich perfume of roses wafted through the open doors, mingled with the sharp odor of rotted vegetation.

Trouble approached the entrance and Allyn put a hand on his shoulder, restraining him. "Let me check it out before we go inside." The Yeti puckered his nose and sniffed the air.

"Can you smell Albert or my friends?"

"Not yet." Allyn moved cautiously into the greenhouse. A vine with thick leaves was wrapped around a post near the door. The vine's curving tendrils extended toward the Yeti and began caressing themselves, beckoning him closer.

Trouble couldn't believe his ears when the plant talked to his grandfather in a seductive, feminine voice. "Hello, Allyn. I've missed you. Won't you come closer so we can touch? You know how I love it when you stroke me."

"What is this thing?" Trouble was amazed. He moved toward the vine to examine it.

Allyn pulled him away just in time. A clamshell with sharp barbs lunged at Trouble and the jaws snapped shut, almost swallowing him.

"Stay close to me and don't touch anything," Allyn warned. "If that meat-eating shrub grabs you, not even I can help. The plant dissolves its prey. An animal turns to syrup in moments."

"Ouch." Trouble felt shocked. He stared at the plant with even more curiosity. "The vine talks in a woman's voice."

"Diana's voice, to be precise." Allyn sounded irritated. "The blasted thing heard Diana use my name once. Now it calls to me every time I enter the conservatory. I haven't had the energy to trim the plant back. It puts up quite a fight when you try to prune its limbs."

"What kind of plant is it?"

"That is a Siren of the Sea, the very creature mentioned in Greek mythology. But it's no myth, as you can see. In ancient times, siren plants grew near the ocean shore and lured sailors closer by singing to them in a woman's voice. Their boat ran aground on submerged rocks. When sailors jumped in the water to push their boat away, the plant ate them for lunch."

"You're kidding. That was for real? I thought it was just a story someone made up to pass the time on a dull evening." Trouble gave the plant a respectful glance.

"A lot of ancient myths have a basis in reality." Allyn brushed thick foliage out of his face and sniffed the air again.

All Trouble could smell was an overpowering scent of roses, like a spilled perfume bottle. "The rose odor in here is suffocating."

Allyn ignored the comment and began walking at a quick pace, using the cane for a crutch so he could go faster.

"What is it?" Trouble called out, trotting after him.

"It isn't just roses I smell," the Yeti said. His breath became labored again, as though the asthma had returned.

"Slow down," Trouble urged. "They can wait a few seconds for us to join them."

"No, they can't." Allyn sounded worried. "You see, it isn't only roses I smell in here. There's fresh blood in the air." The Yeti stopped to catch his breath. "And the scent of a leopard."

Trouble scanned the area, hoping no one was hurt. Then he spotted an object lying on a nearby path. Outlined by a dark stain, the triangular shape was unmistakable. There on the gravel path lay one of Albert's flippers. It had been ripped off his body by a snow leopard's talons. One side of the flipper was a ghastly mess of torn ligaments and muscle.

"Oh no," Trouble groaned. "It can't be true." But it was. He ran to the flipper and gently picked it up, hoping there was some way to restore the wounded limb. Blood trickled on his hand and he turned the severed wing in a vain attempt to preserve the vital fluid. The flipper felt warm and the blood hadn't clotted. The attack on the king penguin seemed a recent event. "This just happened. Albert must be near us."

"The leopard is also nearby," Allyn warned. "Keep silent if you can. And walk softly. In this flickering light, we'll never see the cat until it's too late." He moved forward again, walking so quietly that Trouble couldn't hear a single footstep when he followed.

Trouble carried Albert's flipper as they crept forward, moving through a jungle of plants. It was impossible to see clearly in the blinking illumination. One moment there was brilliant light, blinding them, and the next moment it was black as the ocean bottom, miles deep. Trouble couldn't help brushing against foliage in the dark, despite his grandfather's warning not to touch the plants. At one point, sticky leaves kissed his face and clung like suction cups to his skin. The "kissing" leaves had to be pulled off his cheeks and they left behind painful welts.

Trouble stumbled over the fleshy tentacles of vines sliding along the overgrown walkway. He saw a flash of light and realized the vines were reaching, trying to grab his ankles, just as the "kissing" leaves attacked his face. Desperate to escape, he ran into the sharp thorns of a rose bush, snaring himself in prickly branches. It felt like running into a cactus, with a hundred needles piercing his skin, jabbing nerve endings. He fought not to scream, stuffing the side of a hand in his mouth and biting down.

Allyn came to his rescue and began the tedious process of removing each barbed thorn. "You should be more careful."

"I tried," he whispered. "But those vines wanted to catch me. I had to escape."

"They're harmless," Allyn assured him.

"To you they're harmless, Grandfather. You're strong enough to pull your ankles loose."

"You have a point, Trouble," Allyn admitted. "But please try to be quiet. We're getting close. I can smell it."

"How can you smell anything over those roses?" Trouble asked in frustration. "Their odor is like a whole perfume counter of smashed bottles."

"Yes. They were cultivated for that purpose. Those roses have many times the normal amount of scent." There was another flash of light and Trouble caught a glimpse of Allyn's face. He looked serious and tense.

"I'll show you what the roses are hiding," the Yeti whispered, pointing to long rows of boulders.

The worm's laser pulsed again, revealing the "boulders" were actually enormous plants. Each plant was a giant tulip bulb at the base, high as Trouble. Above his head, the bulbs fanned into rows of pipes, looking like a church organ. However, organ pipes were thicker than the plant's tubes, which were only the width of a garden hose. He heard a gurgling noise rumbling inside the hoses, sounding like bad plumbing in an old house. A creamy liquid oozed from a nozzle at the end of each hose. Hanging above the hose nozzle was a blood-red flower blossom.

Trouble slid between thorny rose bushes for a better look at the weird plants in front of him. He instantly regretted getting closer. Once

Trouble left the perfumed roses, a foul smell enveloped him like a cloud of poison gas. He inhaled a hideous odor familiar to cemetery workers and grave robbers, the stench of a dead body rotted from weeks in a grave, the smell of moldy skin mingled with decomposed organs.

Trouble went into shock. "What are those horrible plants?"

"Those," Allyn explained, "are 'stowns,' a pun on their size, comparable to a large stone or boulder. These Yeti-bred stowns are cousins of the *titan arum*, the world's largest flower. *Titan arums* can grow to twice my height, almost twenty feet tall. In nature, *Titan arums* bloom several times during their forty-year lifetime. The *Titan* plant was originally discovered in the tropical rainforests of Indonesia."

"But why did you grow such awful plants?" Trouble worked hard not to breathe their smell, but it didn't help.

"Why indeed?" Allyn agreed. "Well, because of the bacteria that grows on stown plants. That gurgling you hear is the plant's attempt to wash off the *rhodoferax ferrireducens* bacterium. However, the cleaning doesn't work very well. The bacteria lives by eating stown plants, the same way bacteria eats human flesh in the grave. The smell of rotting bodies is why we had to breed special roses with many times the normal amount of perfume."

Trouble gagged from the putrid odor and cleared his throat. "That's all very fascinating, Grandfather, but you haven't told me why you grow these disgusting plants."

"Ah, yes. That part. We grow them for the electricity provided by the bacteria."

"Can't you get by without electricity? I mean, I didn't see any appliances in your apartment."

"What about the gliding slippers? The magnetic levitation system needs electric power to work – and these plants also need electricity." The Yeti waved a hand to encompass the tangled growth around them.

"The plants?" Trouble asked in confusion.

Allyn nodded. "They need light, a lot of light. We can't bring enough sunlight down here, so we generate it using lasers. Remember that crystal, the one hanging from the worm over this greenhouse?"

"Yes, the broken lens dangling from the giant worm's tail. But why do crystals need electricity?"

"OK," Allyn explained, "the crystal is a laser. Without electricity, the laser would fade out, the way a bell stops ringing. These rows of stown plants are a battery cell, powering the laser. Plus the mag-lev system."

"Oh," Trouble said in exasperation. "Why didn't you say so?"

Allyn gave him a scolding look. “Grandson,” he said sternly, “I can see why you were named Trouble.”

Trouble felt very embarrassed. He tried to recover. “Er, well, thank you for the science lecture.” He wasn’t certain what his grandfather said in reply, but it sounded like a displeased “harrumph.” He felt it was best to leave Allyn alone for a while.

Trouble moved away, trying to spot his friends. It was hard to focus his eyes with that obnoxious smell fouling his mind. That kind of odor belonged to a graveyard night. The image brought chilling fear as he held poor Albert’s flipper. Who else got injured, he wondered? Maybe they were dead.

20

Trouble crouched behind a cluster of rose bushes and scanned the greenhouse. From where he was squatting, he couldn't see Nuru, Tattoo or the wounded Albert. Thorn scratches on his neck itched like a poison ivy rash, adding to his impatience. Trouble felt he must locate his friends. He took a step forward and Allyn's large hand stopped him in mid-stride, hitting Trouble's chest like a football block. He recovered from the stunning collision and stared at the Yeti in surprise. Allyn put a finger to his lips, a reminder to be silent. He gestured along the row of bulbous plants, indicating there was a problem.

Trouble looked down the row of stown plants and was shocked to see a massive leopard, twice the size of Screecher. This snow leopard had curving front teeth, longer and thicker than a rattlesnake's fangs. The powerful cat's bloodstained teeth were chilling proof the carnivore was an experienced killer. Jumping on a quarry's back, the leopard used those razor-like fangs to cut a prey's throat.

Allyn whispered. "She's a mutant, a throwback to the prehistoric saber-toothed tiger. Her name is Styx. She's queen of our snow leopard colony."

"Can you order her to leave?"

"I doubt it. Styx was always our worst problem. She takes orders from no one but Screecher. Only he can control her. Let's watch and wait. Find out why she's here." They moved into the darkest shadows, pressing against roses until Trouble was concerned he'd get snagged by sharp thorns again.

Without warning, the leopard walked straight at Trouble and halted. The cat's nostrils quivered as the leopard plucked each scent from the air and examined it. The cat's head slowly turned until her eyes were staring right at the hiding pair.

Trouble held his breath, hoping Styx couldn't smell anything but overpowering rose perfume and the disgusting odor of stown plants. There was a violent flash of light and Trouble lost all vision. His mind raced. Had the snow leopard spotted them, or was Styx also blinded by the streak of light? When Trouble's eyesight returned, the cat was slinking away, moving down the row of stown plants, her powerful muscles flexing with each stride.

"Come on," Allyn whispered. He quietly stepped on the path, only a few yards behind Styx.

Trouble attempted to move forward and his face almost touched a stown plant. The stown was in a cleansing cycle and made a soft gurgling, trying to wash itself by vomiting sap. Yellow juice poured down the stown pipes, smelling like a dead animal rotting in the sun, a gross odor flooding Trouble's nostrils. He wobbled from lightheadedness, moving even closer to the stown. The plant was coated with electricity-generating bacteria, a charged current of germs sparking on the foliage, covering a thick scum of decaying plant flesh.

"Don't touch the stowns," Allyn hissed. "You'll get bacteria on you. The germs shock you like a million little batteries. You'll lose control of your muscles and start dancing around. Styx will find you in a heartbeat, from all the noise you'll make."

"Why are we near these plants when they're so dangerous?" Trouble whispered.

"We've searched for your friends everywhere else. This is the only spot left to look. The foul odor of the stowns may be the reason Nuru, Tattoo and Albert are hiding back here. Styx can't smell them."

Moving through the stowns was tense, difficult work, made worse by long periods of darkness. When the laser stopped pulsing, they were blinded. They held their position, frozen like a street mime. Trouble's muscles ached from keeping his body in unnatural poses, the tension of waiting for a light flash, followed by a dangerous step. His life became disjointed movements – another strobe of light and a fast step into an unbalanced posture, then freeze, stressing every muscle in his body and tensing every nerve. Ten minutes of that pattern seemed like running a marathon.

Trouble felt soft pressure against his shoulder and jumped with fear. Trouble was worried he'd bumped into a stown plant and gotten bacteria on his arm. Worse yet, Styx might have brushed against him in the dark. But it was Allyn touching him, asking Trouble to look at something.

He craned his neck, stretching to see beyond the stown plants. When a laser blast lit the area, he saw Tattoo and Nuru crumpled on the floor, with Albert lying between them. They seemed lifeless, rag dolls flung on the ground. Not even their chests moved in the act of breathing.

Trouble and Allyn slipped toward the motionless trio, choosing each footstep carefully, trying not to crunch on the gravel. At last, Allyn reached the closest rag doll, a limp shape on the sandy path. The tall Yeti knelt and touched Tattoo's neck, checking for a pulse.

Allyn exhaled in relief. "She's alive." The Yeti moved to Nuru and pressed a finger against the young Sherpa's jugular vein. "Nuru's OK. I think they passed out from the smell."

Trouble could understand losing consciousness from inhaling the putrid odor of the stown plants. He was feeling light-headed himself from breathing the stench. "What about Albert? Is he alive?"

"Albert's in bad shape. Lost a lot of blood. Brave fellow must have tried to protect Tattoo and Nuru. Probably stood in front of them and chattered at Styx, telling her to go home. I'd guess Styx took a swipe at Albert and tore off his flipper."

"Can the penguin be healed?"

Allyn grunted in a sorrowful way. "Don't know." He adjusted his position. "I'll wake your friends." He touched Nuru on the forehead and the young Sherpa stirred a bit.

Trouble knelt down to help, rubbing Tattoo's frozen hands to restore some circulation. Her chilled fingers felt like latex gloves. Allyn and Trouble were so focused they didn't notice Styx approaching.

The leopard was gliding in her sleek, arrogant style when a flash of light highlighted Trouble and Allyn. The presence of a Yeti caused

Styx to approach with caution. She moved only when it was dark and remained motionless during each interval of light. The cat's stealthy movements gave no warning as she got closer.

Allyn began reviving Tattoo, bringing her awake. Trouble rubbed his friend's wrist and called to her softly, unaware of the approaching danger.

Every time the light died, Styx moved, a skilled hunter stalking her prey. There were more pulses of light, followed by long periods of darkness when it was easy for the leopard to close on her victims.

Trouble looked up and saw dagger-like teeth sparkling a few feet away, much too close for escape. Styx was poised to strike, her legs coiled like springs.

"Allyn," Trouble shouted. It was too late.

Styx charged Allyn with blinding speed, trying to sink her long fangs in his throat. The Yeti fought with his walking cane. He jabbed one end in the ground and pointed the other end at Styx, hoping she'd impale herself. The leopard was cunning and shot past the spear-like cane. Allyn struck the cat on her flank, knocking her away, but the leopard's claws raked his arm, opening a terrible wound. Pushed to one side, Styx landed in a stown, her powerful body crushing the plant. Broken stown pipes showered the leopard with bacteria-laden syrup.

Trouble hoped the leopard was disabled. "Styx has germs all over her."

"The bacteria takes time to act." Allyn gritted his teeth, fighting off the pain of his wounded arm.

The leopard's next attack was more cautious. She waited for blood loss to weaken the Yeti. The cat moved like a boxer in a ring, circling her opponent, trying for an advantage. She swiped her claws at Allyn, forcing him to use the wounded arm, draining his strength.

He jumped aside to avoid a vicious swipe and the agile leopard pivoted, shifting her target. The leopard sprang at Tattoo, trying to land on her prone body. Luckily, she rolled away, spinning like a carpet being unrolled to cover a hardwood floor. To protect Tattoo, Allyn jabbed his stick at the leopard, forcing her to abandon her attack on Tattoo and pay attention to the Yeti.

Styx circled Allyn again, thinking she had plenty of time for another attack. In the leopard's mind, time was on her side, but she was wrong. Flesh-rotting bacteria was feeding on sugars from her sweat, growing, worming its way into her skin. The great cat brushed herself with her tail. Then she twisted her neck and bit at her spine, distracted by pain.

Allyn used the moment to strike a powerful blow. He whipped the cane down, hitting the carnivore with a loud crack that echoed through the greenhouse several times.

Knocked to the ground, Styx gave a blood-curdling howl. But the huge leopard rose with twice the fire in her eyes. She charged Allyn without regard for his size or weapon.

The Yeti again tried to impale the leopard. She flew over his stick and knocked him to the earth. Her talons raked his chest and stomach, tearing out his fur, ripping his flesh open.

Nuru was awake now and sprang to his feet, joining the fight. He opened his pocketknife and buried its short blade in the leopard's thick neck. Styx twisted her head around, snapping her powerful jaws at Nuru. Her sharp teeth could've severed his arm, but Nuru anticipated the leopard's reaction and pulled away in time.

Nuru's assault focused the carnivore entirely on him, leaving the cat exposed to attack by another person. Trouble saw the opportunity and raised Allyn's heavy walking stick. He used the cane like a baseball bat, swinging it with all his strength. The cane hit Styx's head with the thunk an axe makes chopping wood. Trouble didn't like striking an animal, but he had to defend his grandfather.

Tattoo joined the battle. She yanked a plant stake from a flowerbed and used it as a spear, jabbing Styx in the side hard enough to make a sickening crunch. A rib was broken and the powerful cat froze in pain. The leopard became a stationary target for the first time in the fight and easy to hit.

Allyn recovered enough to punch Styx in the head with his massive fist, staggering the animal with his blow. Styx dropped like a cut tree and lay there without moving, her tongue lolling out of her mouth. The cat's lungs rose and fell in ragged breathing, indicating the leopard was unconscious and hadn't been killed.

Trouble swung away from the fallen animal and looked at his grandfather, a bloody rug lying on the ground. He rushed to the Yeti and knelt down. "Oh, Allyn, no. Don't die."

"I'll do my best." The Yeti managed a weak smile.

"Isn't there some way we can help you? Is there a hospital with medicine? Where do we take you?"

"The great pyramid," Allyn gasped.

"What?" Trouble bent low to hear his weak voice.

"You must take me to the great pyramid, the healing pyramid, where I cured Nuru's legs."

"Yes, of course." Trouble looked around, bewildered. "Where's this pyramid?"

"Inside the peak of Everest. The mountain's top forms the dome of the healing pyramid."

"But that's a long way," Trouble protested. "You won't make it."

"Yes, I will."

"How?" he begged. "Your wounds …" Trouble couldn't bear to look at them.

"Gather mint, all you can find. Bushels of it. Mint is the Yeti healing herb."

"It'll take too long. We have to get you to the pyramid now." Trouble felt disoriented from the shock of all that had happened.

"There's no point in going to the pyramid without mint. The herb will slow my bleeding. It's high in Vitamin K, allowing my blood to clot around the wounds, so I don't bleed to death."

That was all he needed to hear. Trouble raced along the rows of plants in a desperate search for mint. Tattoo and Nuru split up and went in other directions on the same hunt. Their eyes scoured the ground for oval green leaves, linked by thin runners. Rubbing leaves between finger and thumb released plant oils smelling like breath mints, confirming they'd found the right herb. They called to each other when mint was located, gathering as much of the herb as their arms could hold, uprooting whole plants from the ground. Racing back to Allyn, they covered him in the sweet-smelling herb. He gave them a weak smile of gratitude and began to fall asleep.

Trouble softly touched his face. "Grandpa, wake up. Please. I have to know how we get to the great pyramid."

Allyn moaned, but didn't wake up.

Trouble dared to gently shake him.

"The dumbwaiter," the Yeti whispered.

"What?" Trouble couldn't understand what Allyn meant.

"Dumbwaiter," he repeated. "The bacteria generates electricity, but it also makes iron as a waste byproduct. The dumbwaiter was used to haul away iron. That's why there's a huge mound of iron powder outside Yeti City. A dumbwaiter is like an elevator. Find it and …" His voice trailed off.

Nuru and Tattoo sprinted away, searching for the dumbwaiter. Soon they returned, pushing an ancient cart like the kind used by a migrating nomad family to carry its household goods, pulled by a team of yaks. The yak cart was constructed of rough timbers, stained gray from hauling iron ore. Mineral debris lay strewn over the cargo bed, a dusting of charcoal-colored gravel. The cart's old wheels groaned as the wagon rolled, pushed by Nuru and Tattoo.

She explained what happened. "We found this cart next to the dumbwaiter. Thought we could put Allyn on the wagon, roll him to the dumbwaiter. He's too heavy for us to carry."

"Great idea." Trouble walked around the cart, checking it out. "Can we clean off some of these rocks?"

"Yeah." Nuru stood on tip-toe, sweeping off dirt with his coat sleeve. Even Nuru's long arms had difficulty reaching the center of the tall wagon. The cart was mounted on wheels larger than those used for highway freight trucks. Tattoo helped scrape the bed, brushing away gravel. The pebbles clattered when they hit the ground.

Trouble attempted to lift Allyn's shoulders and failed. "Give me a hand," he grunted.

The trio struggled with the Yeti's heavy body. They felt like a wildlife rescue team, attempting to move a beached whale back into the water without a crane. The only way was to lift a single limb at a time, then grunt his torso atop the cart. By the time they got his massive frame on the wagon, they were exhausted. Yet they couldn't stop to rest. Nuru and Tattoo ran around the vehicle assisting Trouble, heaping mint on his grandfather.

"The mint does seem to help him," Tattoo sighed, looking at deep lines running across Allyn's deflated face.

"I'm glad." Nuru was panting from the effort of lifting Allyn. "But what's going to help us? We need oxygen bottles to reach the top of Everest. You can't even stand on the peak without wearing an oxygen mask. Forget doing anything."

Allyn moved slightly. He mumbled and Trouble leaned closer to hear. "Yes? What is it Grandpa?"

"Stown flower. Eat a stown flower," he muttered. His face looked pale as a white bed sheet.

"He's crazy," Tattoo swore. "It's the blood loss. He doesn't know what he's saying."

"Allyn," Trouble asked, "how can we eat a stown flower when there's bacteria on it?" He didn't mention how the flower smelled. He didn't want to think what a stown might taste like.

"It's safe to eat the flower's crimson tip," Allyn murmured. "Stown flowers give you the lung power of a Yeti. The petals adapt your lungs to heights."

Trouble groaned, thinking of the smell. "But Grandpa ..."

"You can't take me to the great pyramid without it. You'll pass out from lack of oxygen."

"Yes, Allyn." With reluctance, Trouble found a small stown plant and touched the crimson tip of its flower. The rough bud was made from a dozen petals, each with the texture of crepe paper. He pulled his hand away and waited, expecting pain to develop. Nothing happened. Trouble plucked off several petals, but didn't eat any of the flower. Instead, he tossed the scarlet petals in the wagon, to use at a higher elevation. He was stalling, hoping he wouldn't have to eat the horrible smelling flower.

Styx let out a groan and they all jumped. The leopard was twitching in its sleep from bacteria-generated electricity. "Let's get out of here," Tattoo suggested, "before that cat wakes up."

Trouble gently laid Albert on the wagon next to his grandfather and covered the penguin with mint. For a moment, they had the horrible sense of taking the pair of bodies to a cemetery for burial. Then they pushed the cart out of the greenhouse, going toward a crude dumbwaiter they hoped would lift them to the healing chamber of the Yetis. It would certainly be the strangest route anyone ever took to the peak of Mount Everest – and perhaps the most dangerous.

21

The dumbwaiter was quite a different machine from the elevator inside Allyn's mushroom skyscraper, a beautiful crystal bolt that rose by spinning around, threading itself out of the ground. In contrast, the basement dumbwaiter resembled a normal elevator lifted by cables, riding inside a hollow shaft. Also, the dumbwaiter wasn't made of the purest quartz. Instead, the basement lift was a crude wooden box, sized exactly to hold the ore wagon. The cargo elevator felt like a dark shoebox inside, with splinters the size of ice picks jutting from its rough timbers. The floor was littered with sour smelling black powder, gritty and thick. Trouble, Nuru and Tattoo had difficulty rolling the cart inside the dumbwaiter, forcing its wheels across sand-like iron dust covering the floor. When they finished the exhausting effort, they felt upset to discover the wagon fit too snugly, leaving no room for them to ride along.

"The cart uses up the whole elevator. There's no room for us. What are we gonna do?" Tattoo asked. Anxious, her legs jittered in little break dance steps again, like when she first met Trouble.

Puzzled by the dilemma of how they would all fit in the elevator, Nuru removed his cap and scratched his head. "Maybe we can crawl under the wagon and ride there."

Tattoo peered beneath the yak cart. "I'll try sliding behind the axle, see if there's space for three in the back." She squirmed under the wagon and called out, "Yeah, this'll do."

Nuru bent down and stared at Tattoo's bright teeth, the only thing visible in the blackness under the ore wagon. "You sure this is going to work? I mean, once the dumbwaiter starts, there's no way to get out. We're stuck under the wagon."

Tattoo had a suggestion. "You could wait here while I ride up and check things out."

Trouble insisted, "There isn't time for practice runs." He looked at Allyn's pale face. "We gotta go now."

Nuru moaned, "Oh, man."

Trouble shook his head. "We don't have any choice."

"This isn't good," Nuru groaned. But he slid beneath the cart, crawling toward the grinning Tattoo.

"You set?" Trouble put his hand on a switch activating the dumbwaiter.

"Yeah," Tattoo chimed. Nuru silently rolled his eyes and shrugged.

"OK." Trouble pulled a huge lever, like switching train tracks, and the dumbwaiter creaked to life, lurching upward. He dove on the lifting platform, sliding across the black grit and wriggled forward, making sure his feet didn't stick out where they'd be hurt. He spat out a mouthful of foul-tasting iron ore, inhaled when his face hit a clump of black powder.

The dumbwaiter box quickly slid past the basement opening, moving into the dark shaft. All light vanished and Trouble couldn't see a thing. It felt like being buried alive and he fought to relax. It wasn't easy to be calm in the dark. All he could hear was a hollow clanking of chains, like an old ship raising its anchor, dragging a huge weight off the ocean bottom and slowly lifting it upward. The loud racket must be part of the dumbwaiter mechanism, Trouble assumed.

"How long do you think it'll take us to reach the top?" Nuru's voice trembled a bit with fear.

"Don't know," Trouble answered, "but I hope it's soon. I'm ready to get out."

"Yeah," Tattoo grunted.

They rode in silence for a few minutes, with only the wobble of the dumbwaiter reminding them they were moving upward. Unfortunately, there was soon another clue they were rising in altitude – a sudden drop in temperature. The higher they went in the dark box, the colder it got.

"I'm gettin' really chilled," Tattoo said in a frightened voice.

"Me too," Nuru confirmed. "What about you, Trouble?"

"Yeah, I'm cold. We should've eaten some stown flower, like Allyn told us. Maybe I can grab a flower petal. I'll try reaching around the wagon's side." He felt for the edge of the yak cart, tapping the wagon's bottom, groping for its border. His gloved fingers hit the dumbwaiter's wall and Trouble groaned in frustration. The wagon fit so tightly inside the elevator there wasn't room for his gloved hand to reach higher.

"I'll take off my gloves." He tugged at his thick, insulated mittens and was sorry when the arctic environment surrounded his exposed skin. Instantly, cold air stung his bare fingers and stiffened his joints. His hands got even colder when he reached around the wagon's side and teased stray leaves through a slim gap. He tried sticking a leaf in his mouth and was exasperated to taste mint. Trouble put on his gloves, frustrated and upset. "It's no use. I can't reach the stown petals."

Tattoo mumbled through chattering teeth, "Itttt'sss … alll righttt."

Trouble attempted to reassure her. "Hang on, we're almost there." However, he knew they had a serious problem. Sharp chill cut through his parka, penetrating his skin like he was naked. In a few moments, he had goose bumps on his flesh and began shivering. His teeth rattled so much Trouble was afraid of chipping a tooth.

When the shivering quit, Trouble knew things were getting worse, not better. He realized his body was going into shock from the cold. His teeth didn't chatter because there was no blood flowing to his face. Trouble was entering a dangerous medical condition called hypothermia, where blood flowed only to his brain and heart so he could stay alive. With difficulty, he touched a finger to his nose and it felt numb. His ankles and feet had no sensation in them either.

Freezing wasn't his only problem. Altitude sickness added to Trouble's misery, leaving him nauseated. He wanted to vomit, yet his throat couldn't make even a gagging sound. His tongue swelled and felt glued to his mouth.

Worst of all was the struggle to breathe. Normally, climbers on Mount Everest spend weeks letting their lungs adjust to the extreme altitude. They move upward in stages, resting at each of nine camps before ascending further. But the fast elevator ride compressed a gradual one month ascent of Everest into an hour. The thin air was ultra-dry, leeching moisture from his lungs, leaving them chapped and burned. The higher he went, the more Trouble struggled to inhale life-giving air. Each breath contained precious little oxygen. He kept sucking at the atmosphere, but found no air to breathe, as though he were underwater and someone turned off the valve on his scuba tank. Soon Trouble was in danger of passing out.

Minutes later, the dumbwaiter finally stopped moving and light again flooded the cramped box. Trouble could see that Nuru and Tattoo had fainted, unconscious from lack of oxygen. That was certainly understandable to Trouble, who could barely stay awake. Weakened by thin air, he tried to move and discovered his legs were useless rubber bands dangling from his hips. He crawled under the ore wagon's axle and grabbed the cart's side, fighting to pull himself up so he could reach the stown petals. It was a long time before Trouble dragged himself on the ore wagon, leaving his legs hanging off the side.

Where were the stown flowers? He reached for the nearest foliage and shoved leaves in his mouth, but it was only mint. Trouble's eyes were stinging, showing him a hazy world. Without oxygen feeding his brain, he saw no colors and couldn't distinguish red stown flowers from green mint. Everything became a shade of gray, looking like a grainy silent film from the early cinema. After a few deep breaths, tinting returned and Trouble saw a sprinkle of red flower petals scattered across the back of the wagon.

With aching arms, Trouble pulled himself along the yak cart, struggling to avoid his grandfather's injured body. At last he got close enough to reach for the crimson petals. One frustrating attempt to touch a flower followed another. Finally, he grabbed a cluster of petals and shoved them in his mouth. A stown flower proved to be the most horrible food he'd ever eaten. Brussels sprouts were nothing compared to stown blossoms.

Every time he chewed a squishy petal, it felt like biting into an eyeball. Foul-tasting juice squirted around his mouth. He fought against an overpowering urge to spit out the flower. Swallowing a whole petal seemed unthinkable. Trouble kept the lump in his cheek like bubblegum and gradually he felt warmer. Even just sucking on a stown flower helped him adjust to the extreme altitude.

To get more energy, he closed his eyes and tried to swallow. The foul lump stuck in his throat and Trouble gagged, almost spitting out the stinking mash. Swallow, he willed himself. Finally the lump went down with a gulp. In a moment, the effects became apparent and Trouble took his first breath of fresh air in over an hour.

There was no time to relax. He heard a clanking noise from the dumbwaiter and felt the elevator moving again. He needed to pull the wagon out of the box before it left, disappearing into the elevator shaft. Another trip in the dumbwaiter would surely kill his friends.

Trouble wormed off the yak cart and searched for a button to stop the lift. His fingers patted rough stone walls, but he found no controls for halting the machinery. Trouble had an inspiration. He lifted his grandfather's walking stick and wedged the thick cane in the elevator mechanism. There was a wrenching sound as the heavy rod jammed the gears, buying him some time. But the stick was being crushed and wouldn't hold for long.

He grabbed Nuru's arms and yanked with all his might. Trouble pulled again and Nuru's head bobbed off the dumbwaiter, hanging over its raised edge. Finally, he dragged Nuru free and his body thumped on the ground like a sandbag.

Trouble began pulling Tattoo, yanking her arms like he'd done with Nuru. After a few exhausting tugs, Tattoo slid forward until her calves hung under the ore wagon's axle. She was almost free. Trouble pulled with all his might. For a moment, it looked like Tattoo was going to make it. Then her thick hiking boots stuck under the wagon's axle.

There was no time to lose. Fast as he could, Trouble stripped Tattoo's boot laces, pulling the nylon threads from their eyelets. The first trekking shoe slid off and he tossed it away. Trouble ripped Tattoo's other boot off, put his arms around her and tugged with all his strength. They tumbled on the hard rock floor, yet the stinging pain didn't matter. His friends were safe.

There was a sickening crunch and Allyn's cane disappeared, chewed to slivers by the dumbwaiter mechanism. The elevator began moving. Trouble's grandfather was in jeopardy, lying motionless on the ore cart. Trouble yanked on the wagon and it lurched off the dumbwaiter, threatening to run away. He grabbed the wagon's side, pulling on its wooden slats, and managed to stop the cart before it rolled off a ledge. Relieved that he'd halted the wagon, Trouble dared a glance over the edge and got quite a shock.

The cart's front was hanging off a deep canyon, a narrow gorge sliced in the earth. It looked like a giant used a knife to cut the globe open. The canyon's sides were a geology lesson, with one level of striped rock heaped on another. Dramatic colors rippled across the abyss in layers, resembling a cake made from mineral-rich stone instead of dough and frosting.

The rock didn't soften into gradual slopes, eroded by wind and rain. Instead, the canyon's sides plunged straight down, a sharp crack in the earth reaching the planet's core. A scarlet thread shimmered in the bottom of the abyss, a river of molten lava flowing along the canyon's floor. Sulfurous vapors steamed in drifting yellow clouds, like hot air balloons filled with poisonous gas.

When Trouble looked around, he realized they were stranded on the narrow ledge. The dumbwaiter was gone and the pit yawning in front of him offered no chance of escape. He couldn't imagine how to get across a bottomless ditch flooded with red-hot volcanic lava.

22

Trapped on a thin ledge, Trouble spent his time reviving Tattoo and Nuru. He rubbed stown petals on Nuru's rigid face, cold and inflexible as a clothes mannequin in a store. Trouble stepped back and waited. There was no way to put anything in Nuru's mouth because his lips were closed, his jaw clamped shut. Nuru lay on his back, arms splayed wide on each side of his body, the front of his parka smeared with axle grease and iron grit. Gradually, the stown paste spread on Nuru's skin got into his bloodstream and he stirred, opening his lips. Trouble hurried to rip a flower petal in half and drop it inside his friend's mouth.

Asleep, Nuru chewed the petal without thinking and swallowed. The awful flavor woke him instantly. Nuru's voice was so raw that he sounded like a frog talking. He croaked, "What is this stuff?"

"A stown flower. Adjusts your body to high altitude, like Allyn said it would."

"Why couldn't it be chocolate that grows your lungs?" Nuru moaned. He raised himself on his elbows and looked around, feeling dazed. "Where are we?"

"We're on a narrow ledge, high above a canyon. The fall off this cliff is several miles. Listen to the echo when I drop a rock." Trouble rolled a small boulder over the edge and there was an eerie silence, instead of the usual noise when a stone ricochets off the sides of a canyon. After a long pause, they heard a loud sizzling as the granite boulder plunged in lava and evaporated into steam.

Nuru blinked puffy eyes, struggling to see. He leaned over the cliff. "Oh, no. That is several miles."

"Uh huh," Trouble grunted. He wasn't any happier about it than Nuru.

The Sherpa tapped his head, shaking off mental cobwebs. "I passed out in the dumbwaiter. Did we get off in the wrong place and miss the healing pyramid?"

"No. I don't think so."

Nuru looked around in bewilderment and saw nothing. "I don't believe you. We got off in the wrong place. There's no pyramid."

"Yeah, there is," Trouble argued. "Look across the gap. You'll see a giant wall. That slab is one side of the pyramid. Took me a while to recognize the pyramid 'cause it's so large."

Nuru stared over the canyon and his jaw hung open in shock. Across the dark chasm a huge pyramid rose to touch Mount Everest's peak from the inside. The Yeti monument was nested within Everest's dome, the tip of the pyramid touching the mountain's crest like a pillar holding up a roof. Everest's interior arched over the pyramid in a jagged curve, a rough hollow lined with crystallized minerals like the inside of a geode.

In contrast with the mountain's coarse stone lining, the pyramid's sides were flawlessly smooth, coated in dazzling white marble. The triangular shape's walls rose in glassy perfection, flat slabs meeting at a single point, the monument's apex. That distant tip gleamed in pure gold, a cap of precious metal. The crown sparkled in dark hues, the reddish brass color of uncorrupted 24 karat gold.

Nuru bent his neck, craning his head to stare at the pyramid's top, fascinated by its hundred million dollar crown. His mind was fixated on the gold. "I had no idea pyramids looked like this. The ones in movies have steps carved in the sides and the peak is just a crumbly old stone."

"This is how Egyptian pyramids looked before they were stripped by tomb raiders," Trouble explained.

"How do you know?" Nuru acted suspicious.

Trouble rolled his eyes. "My parents are archeologists, remember? All they talk about is the way things looked ten thousand years ago."

"Yeah." Nuru was dreamy. "Do you have any idea how many DVDs I can buy with this gold? I can own all the cool trekking gear I want. We'll live in a mansion. I'll ride a helicopter to the Namche Bazaar instead of spending five days on a yak, snot freezing to my lips." He grabbed Trouble, clamping his fingers into a shoulder. "Do you know what this means?"

"Ouch, let go of me, will ya?" He yanked free of Nuru's hand. "Know what happened to Egyptian grave robbers?"

"They got rich," Nuru insisted.

"Nope. Try again. They were caught and tortured. Thrown off a high cliff so their bodies were impaled on spears. They were left to rot in the sun as a warning."

"Someone got away with the gold then. We can get it now," Nuru argued.

"How? We can't even get off this ledge. In the cyber café, you told me a Yeti carried you to the pyramid's healing chamber. Do you remember how you got across the gorge?"

"It's been a lot of years, Trouble. I was just a little kid," Nuru hedged. He kicked a pebble over the cliff with the toe of his hiking boot.

"Do you remember anything at all?"

"I know it sounds crazy, but I think we walked."

"Walked?" The idea seemed incredible to Trouble. "You just strolled across this chasm?"

"Yeah, walked," he confirmed. "At least I think so."

Trouble thought about it. "There must be a drawbridge somewhere." Half serious, he joked, "I wonder where the secret lever is located, the one you press and poof, a drawbridge falls across the gorge with a thunderous clap."

"Trouble, you've watched too many movies." Nuru laughed, but the idea of a drawbridge stuck in his mind. "Searching for a bridge is worth a try. We don't have any other ideas." Nuru walked away, patting and twisting stones, muttering ancient Sherpa incantations, trying anything he thought might cause a drawbridge to materialize.

Trouble called to Nuru. "You keep searching. I'll try to wake up Tattoo."

"Yeah, sure," Nuru answered without enthusiasm, distracted by his search for a path across the gorge.

Trouble heard Nuru's mittens slapping against granite, beating like a drummer in a rock concert. He shook his head in amazement at Nuru's fixation and reached in the cart for more stown flower petals to use on Tattoo. Despite the toxic odor, he mashed a stown flower in his fist and applied the paste to her lips. Tattoo's mouth twitched, reacting to a goo that smelled like produce rotting in the hot sun. Luckily, some of the mess dribbled on her tongue and was swallowed. She began breathing normally again and her pale face got some color back. It was a good sign. Nuru went through this phase just before waking up.

Behind him, Nuru yelled in an excited voice. "Think I found something."

"What is it?" Trouble asked, turning around.

"Come here," Nuru insisted. "I'll show you."

Assuming Tattoo wouldn't wake up for several minutes, Trouble walked around the cliff face, leaving her alone.

Unfortunately, the stown paste worked quickly on Tattoo. She rolled on her stomach and fought to get up, shaking off a coma of sleep. Unsteady legs didn't keep her from stumbling to her feet in a woozy pushup. Bobbing around the ledge in hesitant steps, she moved like a sleepwalker, edging toward the precipice. She wiped drool from her chin and looked at the red paste on her fingers. Blinking, she noticed Trouble in the distance. "Hey," Tattoo croaked, spitting out flower petal mash. "What'd you put in my mouth? It tastes horrible."

Trouble spun around at the sound of his friend's voice. He saw Tattoo standing on the cliff edge, in danger of falling into a miles-deep gorge. "Don't move," he yelled. "I'm coming to help you." Trouble ran toward her, but he wasn't fast enough.

Tattoo wobbled, taking a step, and discovered there was no ground under her foot. Her mouth opened in an oval of surprise and she twisted in a futile attempt to keep her balance. Tattoo flailed her arms, trying to grab something. Nothing worked. Despite all her efforts, Tattoo fell head-first into the miles-deep chasm.

23

One moment Trouble saw his friend's trekking cap drop from her unsteady head. The next second his stomach twisted, watching her fall off the ledge in slow motion, stiff as a tree cut down in the forest. Tattoo's body spun to horizontal, flat as a desert highway. Trouble expected her to keep falling into the void, but she didn't tumble in the canyon. There was a loud "thunk" and Tattoo hit the unyielding surface of some invisible platform, hard as a sidewalk. The collision knocked her unconscious. Blood ran from a gash on her cheek and her eye swelled like someone punched her in a fight. She was lying face down, suspended as though some enchantment levitated her body in mid-air. He saw nothing visible under Tattoo and she appeared to hang over the gorge by magic.

Trouble had grabbed Tattoo's ankle at the last second, in a desperate attempt to save her. Unfortunately, it didn't work and Tattoo's momentum pulled him off the cliff. He'd fallen into the gorge and was now dangling from Tattoo's foot. Clutching his friend's boot, Trouble swung back and forth like the pendulum on an old-fashioned grandfather clock. He looked down, hoping to discover a foothold to push himself up. Instead, he saw dust spinning downward, floating into empty space. There seemed no way to climb out. Every tug on Tattoo's leg backfired, sliding her off some mysterious platform. He didn't dare pull harder or they'd both tumble into the gorge. Trouble quit trying to climb Tattoo's leg and grabbed her ankle in a fierce grip, hoping Nuru would help them.

Startled they were still alive, Nuru stood nearby with his mouth hanging open from shock. Nuru realized he had to find a way to reach his friends, dangling over the chasm. He tossed a handful of dirt toward the horizontal Tattoo, hoping the dust would reveal more of the outcropping holding her. Some of Nuru's grit fell in the canyon, but most of the dust floated in space, held by the invisible platform. The dirt outlined a path between Tattoo and Nuru. He took a cautious footstep on the dust cloud and it held his weight. He tiptoed on a gritty fog hanging over the chasm like vapor, creeping toward his friends. Tattoo was moaning and jerking her leg, bothered by the heavy weight of Trouble dangling from her ankle.

Trouble gave a frightened laugh. "Seems Tattoo found the drawbridge."

"Yeah. Now we just need to get you on it." Nuru knelt down, offering a hand. With difficulty, he pulled Trouble to safety in a slow, painful drag.

Once on the drawbridge, Trouble rapped the invisible structure with his knuckles. "Solid. Amazing. I don't understand how this was done."

Nuru shrugged. "Who knows? Yetis do a lot of weird things."

Tattoo was awake, nursing her throbbing eye socket with a cold mitten. She rolled over and groaned. "Man, what hit me?"

"You fell." Trouble reached in the wagon for mint, made a compress and handed it to Tattoo. "Hold this on your bruise. Maybe it'll help."

"Thanks," she grunted.

While Tattoo held the mint compress against her face, Trouble scraped at the mysterious drawbridge, leaving a black mark on the invisible surface. "Painted to look like the canyon," he remarked. "Yetis hid the bridge in plain sight. It was here the whole time. We just couldn't see its surface."

"How can they disguise a bridge with paint?" Nuru wondered. "No matter where you stand, this drawbridge looks like the canyon underneath. You can't do that with a painting."

"OK, so they used a Klingon cloaking device," Trouble joked, referring to the *Star Trek* series where space ships are hidden by a mysterious technique. "Anyway, who cares how Yetis do it? We needed to get across so my grandfather can be healed and now we have a bridge."

Nuru was still worried. "How do we know where to step? The drawbridge is narrow. I'd hate to walk off the edge."

"Fill your pockets with soil," Trouble suggested. "Toss a little dirt ahead of you to show the way, like you did before. Tattoo and I will follow, pushing the wagon."

"OK," Nuru agreed. It only took a minute to scrape the cliff, filling every jacket pocket with dirt and gritty stones. Then they began the unnerving process of pushing a heavy wagon across an invisible drawbridge.

"Try not to look down," Nuru advised as they stepped off the ledge.

Of course, Nuru's comment caused both Tattoo and Trouble to gaze downward, where there was nothing but occasional dust specks floating in a dark vacuum.

"I hope this thing doesn't end in the middle," Trouble muttered. He pulled his eyes off the cold emptiness and took a deep breath. Then he tugged on the yak cart and took the first of many steps, hanging in the air with nothing under him.

24

Walking on the invisible bridge was a stressful experience. Their boots never appeared to touch anything solid. Worse, the bridge sagged with each step, giving a false impression they were walking off the edge. The trio placed each footstep carefully, moving like a blind person tapping their cane to cross a busy intersection. No movement felt safe and their anxiety worsened every time the gorge under them bubbled up a volcanic fart, releasing noxious fumes. They were enveloped by a cloud of rotten eggs, the sulfurous odor of lava.

A yellow fog surrounded them in a stinking mist, forcing them to halt. All they could do was wait, coughing and sneezing. Their noses and throats became coated in mucus from allergy reactions. It didn't help to rub itching ears or watery eyes. The terrible odor stuck to the inside of their nostrils, clinging long after the smoke evaporated. Mustard-colored powder dusted their clothing, blending with rusty iron grit, making them look like chimney sweeps at the end of a hard day on the rooftops of London.

The hacking, sniffling journey was made worse by dragging the ore wagon. The invisible walkway seemed only an inch wider than the cart, leaving no room for a mistake. Several times they discovered a wheel rolling off the edge into space and panicked, doing an emergency reverse, pushing hard to stop the heavy wagon from plunging into the canyon. The group took almost an hour to roll their clumsy vehicle across the causeway. Unfortunately, their problems didn't end when they reached the other side. The bridge terminated in a thin ledge running like eyebrows penciled on the pyramid's face. There was very little room for them to move.

Trouble stood on the narrow shelf, feeling like an ant, dwarfed by the huge monument. In front of him, the pyramid rose as a featureless barrier, a wall blank as his mind. He had no idea how to get inside the structure. There didn't seem to be an entrance anywhere he looked. Trouble patted white stone and found the marble smooth as glass and just as rigid. He moved a few feet over and tapped again, with the same result – nothing. No door opened in front of him, no panel slid back revealing a hole. He saw only a seamless expanse of white sheets. Trouble looked for a clue in gaps between marble blocks, but the masonry work appeared perfect. Cracks were so thin Trouble couldn't slide a fingernail between stones.

Nuru explored in the opposite direction, leaving Tattoo to watch over the ore cart. After a few minutes, he called out, "Find anything?"

"Nothing," Trouble answered. His voice echoed around the pyramid, repeating a hollow, "Noth…ing … ing … ing."

"Hey, maybe I found something," Tattoo shouted. Her words bounced off the hard stone walls, repeating her announcement.

Trouble scuttled along the narrow shelf, returning to the wagon. "What'd you find?"

"Your grandfather rolled over and his arm hung off the cart," Tattoo explained. "His hand touched the pyramid and something weird happened."

Nuru joined them. "Do it again," he urged.

"OK." Tattoo tried to lift Allyn's arm and grunted from exertion. "A Yeti's arm weighs a ton. Help me, will you?"

Trouble and Nuru crowded next to Tattoo, squeezing together like a football huddle. They grabbed hold of the Yeti's oversize hand, a meaty glove joined to dinosaur claws. In a collective grunt, they lifted and his wrist felt like a barbell loaded with iron weights. With a lot of work, they got Allyn's thumb pressed against the pyramid.

The Yeti's finger touched stone and the marble block changed color, going from ivory white to ebony black. The pale stone became a dark tablet radiating Yeti hieroglyphs, sketches of scorpions and vipers wriggling like pulsing leeches sucking blood. Lines of symbols rolled upward the way a computer display scrolls through a document, moving from the first page to the last.

Nuru leaned over the hieroglyphs and squinted. "Can't read what it says. Can you?"

Trouble shook his head. "Not really. Seems like a list of names."

"Maybe you have to click on it, like using a computer mouse." Always ready to try something, Tattoo pressed on the display. They felt a vibration under their feet, but the trembling stopped. No entrance appeared in the pyramid's side.

Then Nuru shouted. "Look! The drawbridge is disappearing."

Trouble watched all their carefully placed dirt fall into the canyon. They'd scattered gravel along the bridge to mark their path and the sand dropped in a dusty cyclone, sinking into the gorge. Without brown dirt on it, the drawbridge vanished. He tried to put a foot on the invisible path and felt nothing, no structure at all. The walkway from dumbwaiter to pyramid was gone. "Great," he moaned. "We're trapped here."

"I think that's the idea," Nuru explained. "I'm guessing that touching this list is like entering your e-mail password. You get a few tries and then the system locks you out."

Trouble corrected him. "This pyramid doesn't just lock you out. Use the wrong password and it traps you on this ledge. We need a clue on how to get inside." He turned again to the scrolling list. Trouble was relieved to observe familiar hieroglyphs, symbols he learned from his mother, thinking they were Egyptian. Apparently the drawings were actually Yetish. "I think this row spells Indigo," he exclaimed. "My father's name."

"Try touching it," Tattoo urged.

"Wait," Nuru shouted. "You don't know what'll happen."

"I don't think we can wait." Trouble put his fingertips on Allyn's forehead and his skin felt even colder than before. It was urgent they get inside the pyramid. "We're out of time. I have to try something."

Trouble pressed his hand against the pyramid and again he felt a shuddering under his feet, almost a groaning. He realized the ledge was breaking, cracking like a shattered dinner plate. In the distance, he saw part of the shelf crumble and fall into the gorge. More pieces broke away, spinning downward, vanishing in a haze of vapors at the bottom of the abyss. Every few seconds, another part of the shelf cracked, flaking off the pyramid. Soon there'd be no place to stand.

"Trouble, do something," Tattoo urged.

"Do the wrong thing and we'll fall in that abyss," Nuru cautioned.

"Do nothing and we're dead," Tattoo countered. "Trouble …" She grabbed his shoulder.

"OK, I'm trying. Please be quiet so I can focus. Allyn once said his name in Yetish. It was something like Yerglornamega Ergbish. No, that wasn't right."

Trouble heard another loud crash and he watched the ledge surrounding them disappear. With the next break, they were going to drop into the chasm like people forced to jump off a burning building.

He peered at the hieroglyphs, sweat dripping from his forehead despite the cold air. "Maybe that's Allyn's name. I recognize the symbols. They might spell his name in Yetish."

The ledge under them began to shake and splinters appeared where the shelf attached to the pyramid. The platform was crumbling. Desperate to save their lives, Tattoo reached for the hieroglyphs.

Trouble grabbed her just in time. “No, Tattoo. Use my grandfather’s hand. The pyramid may sense who’s touching it.”

“Good idea.”

They tried to press Allyn’s hand against the drawings, but his name had scrolled too high.

Tattoo shouted, “Pull,” helping them tug Allyn’s arm toward the monument. Together they shoved his palm against hieroglyphs that might spell Allyn’s name. The rumbling changed. This time a low growling came from within the building, instead of under their feet.

Trouble looked up and realized the pyramid was opening in a bizarre way, unlike any door he’d ever seen. He’d expected a sliding panel or a rotating stone, the way a secret door springs open in a late night movie. Instead, the gleaming monument changed shape, collapsing like an umbrella. The diamond-shaped pyramid inverted, becoming a funnel, a mile-deep cone. The hole yawning in front of Trouble exerted a dark pull on him, as though it were dragging him inside. Inside the hole, a road coiled downward, spiraling into the velvet-black pit. A parade of smoking torches lit a fiery path, snaking into the void. Trouble’s eye followed the curving flow of light from his feet to a distant vanishing point, the center of a helix twisting downward like a golden spring.

From somewhere inside the torch-lit cone, a flute played a haunting melody, ancient and mysterious, a musical ghost from the past. Its lilting song teased and warned them at the same time, seeming to say, "Enter me, if you dare."

25

The stained ore wagon waited, sitting motionless at the entrance to the pyramid. The monument was now inverted, turned upside-down to form a deep cone like the crater of a volcano. Spiraling into the funnel-shaped hole flowed a golden pathway. The yak cart's battered wheels squatted on that elegant road, seeming completely out of place, like muddy footprints on a royal carpet. Nuru felt he didn't belong there either. Confused and anxious, he remained frozen beside the ore wagon.

"Come on," Tattoo encouraged her friend, patting him on the back. His muscles felt tense, rigid as wooden planks.

Nuru shook his head. "I don't know about this. I mean, all we did was touch its skin and the pyramid got upset. What's gonna happen when we walk inside? I don't want to get dumped in that hole." He pointed a soot-coated mitten at the deep crater in front of them.

Trouble rolled his eyes in frustration. "Oh, come on. We have to walk inside the pyramid. There's nowhere else to go. We can't leave. The bridge vanished. We need to find the Yeti healing chamber. Maybe it has an exit out of the mountain."

Nuru refused to move, unwilling to take even one step inside the crater.

Trouble nodded toward Allyn. "I need help getting my grandfather to the healing chamber. Look at him." The Yeti's face seemed a rigid mask, as though he were a marble statue, all color drained from his cheeks. No signs of life appeared in the huge body, no motion of his chest in breathing, no pulsing vein in his neck. Next to Allyn, the wounded penguin lay motionless, moaning in pain. Severed muscles and ligaments hung from his torn chest where his arm was missing. "Albert defended you from Styx. He lost a flipper saving your life, Nuru. You've got to help him."

Nuru still wouldn't budge. Reluctantly, Trouble and Tattoo got behind the wagon and gave it a shove, leaning into the tailgate. Moving the yak cart was hard work without their friend's help. In a few steps, they halted and gave Nuru a pleading look.

"All right. I'll do it," he conceded. "I don't like it, but I'll do it." He shuffled to them and shoved against the yak cart.

Together they moved the ore wagon along the golden ramp, spiraling into the pyramid. For a few steps, pushing the cart was tough work, needing a lot of strength. But soon the wheels rolled on their own, gliding down the gentle slope. Soon they had to restrain the yak cart so it didn't run away from them. It was even harder work holding the wagon back.

Nuru called a rest break and they halted. He wiped sweat off his forehead despite the frigid temperature. "My back is killing me from slowing this wagon down. There has to be a better way."

"Man, you aren't kidding," groaned Tattoo.

Trouble walked around the cart and looked at the wheels. "I think I see an easier way to slow this thing down, so it doesn't roll away from us."

"I'm all for it," Tattoo said, holding the wagon. Nuru moved around the yak cart to join her.

"Looks like this wagon has brakes." Trouble pointed to levers on each side of the driver's bench. Pulling on the levers applied drag to the wheels, slowing the wagon's roll.

Nuru looked at the brake levers. "So we can ride on the wagon and steer using the brakes."

"Huh?" Tattoo grunted. "Oh, I see."

"Right," Trouble confirmed. "Use the brake lever on one side and the cart turns that direction. It's like a bobsled, where you ride flat on your stomach. Your head points downhill, feet behind you. Drag a foot and you turn toward that side."

Nuru and Tattoo were delighted to have less work. They hopped on the wagon and it began rolling, picking up speed.

"Hey, wait for me," Trouble shouted, running to catch up. Cold and tired, his hiking boots felt like iron weights strapped to his ankles in training for a marathon. His muscles burned from exhaustion and despite the stown petals, his lungs fought to grab air.

They jerked the wagon to a stop and pulled Trouble onboard, lifting him to the driver's bench. Then they were off, with Nuru and Tattoo tugging brake levers to guide the wagon. The brake levers screeched when applied too hard, but otherwise the ride felt eerily silent. They rolled on, the old yak cart gliding along a spiral track.

Gas-fired torches flamed on both sides of the spiral, lighting the path. The torch heat felt good as they rolled past, warming their cold bodies and thawing their faces, numb from arctic temperatures. The torches smoked with greasy kerosene, making their stomachs queasy like inhaling jet fumes at an airport.

Trouble glanced at the fires and realized every flame highlighted an alcove, a niche recessed in the walls. The alcoves were heaped with precious stones, jewels piled high enough to bring a greedy smile to a pirate. Clearly, this was the Yeti vault, as well as their center of healing. The niches also contained paintings and sculpture. The vault held priceless art objects, like the golden chariots buried with pharaohs in tombs lining Egypt's Valley of the Kings.

In addition to art treasures, there was something else near each torch. But the cart was rolling so fast Trouble couldn't identify the mysterious objects. He had the prickly feeling eyes watched him from inside the alcoves. Once he caught a glimpse of a head and the skin was gray, like the face of a dead person.

Trouble focused on each niche when they passed. He didn't look at the treasures. Instead, Trouble stared at twilight areas where torchlight faded to shadow. Yes, he was certain Yetis were entombed next to the alcoves, their bodies frozen in a block of ice like primitive hunters found in glaciers by explorers. They seemed flash-frozen, caught in life rather than dead fossils. With their eyes wide open, staring at the wagon, the dead Yetis were an alarming sight. Their intense, unblinking stares shined through the heavy ice and Trouble had difficulty swallowing. His palms sweated in the Gortex mittens, yet he couldn't pull away from their faces.

Trouble swung around to get another look at a niche. He realized torches snuffed out after they passed, as though someone were erasing the golden path through the pyramid. The road behind them vanished into darkness. It seemed their trip was one-way only, with no exit. Yet there was nothing they could do about their situation. They had to get inside the healing chamber and hope they could find a way out.

Suddenly the ore wagon squealed to a halt and Trouble pitched forward, almost falling off the cart. "What happened?"

"Can't go any farther," Nuru explained.

Tattoo pointed at bronze doors rising out of darkness, blocking their path. The bronze gates had decorative panels with carved figures. Each panel formed a miniature scene illustrating Yeti history. The top section told a story of Yetis traveling around the world, trading with primitive mankind. There was a caravan of human traders parked at a lake, erecting tents and unpacking yak carts. Nearby, a Yeti goldsmith bartered his ornaments for Chinese silk and paints.

In another panel, a tale of Stonehenge appeared. Yetis were shown helping Neolithic man erect monument stones on the Salisbury plain. A dozen Yetis shouldered one of the sixty-ton Sarsen lintels in place, capping a pair of columns of the inner ring. In the next section, people gathered inside Stonehenge to pray, using the circle of rocks as a prehistoric church, temple or mosque. Yetis were also shown lifting giant pillars to build stone circles at Calcoene in a Brazilian rainforest and Callanish on the West Hebrides Islands.

Another series of carved bronze panels featured Egypt, revealing Yetis teaching medicine at Luxor, on the Nile. A couple of Yetis brewed herbal potions in earthen cauldrons, surrounded by human scribes, taking notes on clay tablets. At center stage, a sick Egyptian lay on a stretcher of woven reeds. Servants carried the limp Egyptian's body, placing their master under a small model of the Yeti pyramid. The final panel showed the person after a curing session, able to sit up and drink from a mug.

Trouble felt encouraged by the hospital theme of the Egyptian panel and hopped off the wagon, intending to swing the massive bronze doors out of their way. "This must be the entrance to the healing chamber. I hope we can get inside."

"Uh, oh. Trouble, we've got company." Nuru sounded afraid.

Trouble's nose was hit by a stench like the worst gym locker room, or being downwind at the zoo during the wrong time of day. He swung around and saw giant trees standing on each side of the wagon.

His eyes swept upward and he realized the shaggy trees were actually legs. Enormous animals surrounded the wagon, one on each side of the cart.

"Elephants," Tattoo whispered.

Nuru corrected her. "No. Wooly mammoths, extinct for thousands of years. Look at those curled tusks. Normal elephants have straight ones." The mammoth's giant ivory tusks looped in coils like razor wire. The ivory was weathered to dirty yellow and scratched from chipping against ice.

One of the mammoths sniffed Tattoo's neck with the tip of its trunk. She felt like a giant slug was crawling on her skin, leaving a trail of slime. "Hey," Tattoo complained, pushing away the trunk. Then she turned pale, worried she'd made the huge animal angry.

Nuru pointed at the hairy beasts looming over the yak cart. "What can we do about them?"

"They're guardians," Trouble guessed. "The mammoths want to know why we're trying to enter the healing chamber."

He examined them more closely. Both wooly mammoths looked like senior citizens, with bald patches on their coarse fur. Bony ribs and shrunken stomachs implied they were badly underfed. Hungry as they were, the pachyderms appeared gentle and curious, not hostile like the leopards. The larger elephant was a male. It seemed they were a childless couple, probably the last descendents in their line.

Trouble felt like he'd seen them before and struggled to remember where he'd met them, haunted by a vague memory that was slow to form in his mind. "Mulanathor and Thalastria," he murmured.

The mammoths looked at each other in surprise and then stared at Trouble. The huge female lumbered toward him in booming footsteps and he fought an urge to run away. When the mammoth stood close, her trunk brushed against Trouble, checking if he was for real.

"Thalastria?" he asked, his body rocking from the shove of her trunk.

The wooly mammoth cocked her head and looked at Trouble with a reddened, sad eye. The beast seemed to nod, acknowledging her name was Thalastria.

He turned to the other mammoth and asked, "Mulanathor?"

The huge male stomped closer, purring roughly. He appeared to agree his name was Mulanathor.

"How'd you know their names?" Tattoo asked.

"Yeah." Nuru was suspicious.

"There's carved wooden statues of mammoths in our antique shop. My mother told me they had names. My dad would never sell the statues. He said one day I'd need them, but he wouldn't tell me why. I didn't realize he meant I'd need their names, not the actual statues." He felt bitter. "My parents kept everything a secret, even my grandfather. They've hidden their lives from me."

"Sorry." Tattoo wanted to console Trouble.

Nuru acted impatient, as usual. "Yeah, well it's good you know the elephants' names. But how do we get inside the healing chamber? It's blocked by these huge gates."

"I don't know." Trouble spoke to Thalastria. "Um, we're here because my grandfather Allyn got hurt. He was attacked by a snow leopard, Styx. Do you know her?"

The elephants' expressions changed at the mention of Styx. They looked angry, their facial muscles tensing like they were going to charge an enemy.

Trouble peeled away mint to expose Allyn's face. "We need to move him into the healing chamber. Can you help us open these doors?"

The pachyderms exchanged glances, like they were considering what to do next. Then Mulanathor wrapped his trunk around Trouble, holding him tight. It felt like being squeezed by a python, caught in a wrestler's lock. He tried not to panic at being lifted twenty feet in the air, dangling above Nuru's and Tattoo's heads. With a sweeping motion, he was dropped on Thalastria's back in a stinging thump. He quickly forgot the pain in his tailbone. Sitting on that high perch was frightening, with nothing to hold but the mammoth's thick fur, coarse as ship's rope. Trouble grabbed a knot of greasy, tangled hair for safety. He tried to be gentle, knowing it would be foolish to upset an elephant when you're riding on her.

Abruptly, Trouble jerked forward when Thalastria shoved against the bronze doors, pressing her head into the cold metal. In slow, ponderous steps, her bulk forced the gates to open. Behind Trouble, Mulanathor grabbed the ore wagon with his trunk, dragging it through the cathedral-sized doors. At last they were entering the sacred healing chamber where Nuru's deformed legs were transformed into healthy limbs. Trouble hoped the same room would also save his grandfather's life. Once inside, maybe he'd find clues telling him how to use the healing chamber's power.

26

Riding the wooly mammoth, Trouble entered the healing chamber on a high perch, close to the room's ceiling. He could almost reach up and touch the vaulted dome, built of glass blocks tinted a yellow hue. Gradually, Trouble realized he was inside the tip of the Yeti pyramid, where its golden crown touched the summit of Mount Everest. The transparent ceiling formed the peak of the great Yeti pyramid, capped by thick glass stained the color of gold.

He didn't know how they reached the monument's top. They must have ridden the ore wagon uphill, despite thinking the twisting path took them down a spiral ramp. Trouble stopped worrying about how the elevator worked, stunned by proof they'd arrived at the Yeti pyramid's pointed tip. He looked through the glass dome and saw a man walking toward the mountain's summit, providing indisputable evidence Trouble was beneath Everest's peak.

He watched in fascination when the mountain climber stepped on the transparent roof of the healing chamber. The mountaineer was making his way up the Hillary Steps, the last major obstacle before completing his ascent of Mount Everest. Trouble watched the man's slow, cautious movements and almost felt his labored breathing. Each motion seemed an agony that left the climber's chest heaving, even though he inhaled oxygen from a bottle. Trouble could make out orange snow leggings on the mountaineer's boots and a red parka with a sponsor's logo. At the crest, the man paused for a quick photograph.

Lingering atop the peak was dangerous and climbers stood there for only a moment. Shifting jet streams sometimes hit Mount Everest's crown with 200 mile per hour winds, blasting away even hard-packed snow. In the thin air, intense sunlight blistered human skin in a few seconds. Despite investing months preparing to climb Everest, mountaineers could only spend a minute at their goal. They'd drained their last oxygen bottle reaching the crest and were forced to descend for more air. By contrast, Trouble could reach up and touch the highest point in the world, the summit of Mount Everest, staying as long as he wished.

But he didn't travel all that way to enjoy the view from the world's highest mountain. Healing Allyn and the penguin took priority over sightseeing, no matter how dramatic the scene. Trouble looked around the healing chamber for clues that might help him use the room's powers. Maybe he'd find a hint in the way the chamber was constructed. The healing chamber's circular floor looked like circles in a target's bull's-eye. Each ring had the width of a Yeti footstep and was made from polished blue stone. That intense color made a striking background canvas for golden symbols adorning the cobalt floor.

Trouble didn't understand the floor's design, but it seemed to be a prehistoric astronomical calendar. Pressed into the stone, gold inlays depicted a rising sun, a crescent moon and a constellation of stars named the Pleiades. These stars mark crop cycles for farmers with their departure from the northern sky in spring, followed by their autumn reappearance. His father once showed him a similar design, the Nebra disc. A relic dating from 1600 B.C., the Nebra disc was considered the oldest realistic star chart ever discovered by archeologists.

Another ancient calendar surrounded Trouble, a drawing etched in fine white lines on the healing chamber's wall. That sketch showed the 7,000 year-old Goseck circle. Like the round-shaped Stonehenge, the Goseck circle formed a calendar for predicting seasons. It seemed likely that the healing chamber was thousands of years old, comparable to the Nebra disc and the Goseck circle. Unfortunately, Trouble felt clueless how these astronomical calendars could assist in healing his grandfather.

Allyn and the king penguin lay under the exact center of the pyramid's roof. Mulanathor had pushed the ore wagon into the middle of the room, at the center of the floor's rings. Thalastria bent over, lowering herself to her knees, allowing Trouble to climb off her back. The elephant used her trunk to assist Trouble's descent and he slid to the ground.

"What happens next?" Tattoo asked.

"I don't know," Trouble admitted. "Nuru, do you remember anything from when you were healed?"

"Not really." Nuru craned his neck to look at the pyramid's ceiling. "That dome looks familiar. Maybe I saw it when I woke up." Nuru pointed at the elephants. "Why don't they help? They know how this healing stuff is done. They've been through it before. Go ahead, Trouble. Talk to the mammoths. Couldn't hurt, could it?"

Trouble shrugged. "Well, here goes. Um, Mulanathor and Thalastria, we need help. We don't know what to do here."

The wooly mammoths looked at each other, then stared at Trouble in bewilderment.

"That didn't do much good. Nuru, don't you remember anything from all those weeks you spent in this chamber?"

"Sorry. I slept most of the time." He felt ashamed and rushed to add, "The Yeti brought me nuts and fruit to eat."

"I'm not going in that basement again, even for food," Tattoo objected.

"No one's asking you to go there," Trouble said, trying to calm Tattoo. He moved to the wagon. "Allyn, can you hear me? Can you tell us what to do?" He got no response and Trouble checked Allyn's pulse. His heart was scarcely beating and he felt cold as the room.

Trouble laid Albert's flipper next to the penguin's wounded chest and lifted his grandfather's hand, moving the wide palm so it covered the penguin's injury. The giant hand with its long claws was spread across the bird's chest and severed flipper. "I guess all we can do is wait." Trouble walked away and stood near Mulanathor.

The healing chamber's lighting changed in a subtle way. The glow around the amphitheater shifted and gradually the room became dimmer at the edges, brighter in the center. Soon they vanished in the dark like a theater audience and the wagon became a spot-lit stage. The illumination changed color to a pulsing, iridescent blue. The light beam grew narrower, highlighting Allyn's hand, lying over the severed flipper. They observed sparking and hissing, a welding that fused the torn skin.

Finally, the welding stopped and the room's lighting returned to normal. Trouble ran to the wagon and looked inside. Albert's flipper seemed restored to his body, but the repair wasn't perfect. A scar of ragged flesh traced the seam between wing and body. The flipper looked like it wouldn't move correctly. Trouble put a hand on Albert's chest and felt relieved that the penguin seemed warmer and his heart beat faster. The bird gave a faint chirp and blinked his eyes, falling asleep again. Trouble stroked his head. "He's OK."

Nuru asked, "The penguin or your grandfather?"

"Just Albert, the penguin."

"Oh, I'm sorry." Nuru put a hand on Trouble's shoulder to console him.

"Me, too," Tattoo added and gave Trouble a hug.

"Thanks." He felt exhausted and began to move away from the ore wagon. Then Trouble saw Allyn's lips stir but no words came out. Trouble bent over the Yeti's face and whispered, "What is it, Grandfather?"

Very faintly, Allyn said, "It takes a Yeti to heal a Yeti."

He repeated the phrase and Trouble cut him off to conserve Allyn's strength. "Yes, I got it. You said that you need another Yeti to heal you. I'll get one as soon as I can." Trouble forced back panic.

"Is there anything we can do?" Nuru asked, moving alongside Trouble.

"No. He needs another Yeti to heal him."

Tattoo had a suggestion. "What about you, Trouble? You're part Yeti. Allyn's your grandfather."

"Yeah, that's an idea," Nuru encouraged him.

"I'm not really a Yeti. I've never done any healing. Allyn had training. I mean, at least he got to watch first," Trouble protested.

Tattoo pressed him. "You got to watch your grandfather heal Albert."

"Oh, yeah, I did. But I don't know what to do."

Tattoo pulled Trouble's hands over Allyn's injured chest. "Just stand there. Maybe the room will do the rest." Tattoo walked away.

Trouble never felt so intimidated in his life. It seemed he'd walked in the operating room of a hospital and had to perform surgery – without going to medical school. Sweat beaded on his forehead as he waited. This can't possibly work, he thought.

Tattoo seemed to have an instinct for Trouble's pessimism. "Think positive. Image healing your grandfather."

"Thanks," he muttered. Trouble fought to clear his mind. He closed his eyes and imagined his grandfather walking again, laughing and joking, splashing water on him from a fountain in Yeti City. When he opened his eyes, the room's lighting had dimmed again and his hands glowed in a spotlight. Unlike the penguin's healing, this time a cold wind blew through the doors of the healing chamber.

Trouble looked through the cathedral doors and was surprised to see everything floodlit. The dormant torches rekindled, their flames burning intensely. He could see the pyramid formed a necropolis, a city of the dead. In the bright torch light, the spiral ramp sliced a path through a glacier filled with deceased Yetis.

Thousands of bodies lay encased in ice tombs, a frozen civilization. The crypts were linked by shiny ribbons connecting Yetis in family trees, showing marriages and offspring. Near the top stood a blank niche, a crypt for one more Yeti, presumably Allyn. Trouble hoped the coffin would go unfilled for a long time.

Trouble closed his eyes and told himself, think healing. Your hands will heal Allyn. He moved his fingers along Allyn's torn chest and stomach, feeling the deep wounds under his grandfather's fur. A jolt like an electrical shock went through Trouble. The icy wind became a storm and beat against his face. He had visions of all the Yetis in the pyramid swirling through the healing chamber like ghosts, whispering strange words, muttering incantations in a haunting rhythm.

Their presence entered Trouble's body like ice melting into his bones. Dead Yetis clamped his hands, pressing them into the gore of Allyn's wounds. Trouble heard sparking and hissing, felt heat like candle flames burning his fingertips. He wished he could see what was happening, but didn't dare look for fear of breaking the spell. He knew his hands moved over the Yeti's torso, sinking into every injury at least once, dipping into cuts and touching warm organs underneath the ruptured skin.

The welding gradually stopped and Trouble could feel bright light return, even through closed eyelids. He opened his eyes and looked at Allyn's torn body. Trouble had done an imperfect job, yet the Yeti looked much better. There were scars and bruises, lumps where there shouldn't be lumps, but every wound seemed improved.

Exhausted, Trouble stepped away, then remembered to check Allyn's temperature. His grandfather felt warmer and his breathing appeared normal. For a moment his lips moved. Trouble thought Allyn said, "thank you," yet he couldn't be certain. He told Allyn, "You're welcome, Grandpa."

There was nothing else he could do. The energy drained from Trouble's body and his legs became rubbery. He staggered to Thalastria and leaned against the mammoth for support. Trouble resisted fatigue for a moment, then slid to the floor and fell in a deep sleep.

27

An hour later, Thalastria used her trunk to gently nudge Trouble awake. He blinked his eyes, looking at the surroundings, trying to remember where he was sitting. His nap had been like a coma, the deepest sleep he'd ever experienced, leaving Trouble disoriented.

"Nuru? Tattoo?" he whispered. When he got no answer, Trouble struggled to his feet, feeling cold and out of breath. He forced himself to pick another stown flower from the ore wagon and eat its rancid tasting petals. Immediately, oxygen flowed into his body, making him feel better.

Then a heavy, wet object pressed against his neck and he jumped in fright. "Oh, it's you, Mulanathor. That was your trunk. You scared me." Trouble wasn't used to being around wooly mammoths, with their enormous size, nearly double the bulk of a normal elephant.

Mulanathor again moved the tip of his trunk against Trouble's neck, getting his attention. The oversize, shaggy elephant turned his head in an unmistakable gesture. The mammoth wanted Trouble to follow him. He lumbered out of the healing chamber and along the golden spiral ramp, the thump of his heavy feet echoing off stone walls like a tired drum. After a short distance, Mulanathor turned into a dark hole, wafting the foul odors of moldy dung and unwashed elephant hide.

Trouble followed in the darkness by grabbing a tuft of fur at the end of the beast's massive tail. It felt like Trouble grabbed a coarse hairbrush with ultra-stiff bristles by the wrong end. The elephant led him along a tunnel, ending in a dimly lit cavern glowing with the fluorescence of the same moss they'd observed during their slide inside the mountain.

Trouble was standing in a grotto where the wooly mammoths lived. Their cave was round, carved out of the mountain by crudely removing stone. The rough quarrying left deep gouge marks in the gray walls, but the floor looked smooth and level. The empty room seemed void of furnishings, a barren amphitheater without decorations. One corner formed a toilet area, badly in need of cleanup. Its foul odor nearly made Trouble vomit.

At the opposite end of the cave, clean water dripped in a trough near food bins. Mulanathor walked to his empty food tray and used his trunk to grab a last remaining wisp of hay. Trouble expected him to eat the straw, but instead, the mammoth led him back to the healing chamber. At the ore wagon, he watched Mulanathor lay the strand of hay between his grandfather and Albert.

"You're telling me they'll be waking up soon and need food to eat. Is that it?" He watched the huge pachyderm, not really expecting an answer. But he got one.

The wooly mammoth nodded his head in a "yes."

"What about you and Thalastria? It looks like you haven't eaten in days, or maybe weeks. Aren't you starved?"

That question brought enthusiastic nods from both elephants.

"Where do you get your food?"

The wooly mammoths looked at Allyn, lying on the wagon.

"Oh, my grandfather brings hay to you. Seems he's forgotten to do that for a long time. Sorry." Trouble assumed Allyn put straw bales on the wagon and sent them to the elephants via the dumbwaiter, which would have been quite a chore for his elderly grandfather.

He thought aloud. "We need to get out of this pyramid and bring back food for everyone." Trouble looked around for his friends and didn't see them. He asked the mammoths, "Where are Nuru and Tattoo?"

His answer came from the entrance of the healing chamber. "Sorry," Nuru apologized. "Tattoo and I went exploring. Figured while you slept, we should look for another exit, since the drawbridge is gone."

"Find one?"

Nuru shook his head. "No. If there's another passageway, it's well hidden."

"Did you explore the cavern where Thalastria and Mulanathor live?"

"Er, no." Nuru looked sheepish.

Tattoo provided an explanation. She pinched her nose, indicating the smell was too gross. "Place needs a little shoveling." Tattoo said it in a quiet voice, not wanting to offend the elephants.

"I know the cave stinks, but people need to get fed, right?"

Tattoo and Nuru exchanged uneasy glances.

"Fed?" Tattoo acted suspicious.

Trouble nodded. "Yes. The mammoths are starving. My grandfather and Albert will also need food soon. And I don't know about you guys, but I'm getting pretty hungry."

"Um, Trouble, where do we find this food?" Tattoo seemed nervous.

"Conservatory," was his one word answer.

"Styx," was Tattoo's one word reply.

"I know. We'll have to chance it."

Tattoo sighed in disgust.

"You got any other ideas?" he asked them.

"No," Nuru admitted. "I don't think it's safer at the Coldery. There's probably leopards all over Yeti City, looking for us. Might as well risk your life for something you care to eat."

"Tattoo?" Trouble wanted to know if she agreed.

"Oh, man," she groaned.

"Was that a yes or a no?"

"It was a yes," Tattoo conceded.

"OK." Trouble left the healing chamber and walked toward the wooly mammoths' lair. But at the entrance to their cave, Mulanathor and Thalastria halted.

Puzzled, Trouble asked the elephants, "What's up?"

Mulanathor answered by wrapping his trunk around Trouble and setting him on Thalastria's back. It felt like being grabbed by a weightlifter and squeezed. Dropped on the elephant's thick hide, Trouble grunted in discomfort. He had no saddle to ride and strained his leg muscles to straddle the elephant's wide back. Trouble watched Thalastria lift Nuru and Tattoo, placing them on Mulanathor's large body.

Tattoo felt bewildered. "What are they doing?"

"Whatever it is, we're going for a ride." Trouble felt equally confused.

Driven by their desire to be fed, the wooly mammoths trudged along the golden spiral. The elephants halted only when they'd reached the pyramid's crumbled ledge and could go no further. Mulanathor surveyed the damage for a moment, then lifted his trunk. He trumpeted a deafening bellow, almost knocking Trouble off Thalastria's back. The braying echoed for several seconds before dying out. When Mulanathor repeated his loud call, Thalastria joined in the trumpeting, forcing Tattoo, Nuru and Trouble to press hands over their ears.

When the ringing echoes died, Trouble looked down and saw a ledge surrounding the pyramid. The outcropping seemed new, as though the shelf never crumbled into the abyss. His shock grew when the wooly mammoths stepped off the ledge into space, scaring Trouble and his companions. The invisible drawbridge seemed restored like the ledge, allowing the elephants to jog across a miles-deep gorge, walking on a transparent surface. Mulanathor and Thalastria acted calm, but the trio riding the wooly mammoths felt terrified during the entire crossing. They were relieved to see earth under them again. At the far end, the elephants lowered Tattoo, Nuru and Trouble to the ground, near the dumbwaiter.

"Uh, I guess this is where we descend into the basement," Tattoo said nervously.

Trouble also felt uneasy about going in the conservatory. But he took a step toward the dumbwaiter, knowing they all needed to eat.

Nuru stopped him. "You wait here, so you can watch over your grandfather and Albert. It doesn't take all three of us to gather food."

"He's right," Tattoo agreed. "There's no point in all of us getting …" Tattoo stopped in mid-sentence and changed what she was going to say. "Er, getting worn out," she continued.

Trouble hesitated. "I don't like this. Why don't you stay here, Tattoo? Nuru and I can go."

"Because Allyn is your grandfather, Trouble, not ours." Nuru was firm. "You need to be in the healing chamber when he wakes up, to look after him. We'll be back soon." Nuru put a firm grip on Tattoo's arm and pressed her toward the dumbwaiter.

"Yeah, we'll bring you food." Tattoo said it with false bravado.

Trouble called to them as they entered the dumbwaiter. "Don't forget to bring hay for the mammoths." When they were gone, Trouble sadly cast advice after them. "Be careful," he whispered.

He rode Thalastria back to the healing chamber. Above them, the gray light of dusk seeped through a clear dome, darkening the room.

Trouble slid off the wooly mammoth and walked to the yak cart where his grandfather and Albert lay. The king penguin had rolled on his side and was snoring. Albert's face looked relaxed and he seemed out of pain. Trouble's grandfather also appeared much better, having more color in his cheeks. The clotted blood and torn fur on his chest had vanished. But a trail of scars showed where Styx's talons raked Allyn's chest. The raised scars were inflamed and probably still hurt.

Trouble covered the reddened scars with crushed mint, hoping the legendary healing plant of the Yetis would work a miracle. Maybe it would complete the healing. He sat down, leaning against Thalastria's leg, trying to find a comfortable position, and waited for his grandfather to wake up.

28

Allyn brushed mint leaves from his chest and his fingers touched scars running across his body like a swollen rash. The cauterized flesh felt bumpy and raw, like burns from getting trapped in a fire. Those scars formed a roadmap of ugly wounds, painful reminders of the leopard's razor-sharp claws. Allyn tried to sit up and winced in pain. "Who performed the healing ceremony?"

Trouble squirmed. "Me."

The Yeti exaggerated. "Oh. You did a good job."

"No, I didn't." Trouble felt uncomfortable taking any credit when his grandfather still felt so much pain.

Allyn's face changed from discomfort to concern. "Trouble, you're not a Yeti. To heal me at all is a miracle."

"I'm part Yeti."

"True." Allyn smiled at Trouble's comment. "Even full Yetis have difficulty with their initial healing. They're never asked to mend someone who is badly wounded on their first attempt. It takes extreme concentration to repair a damaged body. The healing chamber focuses all the spiritual energy of Yetis past, transferring that power through the healer. Did you see them, inside your mind?"

"Yes. I felt ghost-like images taking my hands and pressing them into your wounds."

The Yeti smiled. "Thanks for your hard work."

"Well, maybe I can try again in a little while. You can teach me. I'll learn by repairing Albert."

Allyn shook his head. "I'm afraid not. Albert will have to wait until your father returns – and so will I."

"Why?"

"Oh, it's not that you aren't good enough or anything like that. I'm an experienced healer and Albert's flipper is still not attached correctly. I was too injured myself to focus on him. Fixing Albert will take another major session." Allyn gently probed the sleeping penguin.

Trouble couldn't wait for his grandfather to finish with the king penguin. "Why can't I do a second session on Albert?"

"Because you were in the room when the first one was done." Allyn lifted Albert's flipper, then put it back. "This job was close enough that a human surgeon, a good veterinarian, can finish the operation."

"I'm glad. What about you?"

"I'll have to wait until your father shows up. He's half Yeti."

"But you're in pain."

"There's nothing I can do about it. The Yeti spirits won't return unless you have a new healer, one who wasn't in the room during the first attempt. Even then, you must wait at least a month. Perhaps your father will be here by then."

"He's been gone two years."

"Yes, I know." Allyn lowered his voice. "You've done what you could. Now it's time for you and your friends to go home."

"I can't leave you in this condition."

"Oh, but you must," he insisted. "Your friends are missed. Their entire village is on the mountain, looking for you. I feel their presence and so do the leopards. They grow angrier by the moment. Someone will be killed if you don't leave."

"Who will take care of you?" Trouble asked.

"Mulanathor and Thalastria, the wooly mammoths."

"I don't see how they can take care of you. Mulanathor and Thalastria are old and not all that strong." Trying to be discrete, he said quietly, "Someone forgot to feed them."

The Yeti coughed in embarrassment. "Yes, they have. I'll, er, remind them." Allyn looked around for Nuru and Tattoo. "Your friends – have they gone to the conservatory for food?"

Trouble nodded. "They know to bring hay for the elephants also."

"Good. That gives us time to talk." He noticed Trouble's concerned expression. "Oh, don't worry about Styx attacking them in the conservatory. That stown flower bacteria stings like the devil. The only disinfectant is ice-cold snow. I'm sure Styx is outside, rolling in snow, trying to freeze the bacteria and numb her wounds. She won't be back. Styx will never go in the conservatory again. That area gave her terrible pain and she won't forget it."

"That's a relief." But Trouble didn't feel any better. He was too worried about his grandfather. "Once we go, you won't be able to feed Mulanathor and Thalastria."

"They'll come with us when we leave." He patted Trouble on the back. "Remember the green area, where you chased Albert and he ditched you by swimming under the protective bubble? Mulanathor and Thalastria can graze in the park."

"It's too warm in the park for wooly mammoths," Trouble argued.

"They eat just once a day. They'll be inside the bubble for only a short while."

"Wait a minute. They can't leave the pyramid. A wooly mammoth won't fit in the dumbwaiter."

Allyn looked at his grandson for a moment before the truth dawned. "You rode the dumbwaiter up here? You could have died."

"Um. Sorry. You told us to use it."

"Well, I was in a lot of pain. I meant for you to ride in the freight elevator. It's located near the dumbwaiter. That dumbwaiter is only used to dump iron on the slag heap outside Yeti City. The electricity-generating bacteria is always making iron as part of its natural metabolic process. We can't leave tons of rusting sludge in the conservatory."

"The freight elevator." Trouble felt stunned, recalling the scary experience of riding in the dumbwaiter.

The Yeti once again struggled to rise. "Where's my walking stick, Trouble? Did you put it in the cart?"

"Uh, no," Trouble admitted. "I had to use your walking stick. It was kind of an emergency and your cane …" His voice trailed off.

"No matter. I'll make myself a new one." The Yeti tore a decorative carved beam off the wall of the healing chamber as easily as a human plucks a leaf from a tree. "There, a new cane." He smiled at Trouble, trying to make him feel better, but it didn't work.

"I don't want to leave."

Allyn patted Trouble's head. "I know you don't want to go. And I don't want you to leave. But you have to."

They heard a loud squeak from the ox cart, the irritating sound of its rusty axle. Nuru and Tattoo were returning, towing a load of produce heaped on the wagon. Mounds of green hay lay piled on red carrots and parsnips, pulled from the conservatory garden. Hairy filaments clung to the vegetables, smelling of damp earth like the soil of freshly worked crop beds.

Allyn hobbled forward, greeting Nuru and Tattoo. "Well done," he exclaimed. "You even brought fish for Albert." He poked at a basket. "Good choice. Raw vegetables, nuts, berries of all kinds, very healing – and prudent. There's no wait for things to cook. Let's eat. The mammoths have started, so why should we wait?"

29

Tattoo finished chewing a huge carrot and still felt hungry. She poked through a basket of food to see what looked appealing, sifting leafy parsley sprigs and thick red turnip hunks to find something sweet. She discovered some unusual looking berries that smelled like ripe tangerines. The orange balls tasted like spinach, but they rinsed the bitterness of stown petals from her mouth. With her stomach filled, Tattoo decided to satisfy her curiosity. She didn't know how to address Trouble's grandfather. "Er, Mr. Jones, Yeti sir …"

"Please, call me Allyn."

"Well, ah, Mr. Allyn. We passed a lot of Yetis on the road to the healing chamber. They seemed a little …" Tattoo hesitated. She didn't want to offend Allyn. "Well, anyway, they were inside a block of ice. Why is that?"

"The bodies are frozen to preserve them. Our great pyramid is a necropolis, a city of the dead. The Egyptians imitated us, placing mummified bodies inside hidden tombs. Our city of the dead is like the Egyptian Valley of the Kings."

"How come?" Tattoo mumbled, eating another orange ball.

"Valley of the Kings is a canyon, honeycombed with burial chambers holding deceased royalty, an underground town with crypts instead of houses. Valley of the Kings is where Howard Carter discovered the famous King Tutankhamen. People love King Tut's golden burial mask and his beautiful possessions."

Nuru was awestruck. "You're kidding." He'd always been fascinated with pyramids, especially the treasures hidden inside crypts. "You taught Egyptians how to bury dead royalty?"

"Not quite. Actually, we encountered Egyptian traders and taught them our hieroglyphic alphabet, plus some of our healing techniques. We helped them practice on their sick. One of these Egyptian traders went to the royal court and healed an ill pharaoh, the king at that time. This Pharaoh decided he could become immortal by building a pyramidal healing chamber. He assumed every time he got sick, he'd be cured by going inside the pyramid. The king built a stone pyramid far grander than the simple tent used by a humble trader." Allyn paused to nibble on a stalk of celery.

Nuru couldn't wait for the Yeti to finish eating. "Go on. What happened to the Egyptian king? Did he live forever?"

Allyn wagged his head. "No. As I told Trouble, a healer can only do one session on a patient. A new healer is needed for a second treatment."

"So what happened to this Egyptian guy?"

"The next time he got sick, the Pharaoh died. The king was buried inside his pyramid, starting a fashion trend. From then on, pharaohs competed to build grander pyramids, outdoing the previous king."

"I don't get it. How come they stopped building pyramids?"

Allyn stretched. "Years later, Egypt fell on hard economic times and the pharaohs quit building expensive monuments. They cut their tombs into hillsides instead. It was cheaper and easier. That's why Valley of the Kings got created."

"So you bury Yetis in ice instead of wrapping them like an Egyptian mummy. Why?" Tattoo hoped it wasn't true. She was frightened by mummies with their shriveled faces.

"We use ice because freezing preserves bodies much better than embalming."

"Why does it matter, if they're dead? I mean, they don't feel anything." Nuru stared at Allyn.

Tattoo cringed. "That wasn't very tactful."

"Oh, sorry. I didn't mean it that way. I just thought there must be a reason why their bodies are frozen instead of buried in the ground, like we do."

Allyn didn't seem offended. "An ancient prophecy states one day all Yetis will be gone – except for a last Yeti."

"What happens then?" Trouble asked, feeling anxious.

"The last Yeti will bring a new race to life, using the bodies of our ancestors."

"How?" Nuru acted skeptical.

Allyn shrugged. "I have no idea how it will be done. The prophecy doesn't explain that. However, the written scroll states new Yetis won't be old ones brought back to life, which is good. Many of my colleagues needed a bit of self-improvement." Allyn gave Trouble a wink. "That's a nice way of saying I didn't like them."

Worried, Tattoo asked, "This scroll isn't like the Egyptian *Book of the Dead*, is it? It doesn't have spells for reincarnating mummies so they come to life and walk around? Right?"

"Hardly. There are no prayers or incantations in the scroll. The document was begun as a history, recording what happened to the Yeti race. About a thousand years ago, the scroll developed a life force of its own. A year after the history was finished, the historian unrolled his parchment and realized new lines had been added – to the amazement of the scribe, I dare say. He asked who wrote these words, but no one would admit having penned them."

"What did the words say?" Trouble asked.

"The new words predicted our race would die out, only to be reborn from its dead. Yeti elders read the scroll and were frightened by these words. Angry, they tore off this final page and flung it into the abyss guarding the pyramid. A great wind rushed from the gorge and carried the scrap of paper to a safe hiding place, a secret location revealed to me in a dream. I told your father, Indigo, where to find the missing part of the scroll."

"Dad told me to bring that scrap of paper with me if I ever came to the Himalayas. But he didn't say it was from a Yeti prophecy. He said the fragment was part of an ancient Buddhist scroll and belonged to a monastery near Mount Everest."

Allyn put his arm around his grandson. "Don't be angry at your father, Trouble. That's a lot for a young person to know."

Depressed, Trouble put his head in his hands. He mumbled, "I guess." There was an awkward silence.

After a moment, Tattoo broke the quiet. "How did a Yeti scroll wind up in a Buddhist monastery?"

"I took it there, for safekeeping," Allyn explained. "I was afraid Yeti elders might destroy the scroll. They'd talked about burning the document to prevent it being reunited with the missing prophecy. I traveled to the monastery when I was a boy, only fifty years old." He saw confused looks on their faces and told them, "A fifty-year-old Yeti is like a five-year-old human. Yetis often live to a thousand and people survive to about a hundred."

"Oh, right," Tattoo muttered.

"Is there anything else you wanted explained?" Allyn asked.

Nuru pointed at the glass ceiling. "We watch climbers hiking the summit of Everest. Yet they can't see us inside this healing chamber. Why is that?"

Allyn smiled. "The glass above our heads works like a one-way mirror. All climbers see is a reflection of the ice and snow around them. Normal mirrors are tinted with silver. But this dome uses gold for a reflective surface. Gold, by the way, isn't painted on the glass blocks. The precious metal is evaporated, boiled to a hot mist. Golden steam condenses on cold glass, making a smooth coating for the mirror."

The mention of precious metals prompted Nuru to ask about the golden ramp. "How's it possible that we spiraled down the ramp yet wound up at the top of a pyramid?"

"It's true that the ramp is cone-shaped, like a funnel. But there's an elevator under the ramp, lifting you up. At the top level, you're in the healing chamber." Allyn put his food basket on the floor and wiped his hands, using a bundle of straw for his towel.

"Why is the ramp a spiral?" Trouble intuitively sensed the ramp's twisting shape was important.

"Remember that prophecy I talked about? It states that spirals are key to the recovery of the Yeti race. That's why we built a corkscrew ramp as an approach to the healing chamber."

"What about the drawbridge?" Tattoo wondered. "How does it vanish and reappear?"

"And the crumbling ledge?" Nuru hurried to add.

Allyn raised his hands. "One question at a time. The drawbridge is coated with a living organism. This plant is capable of displaying a picture like a flat panel computer display. When you look at the span, you see a picture of the gorge underneath. You're viewing a photo of the canyon, wrapped around the bridge. That's why the span seems invisible."

"The drawbridge vanished when we couldn't get the right password for entering the pyramid. All the dirt I'd tossed on it fell in the canyon. Why was that?" Trouble asked.

"You triggered the pyramid's burglar alarm system. Enter the wrong password and the drawbridge rotates, dumping everything into the canyon. Good thing you weren't standing on the bridge when it rolled over."

Nuru objected. "That doesn't explain how the broken ledge got repaired. Mulanathor and Thalastria trumpeted their calls and a new ledge appeared, plus the bridge came back."

"A wooly mammoth call is the all clear signal, resetting the burglar alarm system. A new shelf moves out of the pyramid to replace the old one. Yes, I know the ledge appears so fast it seems impossible." Allyn waved his hands. "Enough questions for now. We need some exercise after such a big meal." He patted his stomach. "Maybe you fellows could help me with a chore?"

"Oh, sure," Nuru and Tattoo agreed, not realizing they'd be given a very unpleasant job.

"Good. Nice of you to help an old Yeti, injured in a fight with a leopard." Allyn reminded them he'd saved their lives from Styx. He wanted to make sure they felt committed to doing his chore.

Nuru became suspicious. "What exactly do you want?"

"It's been a while since I helped Mulanathor and Thalastria tidy their room. There's large shovels in the cave. You use them as pooper-scoopers. Push the mammoth's digestive output down the toilet chute and I'll be very grateful." Allyn beamed his most charming smile at them.

Tattoo stifled a groan.

"Come on." Trouble nudged the shocked Nuru. "Let's go. There's no getting out of this one." Trouble grabbed Nuru by the arm and they shuffled toward a highly unpleasant odor steaming from the elephant cave. The wooly mammoths were not only busy eating. They were busy digesting as well.

30

Shoveling elephant dung resulted in weary backs and sore wrists. Trouble, Nuru and Tattoo craved a long soak in a steaming bath. Instead, they got lifted on the backs of grateful wooly mammoths for a ride into Yeti City. Exhausted by the hard work, Tattoo and Nuru's eyelids grew heavy as overstuffed backpacks. They slumped across the wide elephants, napping while the group descended on a freight elevator. The Sherpas continued to sleep, but Trouble stayed wide awake, too upset to doze. He petted Thalastria's coarse neck hair when she stepped over the freight elevator's low wall.

Born in the Great Pyramid, Thalastria and Mulanathor never traveled outside the necropolis, until today. The elephants walked slowly, enjoying their first visit ever to the capital city of the Yetis. The pair of wooly mammoths acted excited by exploring a new world. They lifted their trunks to sniff everything and rolled their eyes to examine each curiosity. At this pace, it would take an hour to reach Allyn's apartment building. Strangely, he didn't seem to be in a hurry to get home, despite his wounds.

Allyn felt guilty. "I should've let them out years ago. They were never happy penned-up. The pyramid is safe from intruders without them."

"They lived inside the pyramid as guards for the healing chamber?" Trouble asked.

"Yes. Mulanathor and Thalastria were raised to protect the sacred healing chamber. They also guarded the pyramid's vault area, with all its treasure. They've gotten a bit lazy about checking the outer regions lately. That's why you got so far inside the pyramid before meeting them. Not their fault, though. Poor things were too hungry to wander about the monument, checking for burglars. Looks like their energy is back, now that they've eaten."

"Will they still have to live in the pyramid?"

Allyn seemed evasive. He didn't really answer the question. "You're right. Mulanathor and Thalastria won't want to stay in the pyramid after this tour. Walking around the city has spoiled them as security guards for Yeti treasures." Allyn smiled, indicating he didn't care if the mammoths ever went back to guard duty.

"It's good they'll be here to protect you, Grandfather."

"From Screecher and his pack?" Allyn gave Trouble a thoughtful look.

"Yes. I'm worried about the leopards. They might attack you."

"I'm concerned, too. That's why Mulanathor and Thalastria will keep me company."

"Will Albert be safe?" Trouble stroked the penguin's head. He still acted groggy from his operation. His short tongue lolled out of his mouth and his eyes floated in a milky haze.

"Albert should go with you."

"Me?" Trouble felt shocked.

"Yes," Allyn insisted.

Trouble stammered. "I can't take a penguin to New York. There's no place for him to live. I'd have to put him in Central Park zoo. He'd be heartbroken to live in a cage."

"Albert needs an operation on that flipper or he won't swim again. Water sports are his love. It would be a shame for him to lose them. When you see Albert playing in the water, you'll understand."

"What will I do with him after he heals from surgery? How will I get him back to you?"

"He can return on your next trip. In the meantime, Albert will assist you in the antique store."

"How can you live without Albert? He helps you."

"Don't worry. I'll care for myself." Allyn changed the subject. "Let me take you on a brief tour of the city, show you a few important places." The Yeti commanded his elephants. "Mulanathor, Thalastria, let's go a bit faster, OK?"

Prodded by Allyn, the wooly mammoths trotted, lumbering across the terrain. Their passengers bounced with each step like riders in an off-roading big wheel truck. Soon they arrived at the outskirts of Yeti City, where the mushroom skyscrapers ended in a boundary hedge of rhododendron bushes. Crimson flowers clustered in groups, their color muted in faded twilight. The elephants walked along a tall hedge until an old trail appeared. Taking the abandoned path, Mulanathor and Thalastria plowed through a narrow opening between plants, shoving rhododendrons aside.

In the distance, Trouble spotted a fleet of old-fashioned sailing vessels on the horizon. He could make out their tall masts and billowing canvas sails. When they grew closer, he realized the ships and their sails weren't real. They were only hollows in the cavern's wall, dwellings carved in the mountain like ancient American Indian communities in Arizona and New Mexico. Unlike North American cliff dwellers, Yetis shaped their caves to resemble sails on a boat mast. Each sail-like cave had a tall pole running up its center, similar to the mast in a sailing vessel. Rope netting fanned down the poles like ship's rigging, completing the nautical look. Trouble assumed Yetis climbed the rope netting to reach a high cave.

"What are the caves for?"

Allyn explained. "This is the first Yeti settlement, where we lived after the Great Migration from Svalbard."

Nuru stretched and yawned. "Svalbard?"

"Svalbard is the Yeti homeland, where we came from. Svalbard is a large island between Iceland and Norway."

Tattoo was awake now also. She rubbed the sleep out of her eyes and asked, "Why'd you leave an island and come to Mount Everest?"

"We didn't have a choice. Thousands of years ago, primitive man moved to Svalbard and drove out the Yetis. We closed the entrances to our cities with avalanches and began a long migration across the Arctic. Some of us went over the North Pole to Canada, spreading along the Rocky Mountains and the Sierra Nevada range, starting Abominable

Snowman stories. In California, they called us Bigfoot. A few Yetis made it all the way to Peru and lived in the Andes, where Peruvians named us the Ukumar-Zupai. But most Yetis came here, to the Himalayas and lived inside Mount Everest."

Trouble asked, "When did you leave the caves and move inside mushroom buildings?"

"The mushroom skyscrapers came much later. After we occupied the mushrooms, we preserved this area as a museum. I suppose you're wondering why we designed the whole thing to look like a fleet of ships when viewed from a distance."

"Well, I was," Trouble admitted. "I thought the ship-like design might be an accident, not really intended."

"Oh, the resemblance was intentional. I wasn't the first restless Yeti, by any means."

"There were others? I mean, you roamed around?" Tattoo wondered.

"Sure, we were great adventurers. When we lived in Svalbard, Yetis sailed to the Mediterranean and traded with Greeks and Phoenicians. We tried to think of the migration from Svalbard as an adventure, like everyone sailing off to explore the world. It's our way of putting a positive spin on being driven out of our homeland. Cheered us up to think of the trip as an adventure, instead of exile. When we get closer, you'll see pictures of Yetis who made the initial migration."

"You had photography thousands of years ago?" Tattoo was suspicious.

"No," Allyn chuckled. "Not photographs – tapestries, drapes woven in the image of Yetis who moved here from Svalbard. The tapestries draped the cave openings as privacy screens. The drapes also form a collective family tree. The tapestries portray Yeti generations, with the youngest members at the top."

Nuru pointed to the bottom layer of caves. "Those cut-outs look like ships. Why don't they have privacy screens like the rest of the caves?"

"They were communal eating areas. We put the kitchens outside, so we could bake pies and casseroles."

"What'd you use for fuel?" Tattoo felt curious.

"We burned yak dung, like Sherpas do today. The kitchen chimneys had charcoal filters to keep smoke from polluting the air. See those copper pipes wound around the chimneys?"

Tattoo nodded. "Sure. You heated water that way, I'd guess. That surprises me. I didn't think Yetis liked hot showers."

Allyn smiled. "True, we like to shower at a pleasant 40° F, which is very cold for humans. Water heated in the chimney pipes wasn't used for bathing. We needed hot water for making herbal teas."

The Yeti continued as tour guide, pointing to a large hole in the ground. The elephants stopped at the hole, so their riders could look into the amphitheater, a mini-football stadium. Coarse granite blocks served as chairs. The seats funneled downward to an open lecture area with a podium. "This is the first Yeti school, kindergarten through college. It's like a one-room schoolhouse on the American prairie." He gestured at a large sandpit next to the teacher's podium, near the center of the amphitheater. Diagrams sketched in the sand by a long stick appeared to be arithmetic exercises.

"The sandpit was your blackboard?" Nuru asked.

"Exactly. Very good." Near the edge of the sandpit was a rack with hundreds of oversize stamps. "The teacher used those large wooden stamps to emboss a lesson on the sand so all the students could see."

"What's that other gadget, the one with wooden beads on wires?" Tattoo wondered.

"That's an old abacus, from Babylonian days, when we did calculations using base 60 arithmetic. We switched to the decimal system centuries ago, with the rest of the world."

They rode the wooly mammoths past the amphitheater and stopped at the cave dwellings, where they dismounted from Mulanathor and Thalastria.

Trouble felt puzzled by this detour, yet relieved to have more time with his grandfather. "Where are we going?"

"I'm taking you to the greatest treasure in Yeti City. In my estimation, it's far more valuable than the jewels we keep in our pyramid." Allyn placed his hand in a niche, unlocking the door to a hidden chamber. "When you walk inside, you'll see why this place is known as the Carousel of Ancient Secrets."

31

Walking into the hidden chamber felt like stepping inside a drained water tank, an empty drum. The bottom looked perfectly round and wide as Columbus Circle in New York, a massive traffic circle that could easily hold a dozen tourist buses. Instead of cars and buses, a giant carousel, coated in dust, filled the hidden chamber. It looked like a race with the animals frozen in mid-stride, their legs poised for a next step that would never happen. Their flying manes seemed flags in a stiff wind, yet not a trace of breeze stirred to chase away the smell of mildew. Glassy eyes stared ahead at a race that never progressed, vision fixated on the next animal in a long chain running around the circle.

Tattoo stepped on the carousel and tenderly ran her hands over wooden skins, fascinated by carved reindeer and polar bears. "I saw pictures of a merry-go-round once. But it had horses and unicorns."

Allyn explained, "Reindeer and polar bears are found on Svalbard. It made us less homesick to see familiar animals on the merry-go-round."

"They could use some paint," Tattoo suggested. Her fingers outlined the bald patch on a polar bear's rump. "Bright colors would bring them to life."

"Yes. Sadly, we don't have paint. We'd have to trade with humans for colorful tints, and that's become too dangerous in recent years." Allyn joined Tattoo on the carousel and it sagged under his weight.

Nuru craned his neck and traced the carousel's tarnished brass poles. They rose from the floor to a ten-story-high ceiling. "Wow, those poles are tall." His voice echoed in the hollow reservoir.

"The poles have to be tall, so we can ride up there." Allyn pointed above their heads. "The space above the merry-go-round is a honeycomb, lined with pigeon holes. Each niche holds a rare document."

"Are secrets hidden in those documents?" Tattoo asked. She loved discovering secrets.

"Yes. Ancient civilizations hid their most valuable knowledge in secret books. At one point in history, most of these documents came to Alexandria and were stored in its great library. But the library burned in 400 A.D. and its manuscripts vanished forever, destroyed by fire. Yet the books haven't disappeared, like archeologists think. We have them here, in this vault."

Trouble looked up and saw thousands of slots holding illuminated manuscripts and scrolls. There were also sewn volumes, animal-hide vellums and rolled parchments tied with ribbon. Trouble strained his eyes in an attempt to see the highest row of documents. "How many books do you have?"

"A million, give or take a few." Allyn sounded proud.

Nuru shook his head in disbelief. "Doesn't make sense. You couldn't copy a million books while the Library of Alexandria burned."

"We didn't."

Trouble looked at his grandfather. Allyn was smiling with amusement at Nuru's skepticism. "How did you save all those books from the fire?"

The Yeti shook his head. "We didn't," he repeated. "Scholars felt heartbroken at the loss of the Alexandrian Library. But they shouldn't have worried." He was gloating now. "After all, the books in that library weren't originals. They were copies."

Tattoo was confused. "Huh? What do you mean?"

"You see, the Library of Alexandria built its inventory by stealing books from unsuspecting tourists. Their documents were seized, then copied. The library kept the originals and tourists had to settle for copies."

Tattoo still felt puzzled. "So how did you get all these manuscripts?"

"The tourists got waylaid twice, first by us and again in Alexandria. Like the library, we kept the originals and gave copies to the tourists."

"That wasn't nice, stealing their books. I'm surprised a Yeti would do that." Nuru gave Allyn a scolding look. Nuru enjoyed playing the critic.

The Yeti coughed in embarrassment. "Yes, well, morality changes over time. Those were the social values of that age. Best not to judge ancient Yetis by our current standards. It's unfair. Besides, we healed the tourists. Every traveler we detained left us healthier than when they arrived. Plus, we made better copies of their books than the Library of Alexandria. In fact, our copies looked so good it was hard to tell them from the original. On the other hand, scribes employed by the library were sloppy. They often made mistakes, substituting the wrong word in a sentence, or worse yet, omitting an entire passage. I suspect they dropped things to speed up their work. Probably got paid by the book, not by the hour."

Allyn could see Nuru wasn't convinced and tried a different approach. "Our conduct, however questionable, did preserve these ancient manuscripts. In contrast, human wars destroyed the Alexandrian Library. Its books would be lost forever if we didn't have them."

Nuru pressed him. "Will you ever give them back?"

Allyn looked away, pained by the thought of losing his precious collection. "When the time is right. We always planned on doing it. We looked for an archeological site to serve as a lost library, some place where all these scrolls could be 'discovered' by humans. In fact, that's one of the reasons I encouraged your father's interest in archeology, Trouble."

"Does my dad know about all these scrolls?" Trouble asked.

"Indigo? He came in here once and took some of my most precious books. Indigo sold them to finance an expedition. After that, I never allowed him in here. I changed the lock so he couldn't get in."

The Yeti looked sadder than Trouble had ever seen him. Uncomfortable, Allyn changed the subject. "Why don't I show you some of the collection? I'll take you to my favorite ancient manuscript." The Yeti put his hand in a wall niche and a panel slid open, revealing an organ keyboard decorated with Yeti hieroglyphs. Allyn sat on a wooden bench in front of the "organ" and flexed his hands, like an artist getting ready for a performance.

Tattoo leaned over the "organ," curious how it worked. "How do you find the book you want?"

"To locate a book, you have to know the catalog number. You could find a manuscript the hard way, by searching through all of them. That might take years, so it's best to remember the catalog ID for your favorites." The Yeti typed a string of numbers and rose from the bench.

"We've only got a few seconds to get aboard the carousel." Allyn walked rather stiffly to the merry-go-round and twisted himself between reindeer. He reclined on a polar bear couch with obvious relief.

Trouble put a foot in a stirrup, mounted a reindeer and waited. Nothing happened. "Something wrong?"

"Just be patient. I know that's hard for you." Allyn teased.

The organ played a lilting melody, like an ancient Celtic folksong. They felt a quick jerk and the carousel began to spin. The merry-go-round turned faster and faster. They rose, blurring past hundreds of scrolls resting in honeycomb niches.

The music was soft enough that Allyn could talk. "This abandoned water reservoir used to be an ideal storage place for documents. It was the perfect environment, just the right temperature. Now the place gets warmer every year, like our planet. Eventually, all the pages will crack and turn to powder. Can't have that happen to something precious, like the original copy of Homer's *Iliad*."

"You turned a hollow water tank into a library? Didn't the dampness cause problems?" Nuru frowned.

"No," the Yeti answered. "This empty reservoir was dry when we found it, after arriving from Svalbard. That was centuries before I was born."

Nuru acted surprised. "Yetis hollowed out Mount Everest. Didn't they?"

Allyn shook his head. "No. We found the mountain pretty much as you see it, except for the mushroom buildings and the basement greenhouses. Even the classroom amphitheater was already here, waiting for us when we arrived. We added mushroom skyscrapers, the pyramid and a conservatory level."

"Then who hollowed out Mount Everest?" Tattoo wondered.

"A different race preceded the Yetis. Life on earth goes back farther than anyone suspects. That's my guess. What do you think?"

"I think if this carousel doesn't stop spinning soon, I'll throw up." Tattoo felt dizzy from whirling around, seeing the world as a colored blur. The turning motion didn't seem to affect the Yeti. He was used to spinning on the carousel.

Allyn advised, "Hang on. We're almost there."

The merry-go-round slowed and the walls became clear-cut instead of blurred by motion. When they came to a stop, Allyn rose from his polar bear couch and helped Tattoo dismount. She felt dizzy and leaned on the Yeti for support. Nuru and Trouble followed, wandering through a forest of animals to the carousel's edge.

"Well, there's my personal favorite," the Yeti announced. "Euclid's *Elements*. Euclid's *Elements* was the number two bestseller of all time, topped only by the Bible. We have a full set of all thirteen volumes, penned in 300 B.C. by the master geometer himself, Euclid of Alexandria. It's the first mathematical text ever created."

"You got an original edition in Alexandria, where Euclid lived?" Nuru asked. It was a natural assumption.

"No. These volumes were a recent acquisition, in my lifetime. We got them from a Benedictine monk, Adelard of Bath, around 1100 A.D."

"How'd a monk get hold of math textbooks from ancient times?" Trouble wondered.

The Yeti explained, "Adelard bought the books on a journey. He disguised himself as a Muslim student, so he could travel through Moorish Spain. There, Adelard stumbled across a strange manuscript collection in Madrid. He felt pulled to buy the books, even though he couldn't read any of the volumes because they were written in Greek. He was captivated by the geometric drawings. Probably assumed they were a form of magic. There were thirteen volumes in the set, a superstitious number."

"Adelard got them from a museum?" Nuru stared at the priceless volumes but didn't dare touch them.

Allyn explained. "Actually, the monk bought Euclid's *Elements* for pennies from a street vendor."

"But how did the textbooks wind up in the hands of Yetis?" Tattoo had to know all the details.

"On his return trip to England, Adelard fell ill crossing the Pyrenees mountains. A Yeti named Jeronymus found the monk lying in a stream, near death. Jeronymus nursed Adelard back to life and copied the manuscripts, keeping the original volumes safe in our library."

"What good are they?" Nuru acted cynical. He sensed the books were worth millions of dollars and wished he could sell them and be rich. "I'm sure nobody ever read them."

"Not true. Euclid's *Elements* were used by geniuses like Isaac Newton to build modern science. The volumes you see here changed the world."

"Wow, that's a neat story." Trouble craned his neck to look upward. The honeycomb of books seemed to rise forever. The collection looked more like a tapestry than a library, specks of color dappling the chambered wall, similar to a modern abstract painted as a giant mural on the side of a building. "There are so many documents here. How do you keep track of them all? Are their names stored in that 'organ' you played?"

"That organ-shaped instrument only controls the merry-go-round. You have to know the catalog number of the book. Otherwise the 'organ,' as you call it, is useless."

"You memorized the numbers for all these books? It doesn't seem possible." Nuru felt doubtful it could be done.

Allyn explained, "I only remember the ID numbers for a few volumes, the ones I personally like. There are thousands of books in our library I'd love to examine. Unfortunately, I don't know their index number. Our librarian died years ago and no one has taken her place. She had a catalog, but it's disappeared. The catalog may be stored in one of these honeycomb slots. I've never had time to find it. Been too busy with my own life. Takes a long time to do things when you get old." He looked sad.

"You've searched for that catalog?" Trouble asked.

"Sure, though not very hard. Last time I came here, I was looking for your mother. Julia spent days in here, researching something. Never told me what it was. She must have found the information because Julia left suddenly. I haven't seen her since."

"Do you know what mom was looking for in the library?" Trouble burned to know the answer. It might give him a clue to finding his parents.

Allyn shrugged. "Wish I did know. Her research had something to do with your dad and where he might be. Julia wouldn't tell me more. She wanted to check out her hunches first, she said. I'm sure Julia was the last person to have the librarian's catalog. Where she left the index, I don't know." He shrugged. "Well, it doesn't matter anyway. We're out of time. We need to get going."

Allyn sighed. He walked to a lever and pulled it. "Yank this thing once when you want to go down. Pull the lever twice and it'll go up a level instead. That's how you do a manual search, when you've forgotten a book's index number."

"OK, got it. Do we need to sit in the same place on the way down?" Trouble wondered.

"No." The Yeti acted puzzled by that question.

"Good," Trouble said. "Then I'll sit next to you, on the polar bear couch."

"Only if you want to."

"I want to," Trouble assured him. "I want to spend as much time with you as I can."

32

Half an hour later, they were again riding Mulanathor and Thalastria through Yeti City, surrounded by mushroom skyscrapers. Allyn described key landmarks along their route as though he expected Trouble to return in a few days. "See that statue of the tall merchant on the corner of the alley?" He pointed at a bearded Yeti with hollow eyes and a hesitant smile, reaching into his knapsack. "That's Ullabor, our first mayor, and he's carved from red jasper. It's the only red stone sculpture in the city, so use Ullabor as a guidepost. The alley to his right leads to the park bench where you sat after chasing Albert through the park." The Yeti leaned over and spoke with emphasis, "Pay close attention now, Trouble. I'm showing you how to locate my apartment building."

"OK, Grandfather." It was hard to concentrate with his stomach tightened from anxiety.

"Everything's going to be all right. You'll find your mother. I'm just giving you directions in case you come back with Indigo. My son was never good at navigation. Indigo constantly got lost trying to find me."

"How often has dad visited you?" Trouble was curious.

"Many times. He got thrown out constantly in the days when there were more Yetis. Each time Indigo made a wrong turn, a Yeti spotted him and he got escorted outside. Your dad is a terrible navigator."

"But why didn't he zoom to your apartment using the magnetic levitation system, those gliding slippers?" Tattoo wondered.

"Yeah," Nuru said. "You only need to key in the address and the shoes do the rest."

"That's true. But the mag-lev system works only on main boulevards. Indigo was trying to hide, slip into Yeti City without being seen. You may have the same problem, for a different reason."

"You're taking us along back alleys where we can hide from leopards, aren't you?" Trouble asked.

Allyn fidgeted. "The cats left."

"But the leopards will be back, right?" Tattoo asserted.

"Possibly," Allyn grunted.

Trouble felt concerned. "Can Mulanathor and Thalastria really protect you? I thought wooly mammoths and saber-tooth tigers were natural enemies."

"The only saber-tooth throwback is Styx. The other leopards are intimidated by the size of these elephants." But the Yeti couldn't look his grandson in the eye.

"You can't fool me, Grandpa. Nuru told me leopards hunt in a pack and are very smart. How long before they find a way to attack these mammoths?"

"A month," he admitted. "I'll keep Mulanathor and Thalastria in the park for only two weeks, so they won't be in danger. Then I'll return them to the pyramid. The drawbridge is locked against leopards. They can't get across the abyss."

"That means after two weeks, you'll have to enter the conservatory alone. When you get food, you'll be in danger," Nuru calculated. "Screecher may go there and bring others with him."

"When I return the elephants to the pyramid, I'll stockpile enough food to last another two weeks. That gives me a month. After my provisions are gone, I'll eat at a nearby Coldery, that place you hated for its unusual method of making ice cream and cookies. I'll be safe there."

Trouble shook his head, "It's risky. I should stay here to help you."

"You can't help me, Trouble. The leopards are too strong and quick. Worse, your human presence might draw them inside Yeti City. You could cause an attack, instead of preventing it."

"But Allyn," he protested.

"No." The Yeti gave Trouble a stern look. Then his face softened. "There's more at stake here than just my life," he whispered. "I can't look for your parents. Only you can find Julia and Indigo. You have a month. Use the time wisely and everything will be fine. Get back sooner if you can."

"Yes, Grandfather." But Trouble didn't like it one bit.

Allyn returned to his role as navigator. "This street," he announced, "is the main boulevard of Yeti City, the only straight path in the entire metropolis. All the other streets curve, so they can go around mushrooms. The main boulevard takes you directly to our city gates. Next time you visit, you won't have to climb through a ventilation shaft to say hello to me."

"Why?" Tattoo asked.

"Because he's going to show us how to open the gates, dummy," Nuru sniped.

"Oh. He should've said so," Tattoo complained, scratching her arms.

The mammoths came to a halt before a door that must have been four stories high. The entry gate resembled a bank vault, with rods jutting from the door, pinning it into rock on all sides. All pins were the thickness of Allyn's massive legs and probably weighed a hundred pounds apiece.

Dirt and leaves lay piled in front of the city gate, implying the door remained shut for years. Allyn got off a wooly mammoth. To unlock the city gates, he turned a wheel. The wheel's many spokes poked through its rim like handles. The Yeti grabbed the handles as he spun the lock, looking like a helmsman steering an old-fashioned sailing vessel. Allyn cranked the wheel many times to move the huge securing rods only an inch. Finally, the barrier was free to open and Trouble felt an icy draft billowing around the edges of the door.

He watched in sorrow when his grandfather attached long chains to collars on the wooly mammoths. Thalastria and Mulanathor pulled on the enormous weight of the vault door. The mammoths strained against the chains, heaving their bulk forward in ponderous steps. Even for those giant elephants, it was quite a task to open the gates of Yeti City. After the gates swung wide, Trouble realized a large chunk of the mountain was attached to the face of each door, camouflaging the entrance. No one standing outside would realize the vault existed. They'd think the doors were just giant boulders lining the base of Mount Everest.

Outside, a moonless night swallowed all light, except for a pale yellow rectangle cast on the snow by the open vault door. There was a brisk wind, adding its chill to the already arctic temperature. Accustomed to the relative warmth of Yeti City, Trouble shivered in the cold, watching the mammoths pull the door shut. The bite of the cold was nothing compared to the ache in his heart. He knew these were his last minutes with his grandfather. The need to protect Allyn added more pressure to Trouble's difficult quest to find his parents. He hoped to return soon, accompanied by Julia and Indigo.

Nuru worried they might not find the city gates upon returning. "How will we recognize these boulders among the other rocks? They all look the same."

Allyn pointed to Yeti hieroglyphs scratched on the boulders. "These symbols confirm you've found the entrance. Come when the moon is full and at its highest point in the sky. Then the moon shines on these drawings. The hieroglyphs only show in moonlight. Otherwise, the symbols are invisible."

"We can't open these doors ourselves. How do we get inside?" Tattoo asked.

"I'll sense that you're here and bring the mammoths to open the city gate."

"How long will that take? After all, you said Mulanathor and Thalastria are going back to the pyramid," Nuru complained.

"You'll only have to wait a few hours."

"A few hours!" Tattoo exclaimed in frustration.

Allyn shrugged. "It's faster – and safer – than climbing two thousand feet up an icy rock face, like you did this time."

"Suppose you don't show up after we wait for hours," Trouble worried. "Isn't there a doorbell we can ring? Or another way inside?"

"Your mother knows all the alternate routes to Yeti City. I showed them to Julia the last time she was here."

"I …" Trouble didn't want to say it, but he had to admit the truth. "I may not find my mother. How do we get inside then?"

"You'll find Julia," the Yeti said firmly. Allyn reached up the elephant's side and patted Trouble's leg. The Yeti turned toward the shivering Tattoo and Nuru, who were freezing in the cold. Allyn handed them stown flower petals. "Here. Eat these and you'll feel warmer."

Nuru and Tattoo took the foul tasting flower petals and hesitated. Finally, the cold won and they crammed stown petals in their mouths. "Um, delicious," Tattoo joked.

"Yuck. Tastes like rotted cauliflower," Nuru complained.

"Well, stown flowers work – that's the best that can be said about them." Allyn patted the flanks of the wooly mammoths. "Come on, Mulanathor and Thalastria. Let's go." Thalastria lifted Allyn in place behind Trouble.

"Hang on tight," Allyn shouted to Nuru and Tattoo. "The mammoths leap across crevasses. Grab their fur or you could tumble off when they land." He held Trouble with one arm and pinched a mound of fur with his other hand. They bounded across a wide crevasse and thumped on the far side with a collective "Ugh."

"Do they have to go so fast?" Nuru grumbled.

"We'll be late if they don't hurry. It's almost midnight," Allyn explained. "We're due at the monastery and it's a long ride."

"Why are we going to the monastery?" Trouble asked, feeling upset.

"We need to learn what the scroll says about your future. There will be an important hint, a warning you must heed, written on the parchment."

"I don't see how a scroll can help me," Trouble objected, bouncing on the elephant as it trotted across the glacier.

The Yeti explained, "You started a long chain of events by coming here. Something new will be written on the scroll. The message is important to your journey. I guarantee it."

33

The trail to the monastery grounds led through a tall arch, tied down by dozens of ropes. Each rope crowded brilliantly colored prayer flags along its length. Most of the handkerchief-sized flags were shredded by years of exposure, reduced to tattered scraps from rippling in the arctic wind. But some flags still carried hand-written messages of hope and compassion for those in need.

Beyond the prayerful gateway lay a building of humble construction, built for practical use and not for creating a dominating impression. The monastery wasn't a seat of power, but a place of gentleness and reflection. At this late hour, well beyond midnight, only one window remained illuminated. The haunting light of butter candles painted flickering shadows on the window glass like dancing spirits, greeting them. The lit window signaled the visitors, letting them know they were welcome no matter how late they arrived.

Allyn brought the wooly mammoths to a stop and dismounted. He searched the area to make certain they hadn't been seen by villagers. Convinced it was safe, he waved for Nuru, Tattoo and Trouble to follow him. They formed a line, their footsteps crunching across a crust of icy snow. Starlight twinkled on the crystallized snow, making the ground sparkle like it was covered in broken glass.

Trouble's grandfather approached a door near the lit window and found the entrance unlocked, as Allyn expected. The tall Yeti bowed low to pass under the doorjamb. He entered the monastery quietly, remaining silent in respect for the sleeping monks.

To the Yeti's sensitive nose, countless smells filled the dark hallway. He detected the odors of meals, spicy incense, candle wax and a hundred different human beings living inside the building. Allyn followed the scent of just one person, an old friend. He led Trouble, Nuru and Tattoo through a twisting series of passages, tiptoeing past closed doors. Finally, the glow of candlelight filled a hallway. Allyn lifted a beaded curtain made of wooden rings, letting Nuru, Tattoo and Trouble enter a room. He followed them into the fluttering illumination of a hundred butter candles.

In the room's center, an elderly monk sat cross-legged on a silk cushion. His shaved head bent forward, resting his chin on his chest, as though in prayer. His skull resembled a shrunken walnut, layered with furrows and dimples. Scarlet and gold silk robes flowed around his narrow body. He was the Abbot or Rinpoche, head of the monastery.

"I expected you," the Abbot whispered. "You've been heavy on my thoughts tonight."

"I'm sorry to intrude at this late hour," Allyn replied.

The Abbot gently waved a hand, dismissing concerns about the time. "You only come when there's an urgent need. Your visits are always in the best interests of everyone, Yergamegalorn Ergabish. Perhaps I should call you Allyn, for the sake of our guests, who do not speak Yetish."

Surprised, Trouble asked, "You've been here before, Grandfather?"

"Several times," he quietly responded.

The Abbot spun on his silk pillow, turning to look at them. The sagging, wrinkled lines of his old face smoothed in a look of relief at seeing Nuru and Tattoo. "The whole village has been on the mountain looking for you. They'll be delighted to learn you are well."

Nuru and Tattoo nodded in acknowledgement. They were too intimidated to speak in the presence of the Abbot.

The old monk looked at Trouble. "You, little monkey, have lived up to your name and caused no end of mischief." The elderly priest gestured to a tray on a low table. "I had food prepared in anticipation of your arrival. I thought you might be hungry after traveling on such a cold night."

Nuru and Tattoo looked at Allyn for permission. He nodded and they fell eagerly on the tray of delicacies, fruits and nuts lacquered in syrup, served inside fried rice cones. Anxious about the future, Trouble stayed near his grandfather and ignored the desserts.

The Abbot gave Trouble a sympathetic look. "Tea, then?" He lifted a small iron pot and poured fragrant liquid in five charcoal-colored bowls, resting on orange saucers. The fragrance of jasmine tea filled the room, heavy and floral, with a lingering sweet bouquet.

Trouble accepted a teacup out of politeness, too stressed to eat or drink.

Allyn sipped from a delicate cup that seemed a thimble in the grip of his massive hand. "You have been well?" he asked the Abbot.

"As well as an elderly man can be. We have in common the problems of old age. But you are far more advanced in years and wisdom than I am."

"Not true," Allyn countered. "Your wisdom is legendary, demonstrated by your anticipation of our arrival."

"Expecting your visit was instinct, not wisdom. My intuition ends with foreseeing your appearance. I wasn't allowed to know your purpose in coming here. So I reflected on how I might help you. What could I possibly give you, other than this scroll?" The Abbot's bony fingers held up a wooden dowel wrapped in parchment. "I'm confused. Why would you seek this ancient treasure? You already know all that's written on it."

Trouble was startled. "How can my grandfather know everything written on the scroll?"

The priest gave him a sympathetic look. "Allyn is the Yeti who fell in a trance and inscribed what is written here, when he was only a small child, almost a thousand years ago."

Shocked, Trouble dropped his porcelain cup and it fell on a cushion, staining the satin fabric with tea. He tried to wipe away the blot, but it was impossible.

The Abbot comforted him. "That cushion can be restored, my friend. But these few minutes are precious. Our time together can't be replaced like a simple pillow. Don't waste your focus on trivial matters like a tea stain. Your shock is understandable. Allyn is too modest. That's why he didn't inform you that he was the scroll's author."

Trouble relaxed. He didn't feel so ashamed of his mistake.

The monk continued. "I've read and re-read the scroll, yet many things still elude me. How will the Yetis be saved? And how can mankind exist without Yetis in our midst, invisible yet omnipresent? Those things I do not know." He shook his head. "But you haven't come all this way to hear an old man's pessimism about this difficult world. How can I help you?"

Allyn looked at Trouble. "We need that scrap of paper you brought from the antique shop, the missing end of the parchment roll."

Trouble unzipped an inner pocket of his jacket and brought out a ragged fragment.

The Yeti nodded. "Thank you. Your arrival began the final cycle in the prophecy I wrote a thousand years ago. When you hold this paper to the scroll, I'm certain something new will appear, an insight meant to guide you on the quest for your missing parents."

Trouble's restless fingers tried to match the paper scrap with the ancient manuscript. When the fragment and scroll touched, a mist appeared out of nowhere, a cloud surrounding the roller. A bright light glowed inside the mist. There was a hiss like a scorching iron running over wet cloth. The mist vanished, leaving the roll healed, mended with the torn end.

Trouble unrolled the repaired scroll, amazed to see the parchment transforming itself. Exotic Yeti symbols danced like a thousand squirming ants, rearranging themselves. When they stopped dancing, the hieroglyphic symbols were gone, replaced by English text. "What does it mean, Grandfather?"

Allyn leaned over the scroll. "I'm not certain," the Yeti hedged. "The message is cryptic. I'll need to study it some more. In any event, your future is not decided. What happens next depends on you, Trouble. It is you who are writing the scroll now."

"Me?" he called out, then regretted his loud voice. "Me?" he whispered.

"Yes," Allyn confirmed. "The last few lines are in your handwriting, not mine."

"That does look like I wrote it," Trouble admitted.

The Abbot smiled. "You're making history. Not an enviable task, is it?"

"No." Trouble handed the scroll to Allyn and wiped sweaty palms on his jacket.

Allyn stood up. "May we borrow this?" He held out the scroll so the Abbot could take it back, if he wished.

The elderly monk declined. "The Yeti prophecy was always yours. We simply guarded it for you."

"Thank you for protecting the scroll." Allyn bowed. "I'm afraid, I must be going."

The Abbot blessed each of his visitors and told them, "Go in love." His arthritic fingers, with their inflamed knuckles, touched their foreheads. When he got to Trouble, the monk added, "May you also go in safety. Be careful. Your path is not an easy one."

34

Trouble felt grateful to leave the Abbot's overheated chambers, even though standing outside in the icy air chilled him. The cold feeling came more from his mood than his body temperature. He looked beyond the shelter of a monastery to the harsh snowscape of Everest, a distant presence in the moonless night. His future goals seemed far away, with little chance of success. The only certainty was the pain of separating from Allyn, his newly discovered grandfather. "What happens next?" Trouble asked, dreading the answer.

Allyn looked sad. "We've already said our good-byes. It's time to take our leave."

"I don't want to go." It wasn't a protest. Trouble knew he had to return to New York, then search for his parents somewhere else in the world. So much was riding on his ability to track down Julia and Indigo. "How will I ever find my parents?" he muttered, not really talking to anyone but himself.

Allyn responded to the question anyway. "The scroll helped you. It gave you an essential clue. What were the last words written on the parchment? You should remember them. You wrote them yourself, with your actions."

The idea that his handwriting etched an ancient scroll still jolted Trouble. It took him a moment to answer his grandfather's question. "The scroll said, 'beware the sign of the rat,' whatever that means." He felt irritated. The last thing he needed was another puzzle to solve.

"Then your path will be marked by the sign of a rat. It isn't a friendly symbol, I'm afraid. That's why the Abbot advised you to be careful. You won't have to look for the sign of the rat, Trouble. The omen will come to you, sooner than you think. Stay alert when you get to New York. There is both good and evil in the sign of a rat. It's vital to know when you're being tricked."

"That sign of the rat business isn't much help, Allyn." Trouble sighed, feeling weary and annoyed.

Thalastria nudged Trouble with her trunk, then gently lifted him on Mulanathor's back. The wooly mammoths jiggled along a narrow trail crusted with ice. Just a few days ago, Trouble rode a yak on the same twisting path. He couldn't believe how much happened since he came to Mount Everest. It seemed his future would be even more packed with surprises, despite having precious few clues.

Allyn pointed along the narrow trail toward Nuru and Tattoo's village. Already lights burned in homes, squares of yellow outlining windows against the purple dawn. People were gathering for another day of searching, organizing today's expedition to find Nuru, Tattoo and Trouble, presumed lost and in danger. Soon, torches made a red gash on the black of night. A long parade of flames wormed along the path, moving like a string of fireflies.

The Yeti reassured Trouble. "I have every confidence in you. You'll pass the first test, I'm sure."

"First test?"

"Your first test will be explaining to Ang Dawa where you, Nuru and Tattoo have been all this time. Now we must part company. From here, you walk toward the village and I return to Yeti City."

The idea of saying goodbye to Allyn was impossibly hard on Trouble. He'd lived three years without his father and two years without his mother. Now he'd only spent a day with a grandfather he might never see again. "I'm not ready to leave."

Allyn sighed. "And I'm not ready to leave you. But it must be done. The villagers are approaching. Soon they'll be able to see me. I can't allow that to happen."

Getting off the elephant's back happened far too quickly. In the next moment, Allyn helped Trouble adjust the straps of a Yeti daypack, built with a bamboo frame wrapped in elegant Chinese silk. The pack looked like it should weigh only a feather, but when he put it on, the bag felt like it contained enough supplies for a month of trekking.

"Geez, this is heavy," he commented, puzzled by the pack's weight.

"Albert," his grandfather explained. "The penguin's sleeping comfortably inside your bag, cozy and warm, with a full stomach. He'll be cranky when he wakes up. I put some dried fish in a pouch for you to feed him on the plane."

"Yes, of course I'll feed him." Hesitating to leave, Trouble fought with his emotions instead of walking away, as he should have done. He stalled for time, unzipping his jacket pocket and removing the blue stone. "My mother sent me this Yeti birth egg and a brief note, mailed from Mount Everest. Is this my father's birth egg?"

Allyn coughed and seemed uncomfortable. "No, I'm afraid we don't craft birth eggs for half-human children. It's not allowed. That's my birth egg."

"Yours?" Trouble was astonished. He held out the stone for Allyn to take back.

Allyn closed Trouble's fist around the egg. "Keep it. It will guide you like a compass. I don't need a Yeti exploring compass. I'm too old for another expedition."

Trouble felt shocked. "My mother sent your birth egg?"

"No, I sent the stone to you. That's why the printing in the note was a bit off from your mother's normal handwriting. I mimicked her style from a research note she left here, after an expedition to Siberia."

"Is my mother dead?"

"I hope not. I don't think harm has come to Julia. I'd feel it. My instincts are good, even though my body is weakened with age. My intuition tells me Julia is confused. She can't find Indigo, yet all the clues point in the same direction, to one place. She went there and found nothing."

"Where did she go?"

"She didn't tell me. Julia was afraid I might be foolish and try to follow her, if she didn't return soon with Indigo."

Trouble sagged. "Another dead end." A thought brightened his outlook. "Maybe you know where my dad went on his expedition?"

"No chance. Indigo is very secretive. Always has been. I can't blame him. Yetis weren't nice to him as a child. He learned to keep everything to himself."

"Is he safe? I mean, do you feel my father's in danger? You said your intuition is strong."

"I have a confusing image of Indigo. He seems trapped. For some reason, Indigo is unable to move toward his goals. It's important to find him. The longer he's trapped, the harder it will be to free him."

"Any other images of my dad?"

"He's in the mountains. Not the Himalayas. Some other part of the globe."

"And you're sure he's all right?"

"Well, not all right. His situation isn't good." Allyn's mood became more anxious. "There's nothing else I can tell you. The villagers are getting too close." Their footsteps were audible. They could hear the crunching of villagers trekking across a frozen crust of snow.

"Go now," Allyn urged. "Nuru and Tattoo will follow you."

Trouble took a step and then another. He turned every few paces, catching a glimpse of Allyn until his grandfather became only a shadow on the mountain. Trouble thought he saw Allyn wave, but couldn't be certain. Then a wooly mammoth lifted the Yeti aboard and the elephants plodded away, taking Allyn home. His grandfather shrank to a hunched silhouette on Mulanathor's furry back, getting smaller each moment. The last members of two nearly extinct species were vanishing into darkness to hide inside Everest.

Trouble's depression was interrupted by shouts of surprise and confusion. The villagers shrieked and hollered after spotting Tattoo, Nuru and Trouble. Plodding torches became waving flares pointing along the trail. Slipping on the icy crust, Sherpas rushed toward the trio, Ang Dawa in front of the group.

35

Nuru, Tattoo and Trouble stumbled down the mountain path, slipping on treacherous ice. Their boots skidded across slick rocks, demanding all their concentration to avoid falling and hurting themselves. When they finally looked up, it seemed a hundred people were approaching, their faces a mixture of relief and fear. Villagers rushing uphill to meet them had an easy time getting traction and moved quickly. In seconds, the pack would be upon them, demanding an explanation for why the trio had been missing. Scrambling in front of the mob, Ang Dawa led the way, an angry expression on his tired face.

"What are we going to tell my dad?" Nuru worried. "He'll kill me if he thinks I went up Everest without him."

Tattoo sulked. "Yeah. I'm gonna be grounded for weeks."

"I've got an idea," Trouble suggested. "Before you found me on the Khumbu Ice Falls, there was an avalanche. We'll tell them we were buried and had to dig out. Agreed?"

Nuru grew desperate as his family approached. He whispered, "Anything's better than the truth. They'll never believe we met a Yeti."

"Sure," Tattoo chimed. "An avalanche is great. They'll be happy we lived instead of angry at us."

Nuru approved. "It's not like I have a better idea." He zipped his parka tight and began limping, exaggerating his sore ankle to get sympathy. Nuru only took a few steps and was engulfed in a bone-crushing hug from his father.

"Where have you been?" Ang Dawa scolded. "Tattoo, Trouble, are you hurt?"

"We're fine, just tired and a bit hungry," Trouble answered.

Nuru's mother, Dooli, threw yak hair blankets over all three of them. Dooli squeezed Nuru's arms, checking for broken bones.

"Mom," Nuru protested, "I'm all right. It's Tattoo that got hurt, but no big deal."

"Hurt?" Dooli shouted in a panicked voice. "Stretcher!"

"Hey, I'm fine," Tattoo protested. She tried to stop the stretcher bearers before they ran any farther. Nobody would listen to her objections. Soon a doctor urged Tattoo to lie on the stretcher so she could be examined.

"Cut it out," Tattoo told the doctor. "I just got hit in the face by a little rock. It'll heal. Ow. What's that?"

"Tetanus injection," the doctor explained, withdrawing the needle from Tattoo's arm.

"Geez, lighten up, will you?" Tattoo felt disgusted at the overkill.

"You're not hurt?" The doctor sounded amazed.

"It was only a small avalanche," Nuru explained. "We went looking for Trouble and found him in the Khumbu Ice Falls. He wanted to do a little exploring, so we walked closer to the West Ridge. Suddenly, bam! An avalanche slammed down. Barely missed us. We got buried and had to dig out. Sorry we worried you so much."

"Oh, we're just happy you're all safe." Dooli sounded relieved.

But Ang Dawa's stern look meant he didn't entirely buy his son's explanation.

Trouble jumped into the conversation, hoping to deflect Ang Dawa's anger toward himself and away from Nuru. "It's all my fault. I didn't think Tattoo and Nuru would follow me. I should have turned around and gone back. They insisted on coming along, for safety reasons. They did a brave thing in making sure I wasn't alone. I'm the one at fault, not them. It won't happen again. I'm leaving today to go home. It was foolish of me to come here. I'm sorry."

Dooli gave Trouble a hug. "You were just looking for your parents."

Ang Dawa thawed. "Well, you learned your lesson. Next time, come later in the year. We'll go on a real expedition, to the very top if you like." He beamed in pride at the idea of standing atop Mount Everest again, as he'd done several times before. Ang Dawa launched into the story of his last ascent as a Sardar, leading a team of mountaineers through an ice storm.

Nuru rolled his eyes. He pulled Trouble's sleeve and whispered, "I've only heard that story a hundred times. You aren't really leaving, are you?"

Trouble nodded. "Yeah. Albert needs surgery and I have to take care of the shop."

"You also have to find that clue," Tattoo urged. "You need to find the sign of the rat, whatever that means. When you find out, e-mail us."

"E-mail? How often do you go to the Cybercafé? It's five days by yak." Trouble felt skeptical.

"We go once a month for supplies," Nuru assured Trouble.

Tattoo corrected Nuru. "Well, not quite that often," She got an elbow in her ribs from Nuru.

"Trouble's coming back in a month anyway," Nuru said. "Allyn will run out of food and we gotta protect him from the leopards."

"I have to find my parents first. Allyn needs another healing session and only my father can do that for him. Finding my dad won't be easy. He could be anywhere, from Siberia to the Amazon. Once he was a month overdue and my mother discovered him in the basement of a museum in St. Petersburg. For all I know, they might be in Africa digging up King Solomon's Mines or searching Mongolia for dinosaur bones."

"So how are you going to look for them?" Tattoo was curious.

"I'll play detective some more and go through their notes again. See if I missed anything the first time. Maybe there'll be a clue in that rat sign stuff."

"Watch out," Nuru warned. "Allyn said the sign of the rat was dangerous."

"Yeah, it's going to jump you when you get back to New York," Tattoo added.

"The rat may also help me. Allyn said the problem was knowing when you're being tricked." Trouble tightened the waist strap on his Yeti knapsack, shifting most of the pack's burden to his hips. The penguin's weight had been cutting into his shoulders. "I'll be careful."

"Right, like you were with the Maoist guerillas," Nuru teased.

"Or trying to cross the Khumbu Ice Falls without a ladder." Tattoo laughed.

"OK, so I need help from friends. Lucky you were there. Maybe I'll get a break and the search will get easier." But Trouble's intuition said the opposite. He knew the next part of his journey would be as dangerous as climbing on Mount Everest.

To be continued in … *Sign of the Rat.*

1496025

Made in the USA